"So, you wanna go som

"Sure," he said eagerly. "Wherever you w...

"That's a good puppy dog," I wanted to say. Instead, I said, "I'm not one for bedrooms. I prefer adventure."

"Adventure?"

"Yes, adventure. I enjoy sex in unusual places. The possibility of getting caught, the thrill of someone else watching, just does something to me."

He grinned. "Sounds kinky."

"I'm not kinky. Being kinky ain't shit."

"Then what are you?"

I smirked. "A freak. A nymphomaniac. A sex fiend. Can you handle that?"

Praise for *Gettin' Buck Wild*

"Steamy stories . . . whew! . . . Be forewarned."
—*Black Issues Book Review*

"Erotica at its absolute best."
—*Urban Spectrum*

Praise for *The Heat Seekers*

"Will keep you engrossed from start to finish."
—*Vibe*

"Seductive."
—*Essence*

"Clever banter and sizzling sex."
—*Publishers Weekly*

Also by Zane

Addicted
The Heat Seekers
The Sex Chronicles: Shattering the Myth
Gettin' Buck Wild: Sex Chronicles II
The Sisters of APF: The Indoctrination of Soror Ride Dick
Shame on It All
Skyscraper

Edited by Zane

Chocolate Flava: The Eroticanoir.com Anthology

nervous

a novel

zane

ATRIA BOOKS

New York London Toronto Sydney

ATRIA BOOKS
1230 Avenue of the Americas
New York, NY 10020

Copyright © 2003 by Zane

For information address Atria Books, 1230 Avenue
of the Americas, New York, NY 10020

ISBN-13: 978-0-7434-7623-2
ISBN-10: 0-7434-7623-9
ISBN-13: 978-0-7434-7624-9 (Pbk)
ISBN-10: 0-7434-7624-7 (Pbk)

First Atria Books trade paperback edition June 2004

20 19 18 17

ATRIA BOOKS is a trademark of Simon & Schuster, Inc.

Manufactured in the United States of America

For information regarding special discounts for bulk purchases, please contact
Simon & Schuster Special Sales at 1-800-456-6798 or business@simonandschuster.com

This book is dedicated to "J"
My latest creation
Mommy loves you dearly and I only pray
That Daddy and I can give you the life you deserve

acknowledgments

Here I go again for the seventh time in three years, which in itself is a blessing. Always ever present in my life and first on my list is the Lord. He is responsible for the air that I breathe and my health, my creativity, and my determination.

Next on my list is my parents, for their continuous support and encouragement, I could never express enough gratitude or pay them back properly for all they have given me. However, I intend to try.

Hubby, what can I say except thanks for loving me, cheering me up when I am down, understanding me when I start flipping out (often in the middle of the night), staying up with the baby late at night so I can either sleep or write or a combination of both, being versatile enough to change a diaper one second and handle a major business decision the next. You might not be a superhero but you are definitely a superman.

To my offspring, Mommy loves you and as you know, when it comes to motherhood, nothing else comes first. Even if that means making the sacrifice of staying up all night working so I can spend quality time with you during the day.

To my family members: Miss Bettye, Carlita, Charmaine, Rick, David, Aunt Rose, Aunt Margaret, Aunt Neet, Miss Maurice and Uncle Snook, Uncle George and Miss Mary, Joyce and Ed and all those I am close to, thanks for the support and love.

To my friends: Pamela Crockett, Esq., Destiny Wood, Lisa Fox, Karen Black, Janet Allen, Sharon Johnson, Dee Mc-Conneaughy, Denise Barrow, Tracy Crockett, Pamela Shannon, MD, Cornelia Williams, and all the rest of you hoochie mommas (just kidding), thanks for all the late night phone conversations, the encouragement, the babysitting, and just having my back in general.

To the special kids in my life: Arianna, Ashley, Jazmin, Adam, Jerlan, Tislem, Indira, Briana, Karlin, Brian, Jr., and Nicholas, remember to stay in school and get a good education because it will all pay off in the end.

To my agent, Sara Camilli, thanks for all the pep talks and more importantly your patience in dealing with such a "drama queen" (inside joke) as a client.

To Malaika Adero, my editor, Carlos Brown, my publicist, Judith Curr, Carolyn Reidy, Demond Jarrett, Louise Burke, Brigitte Smith, Dennis Eulau, Karen Mender, and the rest of the ATRIA/Simon & Schuster crew, thanks for everything and I look forward to a prosperous and long-lasting future.

Thanks to the Strebor Books International staff, the Strebor authors, and all the other authors, booksellers, distributors, book clubs, and everyone else who has supported me throughout my brief but exciting writing career. I guarantee you that the best is yet to come.

I am not going to go on and on since I have books coming out every three months or so (smile). Just know that I love and appreciate everyone.

Peace and Blessings,
Zane

introduction

       I wanted to pen *Nervous* for several reasons. I have always been intrigued by the short story I first wrote by the same name for *The Sex Chronicles: Shattering the Myth*. The complexity of the character drew me to her and so many readers felt a connection with the one known only as "SHE." Many women have two sides to them: the good girl and the bad girl. Most of the time they try to hide the bad girl, not realizing how short life truly is and how at the end of it, there is nothing we can do about regrets and missed opportunities.

       I thought about what was the wildest thing that could ever possibly happen to a woman and thus, Jonquinette Pierce was created. A woman that, in her mind, is a virgin, but she suffers with a split personality disorder. The other woman in her is a whore. The contrast between the two was a delight to write. I also love my character. *Nervous* is the second in a planned five-book series that features the psychiatrist, Dr. Marcella Spencer. *Addicted* was the first. After *Nervous, Vengeance, Torn,* and *Patience* will come. Dr. Spencer will become the main character in one, but I won't reveal which one just yet. You will have to wait and see.

I hope you enjoy reading *Nervous* as much as I enjoyed writing it.

Peace, Blessings, and Love,
Zane

"Life has never been what I expected. I only hope that one day I can live a normal one."

—Jonquinette

"Life is a bitch and then you die. What more do you want, heifer?"

—Jude

nervous

nervous*

For as long as I could remember, I had always been nervous. Nervous about school. Nervous about friends. Nervous about relationships with men. Even nervous about talking to my own mother. I don't know whether it was something deep-rooted inside of me from an early childhood experience or whether it was something that was just meant to be.

I lived in my own little world by the time I was twenty-two years old. I was fresh out of college and working as a project coordinator for a nonprofit organization in Philadelphia. I selected that job because I wouldn't have to deal with too many people on a daily basis. I only had face-to-face dealings with a few of the people from the office, mostly women, and I was very thankful for

---

* Excerpted from *The Sex Chronicles: Shattering the Myth* (Pocket Books, 2002).

that. My daily routine consisted of going to work, stopping off at a carry-out on the way home to pick up dinner, and then retiring to my cozy but cramped one bedroom apartment for the rest of the night.

When it came to dealing with a man on an intellectual level, any man, my palms would get sweaty and my knees would tremble a little. I am not sure how noticeable it was to anybody else, but I was painfully aware of it.

I had managed to make it all the way through my high school and college years without a single boyfriend. But I was not a virgin by far. The weekends were her time. They were the times that SHE came out into the light. SHE was my wild side, the one who craved to be fucked. SHE was one who felt conversation was never needed, nor were games, because SHE knew within five minutes after SHE laid eyes on a man whether SHE wanted to fuck him or not.

SHE first appeared back in my freshman year of college. At that time, I would spend lonely nights in my dorm room masturbating myself to sleep by playing with my nipples and rubbing a sheet or towel between my legs. I imagined having wild, passionate sex with men that had no faces until I climaxed and the sheet or towel was soaking wet with my nectar.

I have always been a pretty girl, above average even, I would say. It was never a question of whether I thought I looked good enough to get a man. I was just too nervous to talk to the men who pursued me. They came in all shapes and sizes and from all walks of life. Most were extremely nice and attractive, but I wanted to wait and give my virginity to the man I would ultimately marry. SHE, though, could not wait.

One cold winter night of my freshman year, I was studying in the university library when SHE saw him. He was average height, about five-nine and not what one would call *foine,* yet attractive. It was his eyes that made him desirable. His eyes seemed to have a passion burning inside of them. SHE sat there, at a table across the room from where he was standing at a bookcase flipping through some pages. SHE could feel her panties becoming damp from the growing desire to feel him inside of her. SHE crossed her legs and moved them back and forth, creating a light friction against her vagina and making her desire even more intense. SHE didn't realize that SHE was simultaneously sucking on the eraser of her pencil and staring at him, until SHE felt him staring back. SHE moved her eyes up from where they had locked on the bulge of his pants to his face and for what seemed like an endless moment, their eyes met. He broke the stare and smiled at her. It was then that SHE noticed he had the softest-looking lips. SHE yearned to draw the bottom one into her mouth and suck on it.

SHE looked back down at the economics books SHE was studying for a brief moment, contemplating her next move. When SHE looked up, he was gone. SHE panicked, quickly scanning the library, until SHE noticed him getting into the elevator. He looked at her and smiled as the doors were closing. Something within her exploded and SHE knew what had to be done. SHE jumped up from the table, leaving her books, coat and purse and ran out the exit door, going down the steps two at a time, hoping to catch up to him before the elevator reached the ground floor.

When SHE reached ground level, it was too late. The elevator was empty and he was gone. SHE went out the front door of the library into the cold, brisk, winter air hoping to catch a glimpse of his red ski jacket. But, SHE saw nothing. As SHE turned around to go back into the library and retrieve her things, with disappointment in her heart, SHE looked up and he was standing there. In fact, SHE bumped right into his chest and could feel her heart pounding in her own as he looked deep into her eyes, up close and personal for the first time.

He opened his mouth to say something, probably to ask her name, but SHE put her finger over his lips. SHE was unsure why she did this, but SHE knew that talking would only ruin the moment. Maybe SHE feared that I would rejoin the situation, bringing with me all my shattered nerves at the thought of a mere conversation with a man. Who knows?

SHE smiled at him, took him by the hand and pulled him back inside the library with her. SHE pushed the button for the elevator. When they got on, instead of pushing the button for the floor where her belongings were, SHE pressed the button for the basement where all the stacks were located. SHE knew it would basically be deserted and dark down there. It was the perfect place for what SHE had in mind.

When the elevator began to descend, SHE took his hand and placed it between her legs. SHE had on a black skirt with a white bodysuit and silk panties underneath. SHE could feel his fingers push the crotch of her bodysuit and panties aside and explore her wetness. He brought his face closer to hers and was about to explore her mouth with his tongue when they reached the basement level and the doors opened.

Just as SHE imagined, the stacks were deserted. He left his backpack right beside the then closed elevator, picked her up and wrapped her legs around his back. He carried her to the rear of the stacks where there were a few scattered desks. He sat her down on top of one of them.

Their clothes came off quickly, both of them ripping at the other's until they were completely naked in the dimly lit room. SHE took one of her fingers and rubbed it against her clit. Then she removed it and put it into his mouth, letting him savor her juice. SHE rubbed the finger against her clit again; this time she brought it to her own mouth to suck the juice off her fingers. Then they began to kiss, both savoring her sweetness at the same time.

He pushed her back onto the desk so that her head was hanging halfway over the rear and her nipples were protruding upward. He suckled them one at a time, not only taking her dark pearls into his mouth but licking the entire breast starting at the base of each one with the tip of his tongue and making light, circular strokes until he reached the hardened prize. SHE was in ecstasy. So many nights had been spent alone rubbing HER nipples between HER fingers and now a man was devouring them just like SHE had yearned for all that time. He took both breasts, one in each hand, pushing them together and then sweeping both nipples into his mouth at the same time. Her moans became louder.

Still palming her breasts, with one hand he made a trail with his tongue down to her belly button, pausing just long enough to take a quick dip into it before moving down to explore between her thighs. Before SHE could even prepare herself for what was about to come, he took her hardened clit into his mouth and began to let it vibrate on the tip of his tongue. SHE came for the first time in a matter of seconds, the intensity of having his mouth touch her there was out of this world.

He continued eating her pussy for the next fifteen minutes or so and SHE came at least five or six more times before he had sated his hunger. Then, he walked around to the other side of the desk, where her head was still hanging over the side, and brought her face-to-face with his delicious-looking dick. SHE hesitated not for a second and took the head of it into her mouth with a heightened desire to know what he tasted like. And there, with her head upside down, SHE sucked a dick for the very first time. SHE held the base of it while he dick-fed her, pushing his manhood in and out of her mouth with increasing speed. SHE relaxed her throat so that he could eventually get it all in. SHE loved every minute of it. As his body began to tremble and his knees began to buckle, SHE was given the added treat of tasting semen and was immediately hooked for life on the scrumptious flavor. SHE lay there, savoring every single drop, and secretly hoping there would be more to come. Never had SHE tasted anything so yummy.

He removed his dick, now a little sore and tender but never the worse for wear, from her throat. After going back to the other side of the table, he pushed his dick deep inside her waiting pussy. SHE could feel her hymen break and realized that virginity was now a thing of her past. He fucked her hard. Considering the way SHE had picked him up and led the way to the basement, he had no idea that this was her first time. He just thought SHE had a tight-ass pussy and he was taken aback at how snugly it fit around his throbbing dick.

He fucked her without mercy because he knew that SHE wanted it that way. SHE was paralyzed at first when he stuck it in, but gradually SHE grew attuned to his rhythm and began to grind her hips, fucking him back. SHE could feel his balls slamming up against her ass and was mesmerized by the sound of his dick invading her pussy, for it was a sound SHE had never heard before. SHE loved it.

After a few more minutes, SHE felt him explode again, this time inside her pussy walls. His sweat trickled off his forehead onto her breasts. Her stomach muscles contracted as he removed his well-satisfied dick from her sweet pussy. He began to say something. SHE intervened saying, "No, please don't!"

SHE got up from the desk, dressed quickly and looked at his dick with the veins bulging in all directions. SHE knew that SHE had to get the hell out of there quickly for SHE was half ashamed of what SHE had done. SHE was even more ashamed at how much SHE enjoyed it.

SHE left him there, in the basement of the library, nude and wondering why the hell SHE insisted on anonymity and silence, hoping that one day he would see her again.

And one day he did, in the student union. SHE walked right past him and pretended SHE didn't recognize him. He turned to go after her and beg her to at least tell him her name. With the same haste SHE had entered his life, SHE exited it. He looked for her and SHE was gone.

Gone like SHE was when all the other men looked for her. SHE always fucked them quickly, in silence, and then left them in awe. There was the man SHE saw in the grocery store line. She patiently waited for him in the parking lot and then fucked him right there in the backseat of his car. There was the gas station attendant SHE took into one of the garage bays and fucked while SHE was waiting for another guy outside to change her tire. There were the two guys SHE saw playing basketball one day at the local park who SHE enticed into the woods and there, on a secluded picnic table, fucked them both. And, of course, there were all the men SHE had picked up at hotel bars, nightclubs and virtually everyplace else over the past five years, the total number of which SHE had lost count of long ago.

Her appetite is insatiable and undeniable. SHE can never get enough when SHE appears. As for me, I am still nervous but hopefully one of these days, SHE and I will become one and settle down with one man who can satisfy both our needs. Until then, SHE will just continue to have her fun, ruling the weekends, and I will continue my boring-ass weekdays. One thing is for sure, though. When I masturbate now, I have multiple orgasms and enjoy my body in ways I never imagined before. Maybe SHE and I have already become one.

prologue

Zoe had seen the young woman a few times before. She always sat in the back of the meeting room, seemingly lurking, and she never said a word to anyone. She just sat there with this deadpan expression on her face and listened to everyone else discuss their addictions.

Brian, a white male in his late fifties, was finishing up his testimonial. "I recognize this as an illness now. I used to think I just got a little carried away with sex at moments. Then it became an obsession. There were times when I couldn't even bring myself to fall asleep without feeling the inside of a woman first. When my wife of many years refused to satisfy my needs, I would resort to paying for sex. I would find myself cruising the avenue to pick up whores. Women that had no issues about giving blow jobs for less than the cost of a tank of low-end gasoline. I realized some of them *had* to carry diseases. How could they not? Still, I was so obsessed with sex that I risked it anyway."

Brian's face became distorted as the first tear fell from his left cheek. One of the moderators, Grace, stood up and walked over to the podium to pat him on the back. While Brian was regaining his composure, Zoe seized the opportunity to survey the young woman's face again. Still nothing. No sign of emotion whatsoever. If it were not for the light fabric of her rayon shirt moving slightly, Zoe would have doubted that she was even breathing.

Brian pulled himself together and continued. "Now I have nothing. Alice left me. My kids are grown, living their own lives, and they hate me too much to even look at me. I spend every single holiday alone. The pain is unbearable. If only I could turn back the hands of time and start over. If only I could make things better."

The sexual addiction meeting had turned highly emotional yet again. Several of the people broke down in tears. Not so much for Brian, but for the pain and anguish they themselves had endured in their lives of turmoil. Zoe rarely cried at the meetings anymore. Her counseling sessions with Dr. Marcella Spencer, a month at a center in Florida run by a friend of the doctor's, and a loving and supportive husband had helped her survive her ordeal. Ironically, Zoe had probably been through more drama than anyone else in the room. Her sexual addition had led to three simultaneous affairs with two of her lovers ending up dead at the hands of a third.

Zoe emerged from her seat and approached Brian. She embraced him and whispered in his ear, "It's going to be all right, Brian. We're all in this together."

Zoe glanced at the back of the room. The young woman had exited as quietly as she had entered. *Damn, she always does that!* Zoe thought.

1

jonquinette

I entered my third floor apartment fighting back tears. It was hot. Extremely hot. I'd forgotten to turn on the air before I'd left that morning.

I tossed my keys onto the coffee table and kicked off my low-heel black pumps. "You knew they were calling for a heat wave today," I said aloud, recalling the morning weather report that I'd neglected. "Why didn't you turn on some air?"

The sole of one of my stockings snagged on a nail in the parquet flooring as I stumbled into my hallway. I adjusted the thermostat to seventy and sighed, praying it wouldn't take long to drop down from the current temperature of eighty-six degrees.

I continued down the hall into my bedroom and collapsed on my king-sized bed. I'd purchased it despite the fact that one person didn't need such a monstrosity to sleep alone. And sleep alone I did. Always.

The red light on my answering machine was blinking. Who could possibly have called? On a Saturday, no less. Normally it would be Momma, but she was out of the country for two weeks. She'd whisked off to Paris to fulfill a lifelong dream. More like fantasy. Momma had a way of fantasizing like no other. One day I hoped she would find whatever it was she was truly searching for. I doubted she would've called more than once at those rates and she'd called three days earlier to inform me that she and her latest romantic conquest had arrived safely.

I rewound the tape and hit play.

"Jon, what's up girl? It's me!" a bubbly, female voice squealed out at me to the point where I felt compelled to adjust the volume.

Me who? I wondered.

"In case you don't know who this is, it's me, Darnetta."

I sat up on the bed. I should've known it was Darnetta. I heard that overanxious voice daily at work. Why was Darnetta calling me at home on a Saturday? We were coworkers but rarely spoke more than two words to each other.

"Jon, I was wondering if you want to hang out tonight. I know we don't usually flow like that, but I have two tickets to this live concert at Club Snatch and everyone else I know has plans already." There was a slight pause. "That's not to say that you're my last choice. I was going to ask you about going out sometime soon anyway and I saw this as the perfect opportunity. You always seem so shy at work. Anyway, give me a call if you can make it. My number is—"

I didn't even bother to listen to the phone number and hit the erase button. Me in a club? No way. That meant a lot of people. That meant a lot of men. No way!

I baked some chicken breasts that I had marinated in Hawaiian flavoring all day. I cut up a few russet potatoes and boiled them along with a pouch of broccoli. While I was waiting for my meal to get done, I pulled some paperwork out of my briefcase and looked over the weekly shipping records for the office supply warehouse where I was head accountant.

The numbers didn't make sense. They were way under target for the week, something that normally only happened around holidays. After all, who orders office supplies for Christmas presents? Most people take vacation the week between Christmas and New Year's anyway. But we were in the middle of August, when there were no holidays.

I'd broken out my calculator and was crunching numbers when my phone rang. I debated about answering for the first three rings. What if Momma was calling back? Maybe something had gone wrong in Paris. I picked it up on the fifth ring, one ring before my answering machine normally kicked in.

"Hello."

"Jon, is that you?"

I didn't utter a word.

"Jon, you there?"

"Yes, I'm here," I replied hesitantly.

"It's me, Darnetta!"

"I kind of figured that."

"I left you a message earlier. Did you get it?"

"Uh . . . yes, I did. Sorry I didn't call you back but I couldn't quite make out the number."

"Cool. It's no problem. Sometimes I talk too loud. I'm working on all that though. So, what's up? You trying to hang out tonight or what? Lil' Z is performing. The show is going to be all that and them some. You feel me?"

"Lil' Z?"

"Yeah, Lil' Z, the rapper. You've never heard of him?"

"Of course I have." I lied again. "He's one of my favorites."

I hoped Darnetta wouldn't ask me to name any of his songs because I'd never heard of the man. Thankfully, she didn't go there.

"So how about it, girl?"

After accidentally knocking over my tea onto some paperwork, I involuntarily blurted out, "Shit!"

"Ooh, Jon, I've never heard you curse before," Darnetta chided. "What else do you do that I don't know about?"

I didn't like her implications. "Huh? What do you mean?"

I felt bad about cursing. I wasn't raised that way but, from time to time, a four-letter word forced its way out before I could push it back down my throat.

"Never mind," Darnetta said. "What about tonight? I really need someone to go with me and I don't want to waste the ticket. They were so hard to come by."

"What about your boyfriend, Darnetta?"

Even though we rarely held conversations at work, *everybody* knew about her boyfriend Logan. He was all she ever talked about—rather, bragged about—in the break room.

"Logan's out of town for the weekend. He went to Durham. *Asshole!* I'm so pissed at him. I told him about this concert weeks ago but he made plans to go hang out with some of his immature friends anyway."

"I see." I rolled my eyes up to the ceiling. Surely there had to be one other person in the entire city of Atlanta Darnetta could get to go with her. "Darnetta, I'm exhausted. I had a lot of errands to run today. Maybe we can go out some other time."

"Aw, Jon, please don't do this to me," Darnetta whined into the phone. "I realize this is short notice, girl, but I guarantee you'll have a good time. Funky music. Free buffet. Fine-ass men."

I couldn't help but laugh. Now I definitely wasn't going.

"Jon, I'm telling you to take a chance and do the damn town with me. What's the problem? Do I stink or something?"

We both giggled.

"Darnetta, it's not you. Really, it isn't. I just don't like going out. Especially to clubs. I don't even recall the last time I've been in one."

"Well, things need to change then. How old are you?"

"Twenty-four. Why?"

"I've never heard of a single, twenty-four-year-old woman that doesn't enjoy going out. You have a man, right?"

Now why did she have to go there? I could never tell her the truth. She could never identify with the fact that I'd never really had a boyfriend. No one would.

"No, no man. I'm kind of between men at present. You know how it is."

"I'm feeling you. That's why this is a great opportunity to meet someone new. There will be a ton of bachelors there tonight, just waiting on a sexy sister like you to grace their presence."

Me, sexy? Who was she trying to fool?

"Darnetta, I appreciate the offer. I can't believe you thought of me, but I really just can't make it. Sorry."

Darnetta sighed into the phone. I could tell she was disgusted. "Fine, Jon. I'm going to let you off the hook this time, but there's one condition."

"A condition?" I asked, still trying to reorganize my papers and dry the damp ones off.

"Yeah, the next time I ask you to hang out with me, no matter where it is or when, you have to agree right this second that you'll go."

"Um, I can't really say if—"

"Jon, I mean it. Agree to go with me next time or I'm going to be highly offended and get an emotional complex thinking I really do stink or something."

I didn't want to hurt her feelings so I agreed. "Okay."

"Okay what?"

"I'll hang out with you the next time you ask."

Darnetta giggled. "All right. Now we're getting somewhere. Well, I better run and get ready for the evening. Even though I've got a man, I'm still trying to be fly as hell when I step up in that bitch. I still have to wash my hair so I'm going to get started."

"Have a good time, Darnetta."

"Oh, I will. You can believe that."

We discussed work for another few minutes before hanging up. Darnetta said that if I changed my mind, I could call back within a couple hours. But that would never happen. There was no way I was going to a club with a bunch of strange men around. They made me nervous.

I ate my dinner and watched some cable. I was completely drained by ten. I took a hot shower, threw on some pajamas, and climbed into my bed with the latest D. V. Bernard novel, *The Last Dream Before Dawn*. The brother is a powerful writer but I didn't make it through ten pages before I passed out.

2

Two Hours Later

jude

What kind of boring sista falls asleep at ten-thirty on a Saturday night? Jon really needed to wake up and smell some strong-ass coffee. We were young, educated, and beautiful. But the way Jon dressed, which I hated, deterred people from figuring out the beautiful part. I was sick and tired of the ugly-ass, wire-rimmed glasses. I'd broken three pairs and Jon still hadn't taken the damn hint. Our vision wasn't that bad anyway. I could see just fine without those stupid glasses. Fuck it. Jon could wear them but I refused to reduce myself to that.

I wasn't about to be bored so I got out of bed, went into the bathroom and glanced into the mirror. As usual, Jon had on some baggy-ass, flannel pajamas that I wouldn't be caught dead in.

I checked out our reflection in the mirror. "Look at us. We're tall; we've got thick, ebony hair; caramel skin as smooth as a baby's bottom; legs for days, and an ass men would weep over. Yet you try to cover us up like we're a nun or some shit. Fuck all that. A body like this is meant to be displayed."

Jon had taken care of the bathing part so that left me with the hair and makeup. I tore the pins out of our hair and let it flow before breaking out the curling iron to hook our ass up. Jon kept buying this cheap lipstick from the dollar store but I found an old tube of L'Oréal behind some jars in the medicine cabinet, mixed the two, and it looked halfway decent.

Pickings were slim in the closet, at least when it came to "whorefits." I selected a black suit and managed to turn it into a somewhat revealing ensemble by going braless and leaving the blazer unbuttoned except for one button at the waistline. I was content. We were showing mucho cleavage and looking damn good.

When I pulled up in front of Club Snatch, it was a madhouse. Finding Darnetta to grab that extra ticket would prove to be damn near impossible. Jon was always fucking things up for us. Darnetta was a cool sista and Jon had no business turning down invites in the first place. I almost fainted when she agreed to accept the next invitation from Darnetta. I couldn't wait to see that.

It wasn't like we had some busy-ass social calendar or some shit. Those stupid sexual addiction meetings didn't count as socializing. Jon never said anything while she was there. Besides, there was nothing for her to say. She didn't know jack.

After circling the block three times, I finally lucked out and spotted someone pulling out of a space. The music was slamming but there were more than a hundred people in line. I was infuriated. I wanted in there bad. Lil' Z was doing the remix of his hit "Baby Got Breastesses for Dayz" and I was all into him. Jon's stupid behind had never even heard of him. That says it all.

Damn, I just love bald heads! That was the first thing that came to mind when I spotted his blue-black ass standing at the end of the line. I could tell he was from Jamaica, Barbados, or some other place Jon refused to take a vacation, even though I'd left numerous pamphlets and brochures around the apartment as hints.

The brotha definitely had my interest as I approached him. I surveyed the area. He was alone. The couple in front of him was locking lips and needed to get a room. Hell, Mr. Fine and I needed to get a room our damn selves, but I had something much better in mind.

I brushed my fingertips over one of his ass cheeks. He was wearing the hell out of some navy slacks and I couldn't resist.

He swung around and glared at me with a pair of sexy, brown, bedroom eyes. He was seemingly pleased with what he saw before him and his eyes dropped down to my exposed breasts. The heat had calmed down from earlier and the cool breeze was making my nipples hard.

He flashed an enormous smile. "What's your name?"

Nice smile, wrong question. *Why must they always ask that?*

"What's in a name?" I replied.

He chuckled. Sexy ass. "I was just trying to be friendly, being that you just felt me up."

He had an accent. Definite plus. I was feeling that. I inched closer to him and grabbed his dick. His *huge* dick. Yes, he was surely from an island; somewhere Mandingos are bred on the regular.

"Trust me. I haven't even begun to feel you up yet."

The line had progressed a few feet, but we remained frozen in place. Two sistas all hoochified for the evening walked up behind us.

"Are you in line?" one of them asked.

"I don't know. Are we?" I asked my prospective lover.

"No, I don't suspect we are." He managed to get the words out even though I was latched on to his dick like a vise. I was so close to him that the sistas couldn't see what I was doing. However, I wouldn't have minded if they watched me tear his ass to shreds and slay his dick, which were my intentions.

I glanced at them. "You can go on around us."

"Thanks!" they yelled out in unison. That meant two less people they had to wait behind. They were elated and it showed.

I looked back into his eyes. "So, you wanna go somewhere?"

"Sure," he said eagerly. "Wherever you want."

"That's a good puppy dog," I wanted to say. Instead, I said, "I'm not one for bedrooms. I prefer adventure."

"Adventure?"

"Yes, adventure. I enjoy sex in unusual places. The possibility of getting caught, the thrill of someone else watching, just does something to me."

He grinned. "Sounds kinky."

"I'm not kinky. Being kinky ain't shit."

"Then what are you?"

I smirked. "A freak. A nymphomaniac. A sex fiend. Can you handle that?"

I let go of his dick and began caressing it.

"Yeah, I can deal with that. Hell yeah, I can. But you still didn't tell me your name. I'm Campbell."

"Nice name."

"I'm glad you think so. I bet your name is also."

He was *really* hung up on the name thing. I hated that. I let go of him and backed away. "Look, I don't care to tell you my name. I just want to fuck. You're either down with that or you're not."

"Damn, where were you like ten years ago when I was in my prime?"

I pouted. "I sincerely hope you're not implying that you're no longer in your prime."

Campbell laughed. "I have a feeling you might be able to revive me."

"Let's find out," I challenged.

I headed in the opposite direction of the entrance with Campbell on my tail, and went down the alley behind the club. There was dim lighting coming from an office window on the third floor.

"It sure is dark down here," Campbell commented.

I took his hand and kept walking. "Afraid of the dark? Don't be scared. I won't bite you." I took him off guard by pushing him up against the building and ripping off his shirt. I could hear the buttons scatter across the concrete. I ran my tongue over one of his nipples and caught it between my teeth for a brief second. "That is, unless you want me to bite you."

"This is incredible," Campbell whispered. "Most women over here act like they're afraid to be themselves sexually. But you, you remind me of the women back home."

I didn't ask where he was from because I didn't give a shit. Besides, no woman could compare to me anyway.

"Do you want to fuck or talk?" I asked nastily.

"Oh, I definitely want to fuck."

"Then shut the hell up!"

I took two steps back, released the button on my blazer, and let it fall to the ground. After I was topless, I inched my skirt up and slid my panties down over my hips. I couldn't see Campbell's eyes but I could make out his silhouette.

He came closer and tried to kiss me, but I stuffed my panties into his mouth. "Maybe now you'll be quiet." I undid his belt and yanked it out of the loops of his pants, ran the end of it over his torso, and walked around him. "Put your hands behind your back."

Campbell followed my orders and I bound his wrists with the belt. I walked back around to face him, undid his zipper, and lowered his pants around his ankles. He wasn't wearing any drawers. *Freak!*

I ran my fingers over his chest and pinched his nipple, damn near drawing blood. "You ready for this?"

He nodded and let out a muffled, "Yes."

"Better be."

I took his shirt and sprawled it on the ground so I could get down on my knees. Then I took the tip of his dick into my mouth and suckled on it. He moaned as his salty precum drizzled out onto my tongue. I took the head out of my mouth and ran the tip of my tongue up and down the middle of his slit, which made him moan even louder.

I could make out the words "Oh shit!" as I fingered his balls and tickled the underside of his dick by placing loud, wet kisses on it.

I didn't feel like sucking his dick, I mean *really sucking it* because it was just too damn huge and I wasn't trying to develop lockjaw. After all, I was still trying to get into the concert.

After standing back up, I asked, "Did you like that?"

He nodded.

I pushed him hard up against the building so he couldn't move, turned around and pressed my pussy slowly onto his dick. He filled me up nicely. I started grinding on him and he seemed like he was gasping for breath. I wasn't taking the panties out his mouth though. I didn't feel like holding a conversation while we were fucking.

Next thing you know, the idiot was coming way too quickly. That wasn't good enough for me. I was determined not to allow him to go soft so I started giving him some hand action immediately. It worked like a charm. Before I knew it, his dick was standing at full attention again.

I didn't want to risk doing it in the same position again. He might've come fast again; even though second nuts are generally harder to bust. I pushed him down on the bare ground, not giving a shit whether his ass got dirty or not and climbed on top of him.

I started riding him and laughed when I saw someone pause at the end of the alley and try to make out what was going on. I moaned loudly to see if the person would be daring enough or nosy enough to venture down there. I was hoping it was a sexy-ass man who I could ride next. I could barely make out a shadow but whoever it was stood there for about thirty more seconds and kept on moving. Too bad!

When Campbell had worn out his usefulness, I retrieved my panties and freed his wrists.

"Damn, woman, that was the shit," he said, trying to regain his normal breathing pattern.

"It was okay. Thanks for the experience."

I started getting dressed while he did the same. The music was still thumping through the walls. Lil' Z was getting buck wild with his jam "Devastated" and since that was his biggest hit at the time, I knew closing time was nearing. So much for finding Darnetta and checking out the party. I'd just have to catch his videos on BET. Besides, I'd gotten what I'd ultimately come for anyway: dick.

"So when can I see you again?" Campbell asked.

Hmph, it never ended!

"See me again?" I asked incredulously. "How about never?"

I walked toward the street.

"Never?" Campbell hissed back at me. He grabbed my elbow and swung me around. "After what we just shared?"

"We shared a fuck. Nothing more. Nothing less."

"Damn, you're cold-blooded."

"Aw, is that supposed to hurt my feelings?" I yanked my arm free. "I said thank you. What else do you want?"

"I want to see you again. I think you're fine and you're definitely sexy. I'd like to see what you could do if we had an all-day fuckathon. So how about it?"

"I can't. I don't want to," I said nastily. He was getting on my nerves. They always did afterward. It was so much easier when I wouldn't let them say anything at all. I might have to rethink my strategy and revert to my old ways.

"Why not?" Campbell wanted to know.

"I don't have to explain myself to you." I laughed in his face and started for my car. "I felt like doing it, you looked enticing at the moment, you served your purpose, and now it's over. Get a life!"

Campbell stopped in his tracks and yelled out, "Bitch!"

I turned and leered at him. "I'm not your bitch. If I were you, I'd just walk away before you make me angry. Trust me. You won't like me when I'm angry."

He must have taken my threat to heart because he started speed-walking in the opposite direction. Good for him because I was serious as shit about it. I took no drama from anyone. Not even Jon, and if she really started tripping, she would have to find that out the hard way.

jonquinette

It happened again. I woke up the next morning on my sofa with my black suit on. My hair was curled and I didn't have on a bra. Plus, I was hurting down there. I was terrified. *Was I insane?*

I ran into the bathroom. The curling iron was on the vanity and the pajamas I'd put on the night before were cut into shreds and stuffed into the wastebasket. I didn't know what was wrong with me.

I jumped into the shower and noticed a foreign smell on my body. Someone else's scent. A man's scent. A different man's scent from the last time and the time before that and the time before that.

I wanted to make the eight o'clock service at church but barely got there before the sermon at the eleven o'clock one. Reverend Townsend preached from his soul. I was always moved by his words. The newest member of the deacon board kept staring at me, making me nervous. He was attractive and appeared to be in his early thirties. I couldn't have handled it if he'd actually said something to me. I didn't want to take the chance that he might approach me after the service, so I stayed long enough to tithe and then left before the recessional.

3

Jonquinette sat on the playground, wishing she was anyplace else but there. Every day her mother dropped her off at school, she dreaded walking up the front steps and through the large metal doors. She loved her teachers and desired to gain knowledge but the way the children bullied her was depressing to a seven-year-old girl.

The teasing never stopped, nor did the names. Retard. Fatty. Ugmo. Jonquinette's self-esteem was nonexistent, having long been destroyed by many students; one in particular. Her name was Brenda Morrison and all the kids adored her or at least pretended to adore her. There was nothing really special about her. She just carried herself and talked about herself like she was unique to the point where all the students started to believe her.

This particular day, Jonquinette was sitting on a bench while all the other second graders enjoyed their recess time after lunch. She was staring at the sky and daydreaming, hoping that a bird would come whisk her away and drop her in a better place. She hated the outfit she had on: a pair of pink capris and a top that had way too many colors in the pattern. She preferred darker colors to match her mood: depressed.

Her mother had spent hours the night before cornrowing her hair for the school week ahead. On Mondays, everyone was always overactive after spending the weekend at parks and playing sports. Jonquinette always kept to herself on weekends. She didn't know how to make friends and since no one ever invited her anywhere, she would just sit on the front porch and watch cars drive by at rare intervals.

Jonquinette couldn't wait until the school day was over. Just three more hours and she could escape. She was lost in her own little world when Brenda marched up to her with three other little girls in tow.

"What are you doing, Fatty?" Brenda hissed at her. "Where's my money?"

Jonquinette shrugged. Every single day Brenda would demand that she give her a quarter. Most days she would manage to sneak into her parents' bedroom and grab a quarter off her father's valet tray. However, it had been an impossible task that morning.

Brenda leaned down and punched her on the arm. "You heard me, Retard. Where's my quarter?"

Jonquinette lowered her eyes to the ground. "I don't have it."

"Excuse me?" Brenda asked angrily. "Did you just say you don't have my money?"

One of the other little girls, Francine, said, "That's what she said, Brenda. You gonna beat her up?"

Brenda glanced around the playground to make sure all the

teachers were occupied, trying to make sure no one was falling off equipment or butting in line at the slide. She turned back to Jonquinette and glared down at her. "No, I'm not gonna beat her up. Not today. I'm just gonna slap her."

Before Jonquinette could block it, Brenda's hand smashed against her left cheek, causing an incredible pain to shoot through her entire body.

All the little girls started laughing and doubling over to hold their stomachs. All except Brenda, who issued a warning. "Tomorrow you better have my money. Two quarters instead of one or I'm gonna beat you up for real."

Jonquinette broke out in tears. How could someone be so cruel? She never bothered any of them and yet they continued to torment her day after day. She turned her eyes back up to the sky, waiting on that magical bird to come swoop her up.

Two minutes later, the tears were gone and anger replaced the sad expression on Jonquinette's face. Jude had had enough.

Brenda and two of her groupies were in the little girls' room cheesing in the mirrors and talking about going to the county carnival that weekend. They didn't even glance at the door when Jude came in. Their mistake.

Jude slipped into a stall and closed the door, not bothering to lock it. She wouldn't be in there but a few seconds. When she came back out, she had the ceramic toilet top in her hands, clutching it like a paddle. By the time they saw Jude bring it up over her head, it was too late. She was already swinging. She nailed Francine right across the stomach first. She screamed and fell down on her knees. Then she went for Rhonda, another student who constantly had Brenda's back. Rhonda tried to duck but Jude stepped on her foot, causing her to stand back up partially to lift her foot and grab her toes. That's when Jude got her across the right shoulder. Rhonda fell to the tile floor but was in too much pain to even voice a scream.

Brenda just stood there at first, wondering if she could make it to the door safely without getting a major beatdown. It was obvious that she couldn't so she resorted to intimidation. "Fatty, you know you're not gonna touch me with that. That would mean I'd have to beat you up every day for the rest of the school year."

Jude let out this horrendous laugh. "You must think you're talking to Jonquinette."

Brenda eyed her with confusion.

"Sorry, Jonquinette's not here right now."

Brenda asked, "What are you talking about?"

"I have a message for you," Jude responded. "Don't ever talk to or touch Jonquinette again or you'll have to deal with me."

With that, Jude slammed the ceramic top across Brenda's head and three teeth popped out of her mouth on impact. She hit her three more times with it: once more across the face, once in the ribs and once on the knee. Brenda lay motionless and Jude was satisfied. She looked in the mirror. While Jonquinette could stand to lose some weight, there were numerous kids her size or larger in second grade.

She stared at her reflection. "Don't worry. I'm here to protect you."

Jonquinette didn't know what was happening. All she knew was that the physical education teacher, Mr. Turner, was restraining her for some reason. They were loading Brenda, Francine, and Rhonda into ambulances in front of the school. There were police cars in front of the building and everyone was glaring at her and shaking their heads.

She saw her parents pull up in their Volvo station wagon and practically jump the curb coming to a halt. The look on their faces as they emerged from the vehicle was frightening.

Jonquinette fell down on her knees and cried.

"What did I do?" she screamed out as her mother approached her with outstretched arms. "I didn't do anything!"

4

July 1987
Summer Vacation

Jonquinette came flying out the front door of her house; excited that the weather was so nice. She'd had her share of cartoons for the morning and craved s   fresh air. Her parents had offered to send her to summer camp t   he couldn't imagine dealing with the same nasty kids during summer vacation that she had to deal with during the school year.

It was sunny but not too hot. She had lost her favorite ball underneath the porch the day before and got down on her knees to see if she could locate it. She spotted it about four feet under the steps and went to find a large enough stick to retrieve it.

After much effort, Jonquinette managed to get the ball out and was elated. She started bouncing it up and down and fell in love with the pastel colors of it all over again. She accidentally bounced it too high and it went over the neighbor's picket fence.

Jonquinette panicked. Mrs. Greer wasn't always the nicest person in the world. Besides, Shadow, her poodle, tended to bark a lot and even though he seemed harmless, Jonquinette wasn't sure whether he was a biter or not.

She didn't see anyone peeking out the windows and Shadow was nowhere in sight so she decided to chance hopping over the fence to get the ball and hopping right back over.

Jonquinette had got it and was climbing back over when Mrs. Greer yanked her front door open and started screaming, "You little wench! What are you doing on my yard?"

Jonquinette hung there with both feet straddling the fence but neither touching the ground. "I'm sorry, Mrs. Greer. I was just getting my ball."

Mrs. Greer came catapulting down the steps. "You have no business in my yard. Not to get a ball or anything else. My yard is my pride and joy. Mr. Greer, God rest his soul, spent his entire life making sure this yard was beautifully kept and I will not have little brats destructing my property."

Jonquinette was at a loss for words as she dismounted the fence. She went to sit on the front steps, lowered her face into her lap, and cried. Mrs. Greer went back into her house and slammed the door.

Jude was sitting on the stoop playing jacks when Mrs. Greer came back out of the house with her pocketbook in one hand and Shadow's leash in the other. She paused halfway down her walkway and leered at Jude. Jude leered right back at her.

"When your parents get home, I want to have a word with them," Mrs. Greer lashed out at Jude. "I'm not going to have any more of your mess."

Jude didn't say a word. Just hissed between her lips as she watched Shadow take a dump on the front yard; the so-called "beautifully kept" front yard.

"Why is it that I can't get a ball off your yard but that little runt can take dumps all over it? Huh, bitch? Why is that?"

Mrs. Greer was shocked and at a loss for something to say for a moment. "Just wait till your parents get home!"

Jude smirked and stuck out her tongue.

After Mrs. Greer and the mutt loaded into her Impala and drove away, Jude grew angrier by the second. "Why do you take crap off people, Jon? That bitch ain't shit!"

In the middle of the night, Mrs. Greer's scream could be heard two blocks away. Jude lay in bed grinning while Mr. and Mrs. Pierce turned on all the lights in the house as a bang came at the door. Fifteen minutes later, they came into the bedroom where Jude still lay amused and sat down on opposite sides of the bed. Jude didn't want to be bothered with the bullshit so she let Jon take back over.

Jon was stunned to see both her parents sitting on her bed. "What's wrong? What happened?"

"Jonquinette, someone poisoned Mrs. Greer's dog, Shadow," her daddy said. "Do you know anything about that?"

"Shadow? No, I don't know anything about it."

Her parents both eyed her suspiciously.

"Are you sure?" her father quizzed again.

"I'm sure. Why would someone do something like that, anyway?"

Her mother said, "Mrs. Greer said you two had an altercation earlier today. Something about you climbing over her fence to get a ball."

"Yes, I did get my ball and she did yell at me but that was it."

"She said you yelled back at her later when she was on the way to the store."

"No, I didn't," Jonquinette said on the brink of tears. "I didn't see her at all after that."

Her parents eyed each other with confused expressions. Finally, her mother patted her on the hand. "Go back to sleep. Everything will be all right."

The next morning, Jonquinette headed back upstairs after breakfast to get dressed for the day. There wasn't much to do but she figured she could ride her bike around the block. She entered her room to find both her parents standing there. Her father had an empty can of rat poison in his hand. "I found this under your bed."

Jonquinette fell on the floor and cried. "I didn't do anything!"

5

Jonquinette sat in the bleachers, faking a muscle spasm as usual. She hated to participate in gym class. It was ironic because at home, she had become obsessed with physical fitness. All of the baby fat was long gone and she had an hourglass shape. Many of the boys that used to tease her in elementary school were now sweating her to go out with them. She was too nervous to even think about the prospect of dating.

Sheila Vale hated Jonquinette but no one truly understood why. Jonquinette kept to herself, tried to concentrate on her studies, and went directly home from school every single day.

Sheila came over to the bleachers, dressed in her gym uniform, and folded her arms over her chest. "So what's supposed to be wrong with you today?"

Jonquinette eyed her. "I have a muscle spasm."

"Again? You don't look like you have a damn thing wrong with you."

Jonquinette didn't respond. She waited for someone to come to her rescue and a few seconds later, someone did.

Mrs. Yates, their teacher, yelled toward them. "Sheila, what are you doing? Leave Jonquinette alone. She's not feeling well."

Sheila smacked her lips and walked off.

After class ended, Jonquinette was in the locker room organizing her locker when she heard several people approach her from behind. She turned to find Sheila and a few of her flunkies staring at her.

Sheila stepped forward. "I don't believe there's a damn thing wrong with you. Take off your clothes."

"Take off my clothes?" Jonquinette asked in disbelief.

"Yes, take them off or I'll take them off for you."

Everyone had gathered around laughing. Not one single girl seemed to be on Jonquinette's side. She looked toward Mrs. Yates' office but she wasn't in there.

"I'm not taking off my clothes, Sheila." Jonquinette slammed her locker, grabbed her bookbag, and tried to get past the group. "Excuse me."

Sheila grabbed her arm. "Maybe you didn't hear me good enough. I said take your clothes off."

Jonquinette started breathing heavily. She saw no way to escape. She blinked twice and then *Jude* glared at Sheila before speaking in a threatening tone. "If you don't get out of my way, I will break every bone in your body. You don't want to fuck with me. Just ask Brenda Morrison."

Fear came over Sheila's face. Everyone had heard about what Jonquinette had done in second grade and many of them had attended the same school. Brenda and the other two girls had never returned to school, but Jonquinette had returned after a week's suspension.

Jude continued, "Now, are you going to move out my way or do I need to start putting foot to ass."

"Damn!" one girl yelled out. "Check out Jonquinette breaking bad."

A roar of laughter engulfed the room. Mrs. Yates came in and said, "Break it up! Next period starts in five minutes!"

The next day, Jude asked for a bathroom pass during her second period calculus class. Instead of going to the bathroom, she headed to the girls' locker room and retrieved the three bottles of hair remover she had placed there earlier that morning.

By the time gym class started, fourth period, the dirt had already been done. It was a particularly sweaty period because Mrs. Yates had them run around the indoor track for an entire thirty minutes. Because one girl misbehaved, they were all being punished.

Jude fell right in with the rest of them, shocking just about everyone there. Not only did she run; she outran all of them for the entire thirty minutes. Jude wanted to show the world their bomb-ass body.

After the thirty minutes were up, Mrs. Yates told them to hit the showers and that's when Jude started acting like Jon again. She went into a stall to change and skipped the shower. For good reason.

"Oh my God!" was the first thing she heard someone yell out. "What happened to your hair?"

Then there was just a bunch of screaming as Jude strolled out of the locker room, laughing her ass off.

•   •   •

Jonquinette found the three empty bottles in her locker the following day. Most of the females in her gym class were no-shows that day. They were all at home wondering what they could do about their baldness. Jonquinette held the bottles in her hands, sat down on the bench, and started crying.

6

After discussing it with her husband, Jason, Zoe had made up her mind to help the young woman who always seemed withdrawn. As always, she showed up for the meeting, lurked in the back of the room, and tried to sneak out without being noticed. This time, Zoe followed her.

She caught up to her in the parking lot, climbing into a late model Honda. "Excuse me? Young lady?" Zoe called out to her.

She stared at Zoe uneasily. "Yes?"

"I was just wondering if you needed anything."

"Anything like what?"

Zoe walked closer to her, proceeding with caution. She didn't want to scare her off by overstepping her boundaries. "It's just that I notice you here every week, but you never say anything."

The woman's eyes dropped to the ground. "Maybe I don't have anything to say."

Zoe forced a smile. "Oh, I don't think that's true at all. You wouldn't come to the meetings if something wasn't bothering you. This is Hotlanta, after all. I wouldn't exactly call a sexual addiction meeting someplace to hang out and enjoy the scenery."

The woman didn't respond or look back up.

"I just wanted you to know that if you ever need someone to talk to, in private, I'm available. Trust me, there's nothing you could tell me that I wouldn't understand. If you knew what I've been through, you would realize that things can always get worse."

The woman fumbled with her keys, hesitating between climbing all the way into the car or standing there. Finally, she said, "What makes you think what you've been through is worse than what I've been through?"

Zoe frowned. That was a good point. As horrid as her life had been, she had no clue what this beautiful young woman had endured in her short life. "You're right. That just tells me that maybe I'm not the one you should be talking to. But, I do have another suggestion."

"What's that?"

Zoe walked all the way up to her and reached into her jacket pocket to retrieve a business card. She handed it to the young woman. "Call her. She's the one who helped me and I'm sure she can help you also. If it weren't for her, I wouldn't be alive today, much less attending these meetings."

The woman eyed Zoe suspiciously before reading the card. "She's really all that, huh?"

"Yes, she is. Just give her a chance. You won't regret it."

"Thank you."

"You're welcome."

No more words were spoken between them. Zoe walked back inside, hearing the woman start the ignition of her Honda and pull off.

7

---

jonquinette

       I sat at my desk staring at the card. Dr. Marcella Spencer, a psychiatrist. Was I ready for that? There had been so many years of questioning. So many blackouts. So much pain.

Darnetta poked her head into my office. "What's up, girl? Can I come in?"

I put the card under my desk pad out of her view. "Sure, I have a moment."

"How's business?" Darnetta asked as she sat down opposite me at the desk.

"Better."

"Thank goodness, because Boss Man has been walking around here beet-red like he might croak any second."

I laughed. "He'll survive. All businesses have slow periods but things are picking up."

Darnetta worked in Accounts Receivable and was very good at collections. I often wondered if people just agreed to pay us so they wouldn't have to listen to her squeaky voice over the phone anymore.

"Well, I'm glad we're shipping more product because he's really been on those of us over in my department about closing out past due invoices. You would've thought his house was about to go into foreclosure or something."

"Trust me when I say that Mr. Wilson has no problem paying his bills. It's his staff members that have to pinch pennies."

"Speaking of which, have you heard anything about raise reviews coming up?"

"No, he'll probably pull that old 'We'll show our appreciation with Christmas bonuses' routine."

Darnetta said, "He's such a joy."

We both laughed.

"So, Jon, you remember what you told me?"

"About what?"

"The next time I ask you to go someplace."

I sighed deeply, not wanting to imagine what would come out of her mouth next. "Yes, I remember."

"Good, because Logan's in a wedding next weekend and I refuse to sit in the pews alone while he stands up for one of his immature, silly little friends. I need someone to keep me company. So how about it?"

She knew she had me. I'd already made a promise. "What time and where?"

Darnetta snickered with delight. "The wedding is Saturday at four, downtown, and I'll pick you up at three. Cool?"

"Sounds like a winner," I lied.

"Great!" Darnetta jumped up and headed for the door. "Well, I'm about to go enjoy what's left of my lunch hour. I can't believe in this day and time we still have to punch time clocks. That is so primal."

I couldn't help but agree. "I know. It doesn't make sense, but Mr. Wilson is old-fashioned in many ways."

"No, he's just plain old. What is he? About a hundred ninety?"

I chuckled. "You better watch yourself. I wouldn't put hidden cameras in the walls past him."

Darnetta eyed the walls, taking me seriously.

"You can relax. He's too cheap to invest in them."

"Whew, you had me going for a second. Catch you later."

"Later."

After she was safely down the hall, I closed my office door, went back to my desk, and retrieved the card from under the desk pad. "Dr. Marcella Spencer, can you really help me?"

I picked up the phone and called to make an appointment.

When I got home, I noticed a U-Haul truck in the parking lot of the complex and wondered if the vacant apartment below me had finally been rented out. There were some college kids living there but they'd broken the lease and moved to the Georgia Tech campus. Thank goodness, because their loud rock music was raking on my nerves.

I was on the second floor landing, not paying attention to where I was going because I was searching through my purse for some Tylenol to take the second I could grab a cup of water to wash it down, when I bumped right into the backend of a floor model television. I stubbed my toe, the same one I'm always prone to banging against something, and yelled out in pain.

A man appeared in the doorway of 2-D. "Oh, no, I'm so sorry. I didn't mean to have this thing out in the hallway so long."

I just stared at him. I tried to say something but I'm not even sure I was actually breathing. He was . . . He was . . .

"Excuse me, Miss. Are you all right?" he asked.

"Yes, I'm fine," I finally managed to say. "I just hit my toe."

"Well, toes can be the source of much pain," he said jokingly.

I forced a smile. "True."

I walked around the television and headed for the stairs leading to the third floor, my floor.

"I'm Mason. Mason Copeland."

"Moving in?"

"Yes. I just decided to check out Atlanta for a while. I'm originally from D.C.——the Chocolate City."

"That's cool. I used to live in Philadelphia when I first graduated from college." I don't know why I asked the next question but I did. "Is your wife home? I'd like to meet her."

"Wife? No, I'm single." He grinned at me and added, "Single and extremely available and accessible."

I cleared my throat. "Well, with all the female singles around here, you won't be for long."

"Are you one of the female singles around here?"

I couldn't prevent the blush. "Um, yeah. I guess so."

"Name?"

"Jonquinette Pierce."

"Jonquinette Pierce. Beautiful name for a beautiful lady."

Another blush. "Thanks, but I really have to go."

I started up the steps.

"Jonquinette?"

I turned and saw his head over the railing.

"Yes?"

"Maybe you can help me get settled in. Aren't neighbors supposed to greet newbies with a pound cake, or a pecan pie, or something?"

I giggled. "I'm not a baker. I can't even make toast without burning it."

He frowned and then laughed. "There's always store-bought."

"Now that's a thought."

I hurried the rest of the way to my apartment. My headache really was tormenting me and I just wanted to take something for it and lie down.

jude

Mason Copeland, huh? I didn't even think so. I just knew that Jon would haul ass the way she always did whenever a man said something to her. How dare she actually flirt with him? I wouldn't have that nonsense. No way.

Granted, the man looked good. Damn good. If I saw a brotha with honey-almond skin, hazel eyes, and dreads, someplace inconspicuous, it would definitely be on. But this Mason, hunk or not, lived right below us and that shit was out of the question. No serious relationships. Just sex and I was the only one entitled to that. Jon was really tripping lately. First calling up that shrink bitch's office. Now she was holding actual conversations with men. Something had to be done. Something would be done. I'd worked too hard for control and I'd do whatever it took to keep things just the way they were.

8

jonquinette

I circled the office building five times in my car, debating about keeping my appointment. I yearned to let go of all the emotions that were balled up inside of me, but talking to a complete stranger about my problems didn't sit quite right with me. No matter what accolades Dr. Marcella Spencer had received, I didn't know her from a hole in the wall and I had a serious enough problem talking to people I actually knew.

I finally parked and got up enough nerve to get out of the car and walk into the building. I caught the elevator up to her floor and located the correct office. There were two other people waiting in front of me. Great. I'd have to sit there and let the anticipation build.

I gave my name to the secretary and she gave me some forms to fill out. That took all of five minutes, leaving me with what turned out to be only a short wait because the two people were waiting on a third to come out of the inner office. He was the "authentic patient" and I stared at him while he exited, wondering how a person that appeared so normal could need a psychiatrist.

Five minutes later, I found myself sitting across an expensive desk from a strikingly beautiful woman. My first thought was why would she go into her chosen profession when she could have been a high-end fashion model or something.

"Jonquinette. Lovely name."

"Thank you."

"What brings you to see me today?"

That was one hell of a good question.

"Dr. Spencer, what's the definition of insanity?" I asked her, unable to meet her eyes with my own. "I know what I've heard."

"What have you heard?"

"That insanity is doing the same thing over and over again expecting a different result."

"Do you believe that?"

"No, not really. I believe that's just something a self-proclaimed prophet made up to sugarcoat the term."

She giggled. "Interesting thought."

I waited for her to get her laugh out and then dropped the bomb.

"I think I'm insane. I think I've been insane for a very long time."

As suspected, Dr. Spencer stopped smiling. "What makes you say that?"

"Strange things. Things I can't remember."

"I'm not following you."

I knew discussing matters would be tremendously complicated but I was shaking like a leaf. I was scared, but the thought of walking out of her office and facing my life the way it had been for the past fifteen years was even worse.

"Nasty, vile things written in my handwriting that I don't remember writing. People accusing me of things I don't recall doing. I mean, all of them can't be mistaken. Right?"

"All of them?" she asked.

"My daddy. People I went to school with. Everyone who's ever accused me of something."

"Could you please elaborate?"

I got up from the chair and started pacing the floor. "I'm sorry. I know this must make zero sense. It doesn't even make sense to me and I'm right in the middle of it."

"Right in the middle of what?"

I smirked. "Hell. Right smack dab in the middle of hell."

"When did people start accusing you of things?"

"Second grade."

"Second grade?"

I sat back down and folded my hands on my lap, trying to prevent them from shaking.

"Yes. It was the day someone beat up Brenda Morrison and two other girls in the bathroom. Brenda had two black eyes, three broken ribs, and a smashed knee. I'll never forget the way she looked when they took her away in the ambulance."

"And they said you did that to them?"

"Yes, but it doesn't make sense. I was terrified of Brenda. She was the biggest bully in the entire school."

"Why do you think they accused you?"

I shrugged my shoulders. "Brenda said I did it. So did the others. She said it was me, but it couldn't have been. They said I followed them into the bathroom from the playground but I don't even remember half of recess that day."

"There were more instances after that one?"

"Several."

"Please tell me about them, Jonquinette. If it isn't too painful."

"It's painful, but that's why I came here." I finally looked Dr. Spencer in the eyes. "There was Mrs. Greer's dog."

"Mrs. Greer?"

"Our next-door neighbor when we lived in Florida. She was the nicest old lady and I swear I'd never do anything to hurt her. I'd never do that. Not ever."

"But someone did?"

"She said I was on the porch complaining about Shadow, her poodle, barking. I never did that. I loved Shadow."

"Whom did she tell that to?"

"My parents. She came over after . . . After . . ." I hesitated.

"After what?"

"After someone poisoned Shadow. It wasn't me. I wouldn't even know where to get any rat poison but—"

"But?"

I lowered my eyes. "My daddy found an empty can under my bed."

"And Shadow was poisoned to death?"

"Yes. Poor thing."

"And the next incident?"

"Seventh grade. Someone put hair remover in the shampoo bottles in the girls' locker room."

"They said you did it?"

"No, no one said I did it that time."

"Then what makes you think you had something to do with it?"

"Three empty bottles of hair remover in my locker."

"Oh, I see."

"It just went on and on until—"

"Until what?"

"Until the really bad things started to happen."

"What sorts of things?"

The tears started falling before I felt them coming.

"I can't do this." I wiped my tears with my bare hand. "I'm sorry but I just can't."

Dr. Spencer got up, walked around the desk, and started caressing my shoulders.

"Jonquinette, please continue. I can't help you unless you confide in me."

"I didn't really come here to discuss my childhood," I whispered.

"Then what did you come here to discuss?"

"The things that are happening to me now."

"Like?"

I was so ashamed, but it had to come out. "The reason I think I'm insane is because I wake up sometimes and I'm wearing clothes I've never seen; my hair is curled instead of up; my glasses are tossed someplace; a couple of times they were even broken. And then there's the other stuff."

"What other stuff?"

I clamped my eyes shut. I'd never felt so degraded. "Dr. Spencer, sometimes there are strange smells on my body, on my breath, all over me. Sometimes there's sticky stuff between my legs and—"

Dr. Spencer sat down on the corner of her desk, facing me, and lifted my chin with her hand so I'd look at her. "Jonquinette, are you telling me that you have sex with men and don't remember it?"

"That's the really crazy part, Dr. Spencer."

"Please, call me Marcella."

"Marcella, I've never been with a man. I've never had sex but—"

"But?"

"Somehow I managed to break my hymen and even contract one venereal disease."

"How do you know that?"

"An OB/GYN told me. My freshman year in college something happened to me. I had gone to the library one day to study and I somehow blacked out. Afterward I went to the campus clinic because I was sore down there and I didn't know why."

"And this has been happening ever since then?"

"Yes, it has."

Admitting it caused an instant breakdown. I grabbed hold of Marcella's arm and began to cry. I buried my head into her chest; She wrapped her other arm around me.

"I'm so afraid," I whimpered. "What's wrong with me? Am I really insane?"

"No, I don't think you're insane," she said reassuringly. "If you were insane, you wouldn't have sought me out to help you. And I will help you, Jonquinette. I promise you that."

9

jude

Jon had lost her fucking mind. I couldn't believe she went up there and told that bitch all of our fucking business. She was going to have to pay for that. And promising that doctor chick that she'd let her continue to help? Not as long as there was one breath left in my body.

To top things off, Jon had the nerve to leave there and go to the grocery store. She knew how much I hated the grocery store. Nothing but a bunch of bratty-ass kids begging their parents for candy, sugar-infested juices, or salty foods.

When I took over, we were walking down the pasta aisle. Of course, there was a hard-headed chap blocking the way. I jerked my cart toward him but he didn't budge. Just glared at me and rolled his eyes. His mother was picking out a box of elbow macaroni.

"Ahem, could you tell your kid to move the hell out my way," I lashed out at her.

She snickered like she couldn't believe I'd actually said that.

"Are you going to move him or should I just knock his ass over with my cart?"

She grabbed her son by the shoulders and pulled him aside. "Move over here, David." She leered at me. "You don't have to be so rude, miss. He's just a child."

I picked up the nearest jar of spaghetti sauce and smashed it on the floor. I leaned down and picked up the lid. There was shattered glass attached to it. I held it up and she hauled ass with her kid in tow. I laughed. That's what she gets, fucking with me.

I smashed a few more jars to get rid of some of the anger Jon had stirred up in me by telling our business. By the time I turned the corner, one of the store managers was rushing to see about the noise.

"You need a cleanup on aisle five," I told him. "Some bratty kid was pitching a fit and his mother allowed him to have a tantrum. If I were you, I'd make them pay for it. It makes no sense."

He shook his head in dismay. "I don't know what's wrong with kids these days."

"Me either. If you hurry, you might be able to catch them up by the registers. She has on this horrid pastel dress and he has on a Teletubbies tee."

"Thank you, miss," he said before taking off for the bank of cash registers.

I smirked. I knew that heifer and her brat were long gone if they had any sense.

I decided to peruse the meat cases since I was already there. It had been ages since Jon had fixed a decent meal. I didn't understand why she didn't like eating out. We made enough money to eat out at least three nights a week, but she was on this cooking-healthy-meals kick. I was so sick of chicken that I didn't know what to do.

I thought back to all the shit Jon had told that doctor. She made it seem like I was a bad person. Like I was in the wrong all those times. Didn't Jon realize that I did all that to protect her? That Brenda Morrison chick in second grade had issues. Always teasing Jon about her clothes and hair. Always glaring down her little aquiline nose at us. That day on the playground, she went too far. She called Jon a fat pig, demanding more money, and I wasn't having that. So yes, I kicked the little slut's ass. Beat the shit out of her and her friends. They deserved it.

Now I will admit that I felt a little bad about poisoning Shadow. He was a cute little poodle, but I had to do it. Mrs. Greer hollered at Jon for no reason about running on her yard to get a ball. I mean, get real. Shadow could take his little dumps all over her yard at will, but Jon couldn't get her ball back? So yes, I told her to make that dog stop barking while I was sitting on the porch. His barking wasn't bothering me that much, but I was trying to play jacks in peace. I really just wanted to get into it with Mrs. Greer after what she had done to Jon. She took it a little too far, though. Talked a little bit too much trash. Sorry, Shadow, wherever you are, but the bitch had to pay.

As for those sluts in seventh grade, they're lucky all they ended up with were bald heads. I started to buy everyone pizza and sprinkle rat poison all over it. The shit had worked so well on Shadow that I knew it would do them all in. But there was a problem. They all hated Jon and she never uttered a word to them. Just cringed up in fear every time they looked in her direction, changed in the stall instead of in front of them, and sat in the bleachers during gym class. I never understood that shit. Jon would take a failing grade instead of participating. Personally, I know for a fact that we could've showed all their asses up. By that time, Jon had started working the hell out of the treadmill we had in the basement at home and drinking water by the gallon. All the baby fat was gone and we were in awesome shape, even back then.

What really pissed me off was Jon talking about my sex life. Something she didn't know jack shit about. Thank goodness she didn't, because I didn't want that doctor bitch knowing how I liked to get my freak on. As far as I was concerned, it was my pussy, not Jon's. I'd do what I wanted with it, when I wanted, and no one was going to stop me.

I was highly disappointed with the selection of steaks. Half of them looked brown or were laden with fat. Someone really needed to report that grocery store. Every time we went in there, the meat looked less than kosher. Even some of the chicken Jon purchased reeked with salmonella.

I picked up a porterhouse steak and started sniffing the package. I didn't want to get home, rip off the plastic, and fall out from the stench.

"Is there something wrong with the meat?"

I glanced to my left and saw this fine specimen of a brotha standing there in a blood-covered apron and paper hat. He was tall with sepia skin and dark eyes.

"Yes, the hell there is something wrong with the meat."

The smile on his face dissolved and he crossed his arms in front of him like I'd just personally insulted him.

"What's wrong with it?"

I tossed the package back into the case and put my hands on my hips. Nobody out attitudes me.

"Every single time I come up in here, the meat looks foul." I pointed a few feet down to the chicken. "Especially the chicken. What's up with all the yellow? Granted, I don't work for the FDA or anything, but damn."

He broke out into laughter. That sort of turned me on.

"I apologize for the quality of the meat, and between me and you, I've been waiting for someone to come in here and tell it like it is." He leaned in closer to me and even though he'd obviously been butchering meat all day, I could still pick up on the faint scent of his cologne. "I keep telling the manager that some of this meat is bad, but he continues to sell it anyway."

I grinned at him. "Well, maybe I'll blow the whistle on them and call one of those investigative television shows or something."

"Maybe you should."

We both laughed. I started squeezing his upper arm because I wanted to know what he was hiding underneath that tacky uniform.

"I wouldn't want to cause you to lose your job, though," I said sarcastically. "What on earth would you do then?"

"I have other talents."

"I bet you do." I eyed him seductively. "Can I see where you butcher your meat?"

"Huh?"

"I said, can I see where you butcher your meat?"

"Umm, we're not supposed to have customers back there."

"So, you'd risk losing your job over bad meat, but you won't risk it over me?" I stuck my bottom lip out. "I'm hurt."

"Aw, don't be that way." He licked his lips and started looking around to see if the coast was clear before taking my hand and leading me to a set of double doors. "I guess it wouldn't harm anything for you to take a look."

We were in the meat locker and just like it appeared in movies, it was cold up in there.

"It's cold as shit!" I exclaimed.

He laughed. "By the way, I'm Lewis."

"So it says on your name tag."

"Since you don't have a name tag, how about telling me yours?"

"You can call me whatever you like, but I'd rather not talk at all." I grabbed him by the back of his neck and slipped my tongue into his mouth briefly. "So what are your other talents?"

"Huh?"

"You said out there that you have other talents." I decided it was high time to see what he was holding, so I grabbed his dick. "Nice. Very nice."

"Thank you." He started palming my tits. "These are nice, too."

"Want to suck them?"

He looked at the door to the freezer. The coast was still clear.

"I might lose my job behind this. You better make this good."

I laughed. "I make everything good, baby."

Jon had on this tired-ass, homely dress, but it was easy to get out of and before long, I was nude and holding on to a vacant meat hook with my hands, surrounded by sides of beef.

Lewis was on his knees with my legs wrapped around his shoulders and his tongue was exploring my pussy.

It felt exhilarating. I threw my head back, closed my eyes, and whispered, "You see, Jon. I run this. This is my party."

Lewis stopped going down on me. "Who the fuck is Jon? I'm Lewis."

I dug my fingernails down into his hair and pushed his head back into my pussy. "Shut the hell up and eat!"

10

---

jonquinette

What a boring week at work. While I enjoyed peace and quiet, it was even a little too much for me. I couldn't wait until my appointment with Dr. Spencer on Monday. Hopefully, this time I could bring myself to tell her more about what had happened to me. It was hard to believe that I was willing to open up like that, but I didn't see any other choice.

I hadn't had any weird smells on me that week. Male smells. But something strange did happen that morning. I was sleeping late since it was Saturday and my phone rang. I grabbed it because I assumed it was Momma. I knew that she was due back late the night before and I was right in my assumption.

"Jonquinette, baby!" she squealed into the phone. "I'm back! Did you miss me?"

"Of course I missed you, Momma."

I really did miss her, too. Even though Momma and I didn't

see each other all the time when she was in Atlanta, it was a source of comfort to know that she was right across town whenever I needed her. Unlike Daddy.

"Did you enjoy Europe?"

"That's the understatement of the century, baby. I had the time of my life."

"That's great, Momma. You deserved it."

"So what have you been doing with yourself? I hope you aren't still cooped up in that apartment every weekend. Life's too short for that."

"I get out and hang with some of my friends whenever I get the chance," I lied. "Most of the time, I bring work home with me and end up buried in that for hours."

"They don't pay you enough to bring your work home, Jonquinette. I still don't know why you wanted to become an accountant. You could've been anything you wanted to be."

"I wanted to be an accountant, Momma, and I'm very satisfied with my job."

She sighed, voicing her disapproval that way. "Well, you're still young, so if you ever want to try another profession, it's never too late."

She had a lot of nerve. All she'd ever been was a housewife, and after she kicked Daddy out, she moved in one sugar daddy after another to cover her bills.

"I'm happy, Momma. Can't you just be happy for me?"

"Whatever you say."

There was a pregnant pause while we both gathered our thoughts.

"Jonquinette, how about dinner tomorrow?"

"I have to go to church."

"Church doesn't last all day. I'm talking tomorrow evening. Say about six at the Ram's Head Tavern over in Buckhead."

I really didn't want to go to dinner with Momma but knew I'd never hear the end of it if I didn't make her happy.

"Okay, Momma. I'll be there."

"Great." She giggled. "I could tell you were sleeping when I called so I'll let you go. See you tomorrow, and don't be late."

"I won't be."

She hung up. Momma had this thing about never saying good-bye. I think it was because her first childhood memory revolved around tragedy. She remembered kissing her grandparents good-bye one morning when they left for the mom-and-pop store they owned on the coast of Miami. They never came back. Two masked gunmen took their lives for a measly thirty-seven dollars. Momma's parents were janitors, but somehow she turned out to be extremely materialistic, along with her two sisters.

I stared up at the ceiling but I knew sleep wouldn't come easily for me again. After five minutes or so, I decided to see if the Saturday morning news was still on. I reached for the remote on my nightstand and hit the power button. After I propped my back up on a bank of pillows, I yawned and eyed the screen. I sat there for two hours, staring at it, wondering when, why, and how I'd written the words "You'll never win" on the television in red lipstick.

After I finally managed to move, I decided to just make the best of it. This wasn't the first time I'd seen something written by my hands that I never wrote. "You'll never win" made no sense to me. Who'll never win what?

I was wiping the words off with paper towels and glass cleaner when a knock came at the door. That irritated me because no one ever came to my door unless they were selling something.

I was stunned when I glanced through the peephole and Mason was standing there.

As soon as I opened the door, he winked at me. "Is this the

apartment of a female single? I hear there are a lot of them around here."

I fought to suppress a laugh. "Um, yeah. I'm a female single."

"Good. I thought I might have the wrong place for a second and I wouldn't want to get attacked by a jealous husband or boyfriend."

"Well, I don't have one of those either."

"My lucky day."

"So how do you like your new place?"

"It's okay." He held out his hands and presented me with an apple pie on a glass plate. "Since I waited around for a week for the welcoming committee to grace me with a pie and no one showed up, I figured I might as well break tradition and welcome myself."

Oh my goodness! Did he really expect me to bring him sweets?

"I apologize," I said sincerely. "If I'd known that you really anticipated me getting you something, I would have."

He chuckled. "I'm just kidding with you, Jonquinette. I'll be honest. I wanted to see you again and I haven't been able to catch you in the hallway so I decided to come up here groveling for attention instead."

I took the pie from him. "Thanks for the pie. Did you bake this?"

"Are you kidding? I can't even boil water."

"Now that I can do."

"You just can't make toast?" he asked jokingly.

"Right. I can't make toast."

He cleared his throat and ducked his head into my apartment. "Nice place."

"Thanks." I knew what he was hinting at, but wasn't sure I was ready to invite a man who wasn't there to fix something inside of my apartment. He didn't appear to have plans to leave until I did, so I said, "Would you like to come in?"

"Thanks. I thought you'd never ask."

I moved out of the way so he could enter and headed toward the kitchen. "Feel free to have a seat. I'll be right back."

I set the pie plate down on the counter and had to lean against it to catch my breath. My knees were wobbling and my hands were suddenly sweating. I ran them under cold water and lathered them with soap, splashing some of the water on my face. At that moment, I wished I'd taken the time to get properly dressed instead of staring at my television screen for so long.

I felt someone behind me and jerked around. Mason was standing there.

"I'm sorry. I didn't mean to startle you, Jonquinette."

"No, you didn't." I turned off the water and reached into the cabinet for a couple of saucers. "I was just going to cut the pie. It looks delicious. Would you like a piece?"

"Absolutely. That pie cost me about ten bucks."

We both laughed.

"I didn't want to get you one of those cheap pies from the grocery store so I went to a bona fide bakery."

The man was determined to make me blush. "I feel so special."

He took his index finger and moved a tress of hair out of my face. "You are special. I can see that already."

Things were going well up until that point. His hands on me. The way he was looking at me. I couldn't take it.

I stepped away from him. "Mason, I just remembered that I have to meet someone in a few minutes."

"Really? You just remembered that, huh?" he asked skeptically. He knew it was a fabrication.

"Yes, my friend. Um, Darnetta. She works with me and I promised her that I'd meet her today."

I did make a promise to Darnetta. Just not for that day.

He looked highly disappointed. "In that case, I guess I better leave."

"Would you like a piece of pie to take with you?"

"No thanks. I've suddenly lost my appetite."

I felt bad as I saw Mason out. I really did think he was nice and he even made me laugh. That was rare. But I couldn't be with him or any other man until I figured out what was going on with me. Hopefully, Dr. Spencer would get me the help that I needed. After all, she'd also made a promise.

11

jude

Meredith Williams Pierce aka Queen Bitch. There was no way I was going to allow Jon to go out to dinner with her. Not the way Jon had been acting lately. I couldn't believe she'd actually flirted with that Mason character the day before. For the second time, no less. If she hadn't kicked his ass out the apartment, I would have for damn sure.

I wasn't used to having to take over so much. I was content to surface when Jon needed protection and from time to time to get my sexual needs taken care of, but surfacing had become a matter of survival. Jon actually thought she could get rid of me. Never!

"Do you like this restaurant, baby?" Queenie asked me, taking a sip of her Pink Pony. "Darryl and I used to come here a lot."

"Who?" I knew who the hell she was talking about. I just felt like starting trouble.

"You remember Darryl."

I took a sip of my lemonade. "Oh, him," I said with contempt. "Wasn't he the one you were doing after Frank and before Brent?"

"Doing?"

"You know what I mean, Momma. Wasn't he the one you were *fucking* between the other two men you were *fucking*?"

She almost choked on her cocktail. "Jonquinette, I don't know what's gotten into you."

I laughed. "The better question is what hasn't gotten into *you*. Or who, to utilize a better term."

"How dare you talk to me like that? I'm your mother." She glanced down at the porterhouse steak on my plate. "When did you start eating red meat again? I thought you were on some health kick."

I was truly enjoying this shit. Fucking with Meredith the Bitch's head was right up there with riding some bomb-ass dick.

"Don't you think you're a little over the hill to be whoring?" I asked her.

She slammed her glass down on the table and all but broke it.

"I don't know what the hell is wrong with you, young lady, but you will not disrespect me in such a fashion. I won't tolerate it."

"I won't tolerate it. I won't tolerate it," I repeated mockingly. "Who says you have a choice?"

She glared at me but I met her gaze with one that made her look away. She got up from the table.

"Jonquinette, I've been out of the country and I thought we should spend some time together catching up, but I don't know what comes over you when you start acting like this. Sometimes you act so evil. It's almost like there's two of you."

I smirked. What an interesting choice of words!

The Queen Bitch started gathering her purse and keys.

"Aw, leaving so soon?" I asked sarcastically. I couldn't wait for her to get the fuck out of my face.

"Jonquinette, maybe we can try this again next weekend when you're feeling better."

She stormed out of the restaurant, passing the waiter toting our tray of food on her way out. He watched her depart and asked, "Will the lady be returning?"

"She's not a lady. She's a whore," I lashed out at him. I waved my finger at the food. "Just wrap all that up and bring me the check."

"Whatever you like, madam."

He was walking away when I observed how tight his ass was. I eyed him up and down as he totaled up the bill over by the bar and came back to the table.

"Here's your check. I'll take it whenever you're ready."

I handed him a fifty. "Keep the change."

He grinned, realizing I'd just given him a healthy tip. "Thanks."

I grabbed his wrist and read his name tag. "By the way, Antoine, what time do you get off?"

He had told me that he was getting off at eight. I intended to get off my damn self by eight-thirty. I was going to kill some time by shopping but the stores closed early on Sunday; all except the personal favorites of people on budgets like Wal-Mart and Target. I went to Wal-Mart because they did have some great buys. Plus, I liked scrutinizing people. I was quite the observer. There were a few fine men in there but all of them were on lockdown with bitches and brats surrounding them. Wimps! They just didn't know what they were missing.

After purchasing some toiletries from the clearance aisle, I left Wal-Mart and headed back to the parking lot of the restaurant. I listened to the latest popular disc jockey on the radio and plotted my course of action in my mind.

When he came out the restaurant, dressed in tight jeans and a leather motorcycle jacket, my pussy was suddenly aflame. I turned off the battery power in my car and climbed out, following him to the side where he was about to mount a shiny red Yamaha Z6 motorcycle.

"Can a sista catch a ride?"

He came across as being shocked when he turned to find me standing there. Then he grinned. "Long time no see."

"Yeah, well, I asked you what time you got off for a reason."

"Look, I'm extremely flattered but I'm kind of seeing someone right now and I'm a brotha who tries to do the right thing."

I pounced on him and flicked the tip of my tongue in his ear. "She'll never know because I'll never tell."

He pushed me away slightly but I could tell he wanted some pussy. They all do.

"Um, maybe some other time. Not tonight."

I ran my fingers across his cheek. "Listen, I'm not trying to pressure you or anything. It's just that when you waited on me in the restaurant earlier, I had this incredible fantasy about you and the next thing I knew, I was experiencing this tremendous orgasm."

He blushed. I had his ass. "Really? What was your fantasy about?"

"Sucking your dick. Riding you. Letting you have your way with me." I leaned closer and whispered, "You look like such a powerful man. I can tell by the bike you ride that you must like powerful things. How about you let me show you some powerful pussy?"

"Powerful pussy?" He chuckled. "Can't say I've ever heard it called that."

"That's because you've probably never had any powerful pussy. I bet you're dealing with some chick that still has a little girl mentality. She more than likely just lays there and lets you tap that ass."

"No, she can do the damn thing when she wants to."

I was getting offended. No one refused to give me dick. No one! I rubbed his dick through his jeans and he grew hard instantly. "I don't want to fall in love. I don't even want you to know my name. Let's just take a little ride on your bike. It's such a beautiful night. I promise it will be fun."

He hesitated briefly and then said, "All right, why not?"

He gave me his spare helmet while he put his on. I climbed on the bike behind him and locked my arms around his waist. We pulled off into the night. I unzipped his pants and took his dick out, jacking him off as we rode. We almost crashed three times before ending up by a lake. It was gorgeous and I wondered why Jon's tired ass had never bothered to check it out before. He cut the engine on his bike and I got off, climbing back on immediately but straddling and facing him.

"You cold?" he asked me. "You can have my jacket if you want."

"No, actually I'm the opposite. I'm very, very hot!" I slid my tongue into his mouth and he reacted.

He reached up under the ugly-ass flower-patterned dress Jon had selected for church that day, slipped his fingers into the elastic of my panties, and started fingering my wetness.

"See how excited you have me?" I asked. "Now you know why I just had to wait for you to get off."

"I'm glad you did."

Just like I'd planned, by eight-thirty I was getting my shit off. I rode him right there on top of his bike and then we both got nude and did it again on the bank of the lake. He never asked my name. Good little puppy dog!

12

jonquinette

I woke up and found myself lying in the middle of my kitchen table. There was a carry out container with a half-eaten steak beside me and I could taste the meat in my mouth. I jumped up and ran to the bathroom to inspect my teeth. There were particles of steak embedded in them. I brushed quickly and thoroughly to rid myself of the aftertaste. What the hell had happened?

I went into my bedroom and discovered it was after ten. I was due into work by nine. I called but Mr. Wilson wasn't in his office so I left him a voice mail, telling him I was too sick to come in.

After hanging up, I immediately called Momma to apologize for not meeting her for dinner as promised the day before.

She answered on the second ring, apparently using her caller

ID. "Jonquinette, I really have nothing to say to you at the present time. I will call you next week."

"Momma, what's wrong?" I asked. "I was just calling to apologize for—"

"As well you should. I still can't believe you spoke to me like that last night."

"Last night? I met you?"

Momma paused. "Don't play dumb with me. You know good and damn well you not only met me but you accused me of being a common whore."

"Momma, I didn't—"

"Don't say another word. I'm busy. I have work to do. Although to hear you tell it, I spend all of my time on my knees or back."

Before I could get something together to say, she hung up on me.

I couldn't wait for my next appointment with Dr. Spencer, which was two days away, so I called and requested to see her that afternoon. By two, I was in her waiting room.

"What's wrong, Jonquinette?" she asked when I finally managed to get into her office.

"Something bad happened last night," I managed to say through tear-drenched eyes.

"Something bad like what?"

"I was supposed to meet my mother for dinner and I went to church and everything was fine but then . . . then I don't know what happened after that."

"You mean you blacked out?"

"Exactly. I must have because I did meet her for dinner. At least, that's what she said."

"And what else did she say?"

"She accused me of calling her names and suggesting she was a whore and who knows what else."

Dr. Spencer propped her elbows on her desk. "But you didn't do any of it?"

"No, I mean yes. I mean, I guess I did. Who else could it have been?"

"Jonquinette, I've done a lot of thinking about you since our first visit. Have you ever considered the fact that you might have multiple personalities?"

I almost fainted. "Once or twice, but that doesn't make sense. Then again, none of this makes sense."

"I really would like to explore that possibility. You have been plagued by these blackouts for a long time and obviously you are doing these things. Too many people have accused you."

I sunk down in the chair. "There was this one incident. When I was younger, in my teens, I heard my parents arguing one night."

"About?" she asked.

"My father was trying to convince my mother that I needed counseling. She wouldn't hear of it."

"So your father felt you needed therapy?"

"Yes, he did. I often wonder if that's what broke them up. I know that I was responsible for part of it. But then there was the other thing . . ."

I lowered my eyes to the floor. I really didn't want to put my parents' business out there that way, but opening up was opening up. I could tell she was waiting for me to continue.

"My mother found out my father was cheating on her. Quite frankly, I never believed it. He seemed so in love with her. But apparently the evidence was there so that, coupled with the tension about me, caused her to throw him out the house."

"So where is your father now?" Dr. Spencer asked.

"He lives in North Carolina. He left home and went back to

his hometown, took over my grandfather's auto shop. He always loved working with his hands and fixing up old cars."

"So that was his career all along?"

"No," I replied. "My father was a computer programmer in Florida. I guess he just wanted a fresh start altogether and my grandfather died shortly after he returned home. The business was there and he just took it over and learned whatever it was he didn't already know."

"Do you still keep in contact with your father?"

That was a difficult question for me to answer. "Yes and no."

"Meaning?"

"He writes me letters but I never answer them."

Dr. Spencer set up on the edge of her seat. "Why don't you respond to them?"

"Because . . . I'm torn. My mother is very dominant and opinionated. If I were to have a father-daughter relationship with him, she would view that as a sign of betrayal."

"So your mother is more important to you than your father?"

I sat there for a moment, pondering the question. "I can't really say that's it. My mother has been there for me more than my father."

"But has that been by choice or circumstances?"

I shrugged. "A little of both. If he really wanted to see me, he could find me. He has my address."

I could feel an anxiety attack coming on and apparently so could Dr. Spencer. "Let's not dwell on that right now," she said. "However, in the future, you might want to consider contacting your father. He may be able to bring some closure to whatever it is that's troubling you."

"I've thought about going to see him," I said honestly. "But I really don't know what I could possibly say to him at this point, being that I've ignored him for so long."

"Are his letters written in a way that makes him seem bitter or just anxious to be a part of your life?"

"He wants to be a part of my life. My father has never been mean to me. Not ever."

We continued talking for another thirty minutes. I felt a little bit better when I left but far from sane. What if there really was another person living inside of me?

13

jude

That fuckin' did it! Those bitches! Okay, if that's the way they wanted to play it, so be it! If one of us was going somewhere, it sure as shit wasn't going to be me!

We were driving home from the psycho bitch's office when I made Jon vanish. Fuck her!

I decided to stop by the mall to do some shopping. Let her figure the shit out when her credit card bill came in. I had a secret place where I hid clothes I purchased behind her back. I rarely did it but I deserved a shopping spree after that bullshit she was talking in the doctor's office.

Things were getting out of hand. People were getting into my business that didn't belong in it and if Jon even thought about reaching out to "Dearest Daddy," I planned to put a stop to that shit immediately.

I stopped by Greenbriar Mall; always a good place to find dick. Even though it was a Monday, there were still quite a few people out shopping or at least window shopping. I found two whorefits in one store and a pair of shoes to match each one in another store. Then I got a salted pretzel and some lemonade from a vendor. I sat on a bench and tried to calm down. It wasn't happening.

On my way home, I passed a mattress store. As usual, the parking lot was abandoned. I'd always wondered how mattress stores could stay in business because they were the only stores I knew of that always had empty parking lots. There were usually only one or two cars and those belonged to employees.

I decided to stop, though, and fuck with whomever was working that day. Why not? There was nothing to do at home. I was going to pretend like I planned to purchase the most expensive mattress set in the store, make the person fill out a bunch of fake paperwork, and then roll out.

I walked in and didn't see a soul. "Hello? Anyone here?" I yelled out. There was no response. "Hey! You taking a dump or something?"

I laughed at the prospect. Some senior citizen dude who hadn't saved up enough money for retirement, sitting on the throne in the back embarrassed because I had caught him taking a shit.

I decided to wait and started checking out the selections. They had some low-end sets. I tried a couple of them out and quickly realized the scam they were running. Game always recognizes game.

The lower-priced mattress sets were so hard and uncomfortable that no one in their right mind would want to sleep on them. Thus, they would be forced, if desperate and not feeling like going someplace else, to pay more money for something better.

Finally, I heard someone emerging from the back. I faced the storeroom door and waited for a hundred-ninety-year-old man to come out. Much to my astonishment, this sexy-ass motherfucker came out instead.

"Sorry," he said. "I didn't hear you come in. I was in the back looking for a product for a customer."

I scanned the store. "A customer? Is said customer invisible?"

He laughed. "No, she's on the phone. Give me a second."

I watched him take a seat at the cheap stainless steel desk and pick up the phone.

"Sorry for the delay, Ms. Gray. We don't have it in stock right now but, if you like, I can special order it for you."

I smirked. How in the hell could an item be out of stock when they never had more than two people in the store at a time?

I eyed him carefully as he concluded his call. He was about six-two with skin the color of dark fudge, had almond-shaped dark eyes, and looked like he could hold his own in a bench-pressing contest.

He hung up the phone and said, "Sorry. How may I help you?"

"That's the third time you've said sorry in the past two minutes. What's there to be sorry for? You're just doing your job."

He shrugged. "True, but my mother raised me to be a gentleman."

"Good for her." I fingered one of the more luxurious sets, a king-sized one. "How much is this?" I could've read the tag but I wanted him to come over to assist me so I could peep out his ass and see if I could spot a hump in the front of his pants.

He fell for it, came over, and read the tag that I was perfectly capable of reading. "This set is twenty-seven hundred."

"Twenty-seven hundred? Does it fuck the people sleeping on it for that price?"

He was taken aback. "Sorry?"

"There you go with 'sorry' again." I rolled my eyes. "Look, um,

Jerry," I said, reading his name badge. "Don't get this twisted but how often does someone really come in here and pay that kind of money for a mattress set? Something to sleep on?"

"I'll admit it happens sporadically but it does happen. Most of the sets we sell go for anywhere between three hundred and eight hundred. Is that the price range you were looking for?"

I stood there, debating about whether or not to go through with my original plan or switch it up. I glanced at the door. "What would happen if we locked the door and tried out the twenty-seven hundred set?"

He blushed. "Excuse me?"

"You heard me."

"Try it out how?"

"By fucking on it, how else?"

He was apprehensive. "Are you serious? You must be kidding."

"No, not at all." I reached over, grabbed his tie, and jerked him toward me. "What's wrong? You don't believe women are capable of going after what or who they want? Men do it all the time."

He chuckled. "True, but most men aren't even brave enough to ask someone to fuck them in the middle of a store in broad daylight."

"Well, that's their problem." I ran my tongue across his cheek, like an animal marking my territory. "So how about it?"

He tried to push me away. "Miss, I don't even know you." He held up his left hand to show me his ring. "Besides, I'm married and extremely faithful."

I giggled. All men are dogs. Some of them just don't know it until you educate them. "What does it mean to be *extremely faithful?*"

"It means I don't even look at other women," he replied.

I let him go and backed away, climbing up on the mattress set and pulling my top over my head. When I reached behind me and starting unclasping my bra, I said, "So, I guess you won't look at my tits then."

He not only was looking, he was staring. I bet his wife had carried three or four kids and had tits hanging down to her belly button. My tatas were pert.

I lifted the side of my skirt, reached beneath the elastic of my panties, and started fingering myself. "Jerry, you know you want this pussy. Come on and get some."

He faltered before stating, "There is something seriously wrong with you."

"No, there's something seriously wrong with you if you don't take advantage of this situation because it will never come your way again."

He was beginning to turn me off but I just loved a challenge and I wasn't about to give up until I got the dick. Besides, Jon deserved to be reprimanded and shown who was controlling things.

I lay down in the middle of the bed, pulled my fingers out my panties, and started licking them. "Damn, I taste *sooo* good. You sure you don't want a taste?"

It was obvious he was thinking about taking advantage of the opportunity. He was looking back and forth between me and the parking lot.

"Oh, come on, Jerry," I said. "No one is going to come in here shopping at this time on a Monday evening. People are stressing over their first day back at work, thinking about what they did over the weekend and wondering why it had to end."

Then he did it. He asked me a stupid fucking question. "Did my wife send you?"

I laughed. "No, I don't know the bitch."

"She's always talking about not trusting me. How do I know you're not one of those, what do they call them, decoys that they have on talk shows all the time?"

I shook my head. "Jerry, you need to get a life. You're a sexy man, I'm a sex fiend, and I want to fuck you. Right here, right now. It's just that simple." I pointed at the door. "Lock it."

He didn't utter a word. Just did as he was instructed. When the door was secure, he came back over to the bed and asked, "Now what?"

"Take off your clothes."

"All of them?"

"No, the pants will do. I just want some dick."

He trembled as he undid his belt and kicked off his shoes. "This is absolutely insane. I can't believe I'm doing this."

"Believe it, Jerry. You're doing it. You're about to fuck a complete stranger at your job. Don't worry. Your secret is safe with me."

"So, what's your name anyway?" he asked as he climbed on the bed beside me.

I smacked my lips. "I don't have a name, Jerry. But if you insist on calling me something, just call me Whore. I think I'd like that."

"You want me to call you Whore?"

"Yes, sure, why not?"

"Look, are you sure you're clean?" He started looking me up and down, like he was doing an examination. "I don't have a condom."

"Jerry, either we're going to shit or get off the pot. Know what I'm saying?" I asked. "I don't believe in condoms. When it's my time, it's my time. But, for the record, yes, I am clean."

I decided there had been enough talking. I felt like a man trying to persuade a virgin to do it for the first time.

"Jerry, just shut the hell up!" I yelled at him. "Now give me my dick!"

• • •

I dominated Jerry for the rest of the evening. It was after closing time when I left the mattress shop and not a single person came up to the door. The phone only rang twice. Before it was over, said and done, Jerry had fucked me six ways from Sunday. We fucked on top of four different mattress sets. I tied him to a brass bed and wore him out on top of a pillowtop set but my knees kept sinking into it too much. For the record, the cheapest set was best for rough-riding.

All of that release of sexual tension was for naught. My anger started all over again when I returned to the apartment and that Mason bastard had left a note for Jon taped to the door. He wanted to know if she would consider going out with him that Saturday. Ironically, he wanted her to go to a wedding with him. I snickered. Could it be the same wedding Jon had promised to attend with Darnetta? Either way, Jon was not about to accept his invite. I made sure of that by ripping up the note. However, if it did come to pass that it was one and same event, I was determined to turn that motherfucker out.

14

jonquinette

I didn't remember a thing after I left Dr. Spencer's office. I also overslept for the second day in a row. The scent was there again when I took a shower. What was truly sad about the entire thing was that I was getting used to the same thing happening to me over and over again. That didn't make it any less frightening, though.

I showed up at the office an hour late. There was no way I was calling in two days in a row. I might have found myself on the unemployment line. The place was already jumping. Thank goodness business had picked back up or we all would have had hell to pay.

Less than two minutes after I sat down at my desk, Darnetta was poking her head in my doorway. "What's up, Jon?"

"Nothing. I just got here." I started shuffling some of the papers around. I really didn't feel like having a long, drawn-out discussion that day. "I have a ton of things to catch up on."

"Are you okay?" she asked. "I heard you called in yesterday."

"I'm fine. I was just a little under the weather."

"Yeah, the rapid temperature changes have been wild lately. Most of my family is sick."

"Well, whatever I had only lasted a day." I started scribbling on a pad, hoping she would take the hint and leave. "So, you busy today?"

Darnetta shrugged her shoulders. "You know me. I work at my own pace so I won't wear myself out."

We both laughed.

She came closer to my desk. "Actually, I just came by to remind you about the wedding this Saturday. There's no way I'm letting you back out."

I felt my heart flutter. I was not looking forward to being around a bunch of strangers. "I wouldn't dream of backing out," I said.

"Good. We're going to have a ball."

I sat my pen down. "Darnetta, I hate to be rude but I really have to take care of some of this stuff."

She flicked her hand in my direction. "Hey, I hear you, girl. I'm going to get back to my desk before Big Brother comes looking for me."

"Thanks for the reminder."

"I will be reminding you the rest of the week," she said. "Have you decided what you're going to wear?"

I shook my head. "No, I haven't a clue. I'll come up with something."

Darnetta eyed me uncomfortably. "Might I make a suggestion? Why don't you try something a little more provocative than usual? You're a beautiful woman. You should emphasize it more."

I couldn't come up with a response that made sense to me so I didn't respond at all.

"I'll catch you later, Jon," Darnetta said as she left.

The amount of work that had piled up on my desk during one day of absence was unbelievable. It was so bad that I ended up taking some work home with me. That wasn't a problem since I had no plans anyway. Not that I ever did.

There was a note on my door. It was Mason asking if I had made up my mind. I had no idea what he was talking about. I started to go knock on his door but decided against it. I had nothing to offer him. It was ironic. I had finally found a man that I was somewhat interested in, at least I wanted to get to know him better, and I was too messed up in the head to even deal with the situation.

It had been a long time since I had masturbated. Yet, that night I found myself lying in bed fantasizing about Mason. As I caressed my breasts and squeezed my thighs around the towel placed between my legs to create friction on my clit, I imagined Mason making passionate love to me.

15

jonquinette

Darnetta showed up at my apartment fifteen minutes early. I was ready but I didn't have my hair done. I let her in and ran into the bathroom to throw it up in my habitual bun.

"Jon, do you need some help?" Darnetta yelled from the living room.

"No, I'm fine." I glimpsed in the mirror and thought about applying some makeup. Then I thought better of it. I wasn't trying to meet anyone so why try to enhance my appearance.

I just smeared some lip gloss across my lips so they wouldn't chap and told Darnetta that I was ready to go.

When we got to the church, it was packed. I had never been to that particular church but I had heard a lot about it. Apparently, it had one of the biggest congregations in the city. At least half of them must have been present, which led me to believe that the groom was very active in the church.

"Darnetta, thanks for inviting me," I said after we were seated in a pew.

"No problem. Thank you for coming. Since Logan's in the wedding, I didn't want to sit out here by myself."

The processional music started and I was dazed when the groom and best man walked out from the pastor's study and took their places at the altar. Mason was the best man.

I exhaled a deep breath and Darnetta stared at me. "Something wrong?"

"No, it's just funny because the best man just moved into my building a little while ago."

"Oh, you mean Mason?"

"You know him?"

"I didn't until last night. I met him at the rehearsal dinner. Girl, he's too fine and nice as hell. You need to jump on him."

I blushed. "No, he's just a neighbor but I hope he and I can become good friends."

"Friends?" Darnetta asked. "You need to be friends and lovers. I asked him if he had a woman last night and he said no. You better snatch him up before someone else does."

I shifted uncomfortably in my seat. "Um, I'm not really looking for a man right now. Work is keeping me pretty busy."

"Forget that stupid job. Besides, it can't keep you warm at night or blow your back out. Know what I'm saying?"

Darnetta laughed and I faked a smile. We both got quiet as the rest of the wedding party marched in from the back of the church.

The wedding ceremony was beautiful. When the minister pronounced them man and wife, I almost cried. The couple was extremely cute together. Smitty and Robin had met in college and dated on and off for more than six years before deciding to tie the knot. At the reception afterward, many people stood to toast them and reflect on funny times the two of them had been through. I had trouble hearing some of them because Darnetta was too busy acting jealous about the bridesmaid that Logan had to escort throughout the entire evening. I tried to tell her that it was no big deal. I had never had a man and even I knew that. He was simply doing what he was supposed to do; escorting the woman down the aisle and into the reception as well as sitting beside her at the head table. When they had the first dance and the wedding party joined in, I could feel the steam emitting off Darnetta when Logan had his arm dangling from the woman's waist.

The caterer had it going on. The food was delicious. They served gulf shrimp cocktail, blue crab claws, lobster bisque, smoked salmon, antipasto, shrimp and scallops scampi and veal chops. I was so stuffed that I thought I would burst out of my dress by the time they served the cake, which was incredible as well.

Mason had spotted me during the ceremony. I lowered my eyes in shame. Why, I don't know. I just felt embarrassed to run into him there. During the greeting line on the way out of the church, I paused just long enough to shake his hand. He pulled it up to his mouth and kissed it gently. Then he leaned in closer to me and whispered, "We'll talk at the reception."

The reception was more than halfway over and he hadn't said a word to me. I found myself wondering if he had a woman present after all. The maid of honor, who he had to escort, was not eye-catching at all but that didn't mean she lacked a great personality.

Darnetta was elated when Logan finally rescued her from the table where we were seated.

"Logan, you remember Jonquinette that works with me," Darnetta stated, even though I had never met the man before. I had only heard about him day in and day out and seen his picture.

"No, I don't recall having met," he replied. "But it sure is a pleasure."

I stood up and shook his hand. "It's nice to meet you, Logan. I've heard so much about you."

Logan was extremely attractive and seemed nice enough. Darnetta was a lucky girl. "Jonquinette, you don't mind if I steal Darnetta away for a dance, do you?" he asked. "I won't keep her long."

"No, take your time," I said. "She's wanted to dance with you all evening," I lied. She really had wanted to wring his neck all evening.

As they walked away, I sat back down at the table and scanned the room searching for Mason. After spotting the maid of honor among a group of women on the dance floor getting their boogie on together in their stocking feet, I imagined him off in a quiet corner flirting with one of the many gorgeous women in attendance.

I jumped when I felt a hand on my shoulder. Mason chuckled and took Darnetta's unoccupied seat next to me.

"I'm sorry, Jonquinette. I didn't mean to startle you."

I laughed timidly. "I'm okay."

We sat there in silence for a moment while we both gathered our thoughts.

"Nice wedding," I said finally. "I was surprised to see you here."

"Really?" he asked with an expression of bewilderment on his face. "I don't know why. After all, I did invite you. I'm just sorry you never responded to my note."

"Your note? You must be confused."

He smirked and shook his head. "I'm not confused at all. You mean to tell me that you didn't get the note I stuck on your door earlier this week asking you to be my date?"

I was at a loss for words and didn't want to panic. It could have blown away or some bad kid could have taken it off the door. I didn't want to think the worst.

"Mason, I didn't receive your note. Thanks for the invitation though."

He played with the stem of Darnetta's champagne glass. "Can I ask you something?"

"Sure."

"If you had gotten it, would you have said yes?"

"No."

He sighed deeply. "That's disappointing. I had hoped that you would."

"I didn't mean it like that," I said, trying to correct myself and spare his feelings. "Darnetta had asked me to come with her first and I promised that I would. She and I work together and I never would have heard the end of it if I had backed out on her."

He seemed reassured. "Good, I understand. So you would have said yes if it weren't for that?" he asked, continuing to probe.

"Absolutely." That wasn't true but it didn't matter at that point. I would have been too nervous to go out on a date with Mason, especially to a wedding.

The band slowed the music down and the group of women on the dance floor took their seats, leaving only couples who embraced each other intimately.

"Jonquinette, may I have this dance?" Mason asked, extending his hand to me.

I had never danced with a man before, not ever. But something was different. I really liked Mason.

"I would like that," I said, taking his hand and allowing him to lead me to the dance floor. When he placed his hands on my waist, I shivered. "I have to warn you. I'm not a very good dancer."

He grinned. "There's nothing to it. Just go with the music."

We danced to "Ribbon in the Sky," one of my all-time favorite songs. Mason placed his cheek on mine and I almost lost it. It felt so wonderful. I could feel his dick pressing up against me and that felt wonderful also. I had never experienced even that before.

We remained on the dance floor for three songs. Then Smitty, the groom, came over and tapped Mason on the shoulder.

"Mason, can I holler at you for a few before Robin and I leave for the honeymoon?"

Mason looked torn but said, "Sure, man. By the way, this is Jonquinette. Jonquinette, this is Smitty."

We shook hands.

"Jonquinette, as in your neighbor?" Smitty asked Mason.

"One and the same," Mason replied.

"Aw, so she ended up at the wedding anyway." Smitty eyed me up and down. "I can see why Mason is so taken with you."

I was blushing horribly. Mason had obviously been talking about me to at least one of his friends. I was flattered beyond comprehension.

"Thank you," I managed to get out of my mouth somehow.

"I won't keep him long," Smitty said. "I just need Mason to hold down the fort for me while I'm gone so we need to go over a few things."

"Where are you honeymooning?" I asked.

"The Caymans," Smitty said. "Robin and I have always wanted to have an escapade over there."

Before I knew it, Mason pulled me to him and brushed his lips across mine. "I'll be right back. Don't go anywhere."

I watched them walk outside and then I headed for the ladies' room to pull myself together. That kiss had set my insides on fire.

jude

I sat in the bathroom stall, pissed off. Jon was actually considering dating that fool. I could tell that any day she would be giving up the drawers. I couldn't and wouldn't tolerate it. Something drastic had to be done.

I had hoped, if it did turn out to be the same wedding, that Mason would have been there with some other bitch so Jon could see he was just another playa after a quick lay. But no, he had to be there alone and all up on her like her pussy was embedded with gold.

I came out of the stall and glanced in the mirror as I washed my hands. "What to do? What to do?" I asked my reflection. Then my question was answered when two of the bridesmaids walked in talking about my next victim.

"Damn, that Logan sure is fine," one of them said.

"Yeah, but you can forget it," the other one replied. "He's been dating that Darnetta chick for ages."

"Hmph, that doesn't mean he doesn't fool around. I was flirting with him at the rehearsal last night and he was feeling me. I could tell."

I pretended to be fixing my hair so I could hang back long enough to hear their conversation.

"Kassie, he wasn't feeling you."

"Alicia, look hoe, I know when a man is feeling me and I'm telling you, if I wanted some, I could get it."

"That may be true because I don't know many men that would turn down free sex. But, after you do him, then what? He goes right back to Darnetta and leaves you ass out."

"I'm not trying to fall in love with Logan. I'm just curious, that's all."

Alicia cleared her throat and looked in my direction. I turned at them and grinned. "You ladies have a good evening."

When I was walking out the bathroom door, I heard Alicia ask Kassie, "How do you know that's not one of Darnetta's girls or something? Talking about that man like that."

I laughed. That's what the bitches deserved. They needed some gossip etiquette training. You never spread your dirt in front of other people because you never know who knows who.

Ironically, I passed Darnetta as she was headed into the very same bathroom. "Jon, there you are. I was looking for you. How are things going with Mason? I saw you on the dance floor getting your freak on."

That Darnetta trick could get on my nerves at times with her babbling but all in all she was cool. At least she had a life. I should have felt guilty for what I was contemplating. Not!

"Mason and I are getting along just fine," I responded. "He had to go talk to Smitty about some things but we'll be back on the dance floor getting our freak on again soon."

Darnetta giggled. "Good for you, girl. I'm glad to see that you're loosening up." She slapped me on the shoulder. "Let me get in here before I pee on myself."

I watched her go into the ladies' room and then I went on a hunt. The window of opportunity was a small one. I had to make it work.

I spotted Logan by the back exit door smoking a cigarette. Another brother was standing there for a second but he put his cigarette out and walked away. The reception was being held at a conference center so in addition to the large room where the gathering was actually held, there were numerous smaller rooms.

I walked up to Logan, took his hand, and pulled him toward one.

"Jonquinette, what's going on?" he asked, confused.

"Just come with me," I instructed.

"Did Darnetta send you to get me? Is she all right?"

"Darnetta's fine. Just come."

I tried a couple of the doorknobs until I found one that was unlocked and pulled Logan inside. It was empty except for two tables, a few scattered chairs, and a helium tank that had been used to blow up the balloons for the reception.

"Jonquinette, what's going on?" he asked for the second time.

"Just come," I said for the third time. "That's all I want you to do. Just come."

He finally got the hint. "Um, I'm sorry but I don't know you like that. Besides, I'm dating Darnetta. You know that."

Hmph, the fool was determined to play hard to get. No man could resist me and he was an idiot for even trying. I pushed him onto a table and locked the door.

"Listen to me, Logan. I'm quite aware that you're dating Darnetta. I'm also quite aware that you're a man. All men love pussy. At least real men do."

I lowered his tuxedo jacket off his shoulders just enough to constrict his arm movement and then I started undoing his cummerbund.

"You love pussy, Logan?"

"Yes, but—"

I put my fingers to his lips. "Then shut the hell up!"

I ran my fingers through his curly brown hair with one hand while I caressed his dick through his pants with the other. "You have that exotic look that I adore. Are you from an island or something?"

"No, I'm from right here in Atlanta. My momma has some Cherokee in her, though."

"Well, all I can say is that you're so fine that I couldn't leave here tonight without feeling your dick inside me."

I knew I had his ass then. Men suck up compliments and can't get enough of them.

"Damn!" he exclaimed. "I thought you were shy. That's what Darnetta said."

"Darnetta doesn't know a damn thing about me except what she sees at work. Women who are true dick connoisseurs like me don't have to advertise it. We keep our business private. That's why you never have to worry about anything that transpires within these walls leaving here."

I hooked my foot around a chair and pulled it closer so I could sit down. Then I undid the clasp on his pants and yanked his zipper. Time was of the essence so I plunged right in the second I had his dick in clear view. It was a scrumptious dick, too.

Someone came and knocked at the door. We both fell silent until we heard footsteps walking away down the hall.

Logan whispered, "Oh, no! We have to come to our senses!"

I glanced up at him and said, "Sense this." Then I deep throated him again.

He was right, though. My purpose was more about self-preservation than sex. So I pushed him back until he lay flat on the table, slipped off my panties, and mounted him. I rode him fast and quick for a few minutes, gathered my things together and headed for the door.

Logan looked dumbfounded. "What was that all about?"

I turned around. "Just something I wanted and I always get what I want."

He shook his head in dismay. "Are you going to tell Darnetta?"

I smirked. "Why would I do that? Just tell Darnetta and Mason that I fell ill and decided to catch a cab home. I've had enough of this event to last me a lifetime."

I walked out the room, found the rear exit, and jetted. After getting settled in the back of a cab that I flagged down, I couldn't help but laugh. Let Jon try to get closer to Mason. I already had my game in order.

16

jonquinette

I woke up lying in the middle of my living room floor. My head was splitting from a migraine and I was wearing only a bra and panties. I didn't remember anything: leaving the wedding, the ride home, nothing. I wondered if I had done something crazy in front of Darnetta. Heaven forbid I had done something ridiculous in front of Mason.

I debated about calling Darnetta to make sure she'd gotten home okay and to snoop around about what had happened. Then I glanced at the clock and realized it was after two o'clock in the morning. I wouldn't call anyone's house that late. Not in a million years.

I decided to go to bed and deal with whatever happened in the morning. I had just crawled under my covers when a knock came at the door. Startled, I sat up in the bed and listened to see if I was imagining things. Another knock came; this time louder.

I got up, threw on a robe and went to look out the peephole. Oh no! It was Mason. He must have heard me moving around because he said, "Jonquinette, I know you're home. Can we talk?"

I spoke softly through the door. "Mason, it's really late. Can we do this tomorrow?"

"I just wanted to make sure that you're okay. Logan said you weren't feeling well and that's why you left the wedding so suddenly."

Logan? What in the world did Logan have to do with anything? Other than a brief introduction, I hadn't spoken five words to him.

"Um, I do have a migraine but I'll be fine."

"You sure?"

"Yes, positive. Have a good night."

I glanced through the peephole again and noticed he was still standing there staring at my door. He took a deep breath, started to walk away, and then hesitated. "Jonquinette, can you just open the door for one second? I'd feel a lot better if I could just see you. It'll give me peace of mind."

I decided there was nothing to lose. After fingering my hair and straightening up my robe, I inched the door open. "See, I'm fine, Mason."

He chuckled. "It would help me out if I could see more than your eyeballs."

I opened the door completely. "Is this better?"

He eyed me up and down and I tightened my robe around my chest.

"Definitely better. Well, you look okay," he said. He touched my forehead with his palm. "No fever. Are you sure you don't need to see a doctor?"

"I'm sure. It was a long day and I just overdid it some. I have a history of anemia so my iron is probably low. I forgot to take my tablet earlier."

Mason took me completely off guard by grabbing me into his arms and kissing me. He slipped his tongue into my mouth and at first I didn't know how to react. Then something came alive inside me and I responded. It was the first time I had truly kissed a man and it felt great. He was gentle yet powerful and his arms around my waist made me feel comfortably at ease. For once, I wasn't nervous.

He pushed me backward into my apartment and against the wall as the intensity of our kiss grew. It lasted for a good five minutes until . . .

. . . he grabbed my left breast and I freaked out.

I manuevered myself away from him. "I'm sorry, Mason. I can't do this."

He grinned at me and said, "I didn't mean to rush you. We can take our time getting to know each other."

I grinned back at him. "I'd like that. I'd like that very much."

"So how about we start with a real date. Not one where we just happen to end up in the same place but one where we actually leave here together and come back here together."

"That sounds original."

We both laughed.

"Dinner. Tomorrow night. Seven o'clock. How does that sound?"

"Like a winning proposition."

Mason kissed me on the forehead. "Good night."

"Good night."

I climbed back into bed and fell asleep dreaming about Mason.

jude

BITCH!

17

November 1994
Tenth Grade
Pembroke Pines, Florida

Henry Pierce paced the kitchen floor, waiting for his wife to come back inside from the garage. Meredith came in carrying a large turkey that she had retrieved from the chest freezer.

"This turkey's a little small but I think we'll make do," she said.

"How many people do we have coming over for Thanksgiving dinner?" Henry asked.

"About a dozen."

Henry sighed and sat down at the table. "Why is it that everyone always gathers at our house for holiday dinners? Don't they ever entertain at their homes?"

"Henry, that's not fair. You know my family members entertain from time to time. It's just that we live in the most central location and that makes it easier for everyone to get together."

Henry smirked. "If you say so, but I think it has more to do with us footing the grocery bill than anything else."

Meredith didn't comment. They both knew it was a true statement. While Meredith tried to act as if she "came from money,"
that couldn't have been further from the truth. She'd grown up
dirt-poor, the daughter of two janitors who favored being ad-
dressed as environmental engineers. She had two older sisters
who were golddiggers, which explained why Meredith was one
herself. Unfortunately, her sisters hadn't landed a wealthy man.
Meredith seduced Henry one night while he was too drunk to
know better, they had a whirlwind romance, and were forced to
marry after Meredith became pregnant.

Henry had long recovered from the fact that Meredith had
trapped him by lying and saying she was on the pill. After it was all
over, said and done, he found out that she'd never taken a birth
control pill, rather less had a prescription for one, in her entire
life. Henry wasn't rich by anyone's standards but compared to
Meredith's family, he was Donald Trump.

"Whatever, Meredith," Henry said. "That's not what I want to
talk to you about anyway."

Meredith put the turkey in the sink and ran hot water over it
to begin thawing it out for dinner the next day. "Well, we have to
talk while I'm cooking. It's getting late and I still have to rinse my
greens and get them on, cut up the potatoes for my salad tomorrow, and bake a couple of pumpkin pies."

"Good grief! You act like we're feeding an army!"

Meredith snickered. "Hell, Henry, you know how my family
eats."

Henry cleared his throat and pulled his chair up closer to the
table so he could rest his elbows. "Meredith, we need to have a serious talk about Jonquinette."

Meredith paused and stood still before facing him, leaning her
hips against the sink. "What about her?"

"We can't keep ignoring her behavior. All these years, we've
made excuses for her actions but something has to be done imme-

diately before it gets out of hand. I don't even know what I'm say-ing. Things have already gotten out of hand and you're not helping matters any."

Meredith said, "Jonquinette's just fine. She's the typical teenage girl. Her hormones are raging and she's going through major changes."

Henry shook his head. He stood up and grabbed Meredith by the shoulders. "Jonquinette's anything but typical, Meredith. You and I both know it."

Meredith yanked herself free in anger. "I refuse to stand here and listen to this nonsense."

Henry got a glass out of the cabinet, turned on the faucet, and filled it with cool water. He took a sip and contemplated his next move. "Meredith, I wanted to believe Jonquinette was normal just as much as you. Hell, even more. But we've got to get her some help."

"Help? What kind of help?"

"She needs to see a specialist. A psychiatrist."

"You've lost your damn mind," Meredith said. "Jonquinette isn't crazy; you are."

"Now, Meredith, I'm not saying the girl is crazy. I'm saying, at the very least, she's extremely confused." Henry started pacing the floor. "There's just something that doesn't sit right about all of this."

"The only thing Jonquinette needs is a decent boyfriend. She's at the age where she should start dating." Meredith turned on the oven and then sat down at the table. "If you really want to do something for Jonquinette, spend more time with her. She still has to log another thirty hours of driving with her learner's per-mit before she can get her license in January. She also needs to im-prove her computer science grade and being that you're a programmer, I would think you could help her out with that."

Henry didn't appreciate the sarcasm lingering in Meredith's voice. "This isn't about driving or some damn computer. This is about doing something before Jonquinette seriously hurts herself or someone else."

"Where is this all coming from?" Meredith asked apprehensively. "Granted, she's had episodes in the past but nothing lately."

Henry lowered his eyes to the floor.

"Henry, nothing lately, right?"

"I guess not," he replied. "I just have this gut feeling that this is the calm before the storm."

Meredith got up and touched his hand. "Henry Pierce, you and I have been through hell together over the past two decades and we've always survived. We'll survive this, too, whatever it is."

Henry hugged Meredith snugly. "I love both of you so much. I just want us to have a happy family."

"We do have a happy family, Henry."

"If you say so, but—"

Meredith pulled away from his embrace and glared at him. "But what?"

"I still plan to call someone on Monday. Just to see what they say."

"Someone like who?"

Henry shrugged. "I guess I'll start with the Health and Human Services Department. They should be able to recommend someone."

Meredith rolled her eyes and slammed a pot down on the stove. She didn't say another word.

Jonquinette tiptoed back upstairs without either one of them knowing she'd heard the entire conversation.

18

Thanksgiving Day, 1994
Three A.M.

          Jude had waited until both Henry and Meredith were fast asleep before sneaking out of bed. She threw on a pair of jeans, a tee shirt, and a pair of raggedy sneakers and then eased her way out of the house into the garage. She winced when she pushed the button for the door to rise. It was a dicey move because there was a noisy vibration. Her room was directly over the garage and she always heard it but wasn't sure whether it was audible in the master bedroom.

She waited for a minute to see if she heard any movement. There was nothing, so she unlocked Henry's Lincoln Town Car and eased behind the wheel. She was elated that he always kept an extra set of keys in the kitchen drawer. It made things so much easier for her.

She put the car in reverse without starting the engine and coasted out the driveway onto the street where she turned it over.

She grinned as she headed off into the darkness. "I'll fix your ass but good," she whispered.

Jude knew exactly where to go: a strip downtown that was heavily populated with strip clubs and prostitutes lining the sidewalk. She had two hundred dollars and some change; Jonquinette's life savings. She hoped it would be enough.

One P.M.

Jude stayed up in the bedroom for most of the morning, pretending Jonquinette was studying computer science. But Jude didn't give a fuck about computer science. She did like going into chat rooms, though; particularly those where people talked about sex and nothing but sex. One such room was called "Freaky Black People." It was her personal favorite.

She'd had cyber sex with countless men, most of whom thought she was a twenty-five-year-old nurse from Raleigh, North Carolina, instead of a fifteen-year-old high school student. Stupid idiots, as far as she was concerned.

Even Jude was shocked that so many freaks were online Thanksgiving Day. She assumed they all had family plans but their addiction to chat rooms must have superseded them.

Jude was just bored stiff and waiting for the fireworks to initiate later that day. She still had a few hours before the festivities so she started teasing around with one of the men in the chat room who had the screen name "Slanging Dick." His profile boasted that he could lick a woman's belly button from the inside. *Nasty bastard,* Jude thought. *Just my type of man.*

Jude had yet to have actual intercourse but it was only a matter of time, as far as she was concerned. Jonquinette led such a lackluster life that there wasn't a single boy she spent time around that interested her. The boys at school were all revolting. Plus they were just that: boys. Jude yearned for a man.

A few of the men online had tried to coax her into offline meetings. One of them almost had her, a smooth talker who went by "DreamLvr4U." She was all ready to meet up with him until she found out he wanted to rendezvous at a raunchy hotel instead of one of the fancy ones he always talked about doing the nasty with her in. She also found out, from another woman in the chat room who had actually met him and had sex with him offline, that he had the dick of an eight-year-old. She wasn't sure if "BombAzz-Puddy" was lying or not, but she wasn't taking any chances or wasting her time. Besides, Bomb also informed her that Dream looked nothing like the photo he was emailing to women in the room. She said the photo must've been more than a decade old and that he was really closer to forty instead of the thirty-year-old he claimed to be.

Jude, whose screen name was Hot CUMmodity sent Slanging Dick an invitation to a private chat so she could cyber him. *What the hell,* she thought. *Practice makes perfect. Even if the practice isn't real.*

They entered a private room and it was on:

Hot CUMmodity: What's up, love?

Slanging Dick: Nothing much. Just waiting to see what you're working with. Do you cyber much?

Hot CUMmodity: A little here and a little there but nothing beats the real thing.

Slanging Dick: Amen to that. Cyber sex is cool, though. At least it's safer.

Hot CUMmodity: Yeah, it's safer than phone sex.

Slanging Dick: Phone sex?

Hot CUMmodity: Yeah, you should always wear a condom when you have phone sex so you don't catch hearing aids.

Slanging Dick: LOL—you're a wild girl.

Hot CUMmodity: So your profile said you can lick a woman's belly button from the inside.

Slanging Dick: All night long and my dick's so long you can feel it in your throat.

Hot CUMmodity: Damn, how big is it?

Slanging Dick: How big do you want it to be?

Hot CUMmodity: Big enough to satisfy me in all three holes.

Slanging Dick: Damn! So you like it in the ass, huh?

Hot CUMmodity: Ooh, yeah! I love it in the ass. In fact, let me show you my ass right now. I'm lying here naked on top of my bed fingering myself as you come into the room.

Slanging Dick: Umm, yeah, I can see you. Describe yourself.

Hot CUMmodity: I'm five-ten, caramel, I have long flowing dark hair and large bedroom eyes, and a body that screams, "Cum fuck me!"

Slanging Dick: Oh, my!

Hot CUMmodity: Describe yourself to me.

Slanging Dick: I'm six-eight, light-skinned, bowlegged and I wear my hair low, I'm clean-shaven, and I have a big-ass dick.

Hot CUMmodity: Yummy, I just love tall men. Let me turn over and prop my ass up on a pillow so you can get a better look at it. Can you see my anus now?

Slanging Dick: Yeah, I see it. Lick your finger and run it up and down your crack. Get that ass ripe for me.

Hot CUMmodity: I'm licking my finger. Now I'm running it up and down the middle of my ass. Oh, my bad, I accidentally slipped it in. It feels so good but your dick would feel better.

Slanging Dick: Well, get ready for it because here it CUMS!

Hot CUMmodity: Um, yeah, that's it, baby. Slide it right up in there, slowly so I can get used to it.

Slanging Dick: I'm pushing my dick into your ass inch by muthafuckin' inch. How does that feel?

Hot CUMmodity: Awesome. Give it all to me. Fuck it. I can't wait anymore.

Slanging Dick: I'm shoving it all the way in. Take this shit, raw dog, you whore.

Hot CUMmodity: I like it when a man talks dirty to me. Talk dirty to me some more.

Slanging Dick: Okay, bitch! Take all this dick up that black hole of yours!

Hot CUMmodity: Uh, yeah, you're ripping it up now. I can feel your balls slapping up against the back of my thighs.

Slanging Dick: Ooh, I'm yanking your head back by your hair, forcing your ass further onto my dick. Take this pain, bitch!

Hot CUMmodity: I'm fingering myself and feeding my pussy to you. How do I taste?

Slanging Dick: Like chicken.

Hot CUMmodity: Cum for me, baby!

Slanging Dick: I'm not ready to cum yet. I'm yanking my dick out your ass and ramming it into your pussy. I'm gonna fuck you doggy-style.

Hot CUMmodity: That's my fav!

Slanging Dick: Uh, yeah, mine too. Work this dick over, whore!

Hot CUMmodity: Mammacita's working it, Boo!

Slanging Dick: I want you to cum all over this dick.

Hot CUMmodity: Grab my ass cheeks and dig your nails into them.

Slanging Dick: Oh, yeah! How's that?

Hot CUMmodity: That's it, Poppi! I'm cumming already. I can feel it trickling down the inside of my thighs onto the sheets.

Slanging Dick: I'm fingering your ass. Does that make it better for you?

Hot CUMmodity: Yeah, but stick three fingers inside me instead of just one.

Slanging Dick: I wanna taste you, bitch!

Hot CUMmodity: Only if I can taste you, too!

Slanging Dick: I'm pulling my dick out your pussy and laying down on the bed. Climb on my face. Lay that sweet pussy right on my hungry mouth.

Hot CUMmodity: I'm lowering myself onto you. My pussy's so sticky with my cum.

Slanging Dick: We 69ing?

Hot CUMmodity: Absolutely. I'm taking your dick into my mouth at the same time I'm sitting on your face.

Slanging Dick: Umm, your pussy is so sweet.

Hot CUMmodity: I'm licking my pussy juice off your dick. You're right. It is sweet.

Slanging Dick: Umm, damn skippy!

Hot CUMmodity: I deep throat you and I feel you cumming in my mouth.

Slanging Dick: Is it good to you, baby?

Hot CUMmodity: The best! I cum in your mouth and then climb off your face.

Slanging Dick: Oh, shit! @@@@ That was some bomb pussy.

Hot CUMmodity: I have to go now. Thanks for the dick,
    Boo. Kisses all over your body.

Four P.M.

The house was packed with relatives, all of whom Jude hated.
She'd put on a plaid wool skirt and long-sleeved sweater; just the
variety of boring outfit Jonquinette would've selected.

Meredith was in her element, showing off for her family and
pretending like she was the shit. When she asked Jonquinette to
help her set the table, Jude plastered on a bogus smile and com-
plied. She wanted to stay downstairs because she didn't want to
jeopardize missing the action once the doorbell rang.

By four-thirty, when they all actually sat down to eat, Jude
was getting edgy. "The bitch" was late.

Benjamin, Jonquinette's twelve-year-old cousin, was making
Jude queasy by chewing with his mouth open. Jude wanted to
reach across the table and slap him. Instead, she just grinned at
him and redirected her eyes elsewhere. When he let out a loud
belch, Jude cleared her throat. *That sorry motherfucker has no home
training whatsoever,* she thought. Then again, she shouldn't have
been surprised considering his mother, Meredith's sister Elaine,
had no home training her damn self.

By five, Jude was absolutely enraged. She was ready to go scour
the streets for "the bitch" and strangle her with her bare hands.

At five-fifteen, the doorbell finally rang. Jude jumped up and
said, "I'll get it. You all finish your dessert."

Meredith called after her as she headed out into the foyer. "I
wonder who it could be. Everyone's already here."

Jude yanked the front door open and glared angrily at "the
bitch." She whispered, "Don't you own a watch?"

"The bitch" came back at her. "Yeah, but I had three dudes
come by in a van and they were loaded with cash. Shit, you only

gave me two hundred. Don't get to tripping on me or I'll turn right back around."

Jude decided to swallow the words in her throat. At the moment, other things were more important.

Meredith decided to come out of the dining room to investigate. She was shocked when she saw the slut standing in her doorway. The woman gave the impression of being a streetwalker. She had on a taut spandex skirt that was so undersized you could see the crotch of her red lace underwear, a pair of stilettos and a halter top in the middle of November.

"Who the hell are you?" Meredith demanded to know.

Jude winked at "the bitch," letting her know it was time to get the show on the road.

"Um, I'm looking for Henry," she said. "Henry Pierce. Does he live here?"

Meredith came closer to the door. "Henry's my husband. Who are you?"

"The bitch" grimaced and then laughed in Meredith's face. "I'm Henry's mistress."

"Momma . . ." Jude cried, starting the performance she'd planned all along. "Daddy has a mistress?"

Meredith coughed, trying to prevent herself from choking on her own saliva. "Of course, he doesn't. This *woman* is obviously mistaken." She eyed the hooker and said, "You've apparently got the wrong house."

"The bitch" asked, "Is this 12709 Spring Valley Lane?"

"Yes, it is," Jude quickly responded. When she noticed no one else was coming out of the dining room, she got louder so they could hear the commotion. "You did say you were looking for Henry Pierce, didn't you?" she yelled.

Henry obviously heard that because he appeared around the corner less than ten seconds later asking, "Who's at the door?"

"The bitch" eyed Jude, trying to make sure he was the right person because she'd never seen him.

Jude decided to confirm it by running up to Henry and throwing her arms around his neck. "Daddy, say it isn't so! Say she's lying!"

"Who's lying?" Henry asked.

Meredith glowered at Henry and said, "Your *mistress* is at the door."

"My what?" Henry bellowed.

It gradually became Noah's Ark up in the Pierce household as their guests came into the living room in pairs. No one wanted to be considered nosy but, at the same time, no one wanted to miss a single word of what was about to go down.

"The bitch" came farther into the house uninvited and threw herself down at Henry's feet, grabbing onto one of his calves. "Henry, please come be with me."

"What? What the fuck are you talking about?" Henry was panic-stricken. "I don't know you."

"The bitch" got up and placed her hands on her hips in anger. "Oh, so you're just going to play me like that, huh?" She turned to Meredith. "My name's Mahagony and I'm carrying your husband's child."

Meredith threw her hands up in the air in alarm and looked at Henry. "Damn, Henry, she's pregnant too?" Meredith was totally embarrassed. She couldn't believe all of this was happening in front of her family members. She switched her attention to Mahagony. "It's Thanksgiving. Couldn't you have had the decency to at least wait until tomorrow? We have guests."

Mahagony said, "I don't give a damn about your guests. Your husband paid me for sex, *at first*. Then it became more than that. I started being with him for free and we fell in love. Why should I have to spend my holidays alone? I belong here just as much as you do. Even more, probably, because I'm the one satisfying his needs."

Henry seized Mahagony and started pushing her toward the door. "I don't know what kind of game you're running but you need to get the hell out of this house right now."

Meredith's sister, Elaine, Miss Know-It-All, was the first family member to jump into the mix. "Henry, how could you do this to Meredith? She's been faithful to you all these years and treated you like gold. You filthy bastard!"

Mahagony pulled away from Henry and spit in his face. "That's right! You are a filthy bastard!"

Meredith couldn't take it anymore. She broke out in tears and ran upstairs. Both of her sisters followed her.

The rest of the family stood around in silence, regarding Henry with expressions that ran the breadth from anger to pure repugnance.

Jude really laid it on thick by burying her head in a pillow from the sofa and sobbing. She was in actuality laughing and grinning from ear to ear but they all thought she was overcome with emotion. One of her uncles came over and started patting her on the back. "It's going to be okay, Jonquinette."

Henry finally broke out of the state of shock he'd gone into when Meredith took off up the stairs. He became physical and dragged Mahagony out the door onto the porch. He told her, "Don't ever come around here again or I'm calling the police. You're obviously some hopeless whore who thinks she can achieve something from doing this. Well, you're not getting a damn thing except locked up if you don't leave."

Henry came back in and slammed the door in her face.

Everyone could hear her outside screaming, "You bastard! I should call the police on you! You're gonna take care of me and this baby! I'm taking you to court! You hear me, Henry! Do you hear me, you bastard!"

Jude got up from the couch, wiping fake tears and announced, "I'm going to lie down!"

No one paid much attention to her as she eased upstairs. They were all too busy preparing to rip Henry a new asshole for mistreating the precious Meredith.

Ten P.M.

Jonquinette woke up and wondered why it was so quiet in the house. She noticed that it was dark outside and couldn't believe it when she saw that it was ten o'clock on her digital alarm clock. She couldn't have possibly slept through the entire Thanksgiving.

She got up and went into the bathroom to wash her face. When she glimpsed in the mirror, she couldn't remember putting on the outfit she was wearing. There was a sheer layer of lip gloss on her lips. She didn't recall putting that on either.

As she went down the hall toward the steps, she paused to look into her parents' bedroom. There were clothes strewn everywhere and evidence of a struggle. Jonquinette grew scared. *Had something bad happened? Had there been an intruder or something?*

Jonquinette tiptoed downstairs and was relieved when she saw her aunt Elaine and aunt Louise sitting on the couch with her mother between them.

"Momma," she called out. "What's going on? Where's everyone else?"

Her mother didn't answer. Instead, she broke out in tears.

Elaine hopped up and came over to Jonquinette. "Don't worry. It's going to be fine. You and your mother still have each other."

At that point, Jonquinette's knees went weak. "Where's my daddy?" she asked.

Elaine cradled Jonquinette's face in her hands. "He's gone."

"Gone." Jonquinette started crying. "He died?"

"No, child. In light of what happened earlier today, your mother thought it best that he leave. He took some things with him and, who knows, maybe one day they can reconcile."

Meredith yelled out in anger, "Don't lie to her! There's not going to be any damn reconciliation! He cheated on me with a hooker! A hooker! I hope he burns in hell!"

Louise patted Meredith on the back. "If there's any justice in this world, he will burn in hell for all eternity."

Jonquinette didn't know what to say, so she didn't say one single word.

19

---

jonquinette

I heard the knock at my door and debated. I wanted to go out with Mason so bad but, in all fairness, how could I allow him to become involved with a basket case like me?

He knocked again and I realized he wasn't going away. It was seven on the dot and we had a date. I couldn't believe I was going on an actual date: my first for all intents and purposes.

I smoothed out the cream dress I had selected to wear, one last time, hoping it wasn't too wrinkled. Then I opened the door.

"Hey, Mason."

"Hey, Jonquinette." He was standing there looking as attractive as ever. "You all set to go?" he asked.

"Um . . ." I was too caught up in his hazel eyes to come up with an answer at first. Then I realized I couldn't go through with it. "Actually, could you step inside for a moment? I really need to talk about something important with you."

"No, no, no," Mason said, shaking his head so his dreadlocks swung from side to side. "Don't do this to me again, Jonquinette. Don't cancel out on our date."

"Could you please just come in?" Grudgingly, he came inside but stood right inside the door and didn't venture any farther. "Mason, there are a lot of things you don't know about me."

He grinned, as if to say "is that all?"

"I'm sure. There are tons of things we don't know about each other," he said. "That's the whole rationale behind dating—getting to know each other better."

"You don't understand." I diverted my eyes from him. "I have some issues that I need to work through before I can get caught up with someone."

"Okay, I'll bite." He crossed him arms in front of him and sighed. "What kind of issues?"

I turned my back on him and went to sit down on the couch. "This is extremely complicated for me."

After closing my front door, coming into the living room and sitting down beside me, Mason said, "Take your time."

How could I put it without making myself sound insane?

"Let's just say that I have a lot of emotional baggage that I'm hauling around with me."

"Don't we all?" Mason asked. He reached for me and gently rubbed my shoulder. "Jonquinette, I don't profess to be some sort of saint. I've had troubled relationships in my past. I'm not about to give up on finding Ms. Right, though. Life is short and I intend to share mine with someone."

"So you're looking for a serious relationship?" I asked, because I knew that if I entered into any type of relationship at that point in my life, it would have to be a committed one. Dating numerous men was definitely out of the question. Besides, Mason was the only man I had ever been willing to take the risk for anyway.

"Eventually," he responded. He slid his hand all the way down my arm and took my hand. "I won't lie to you or attempt to deceive you. No one ever knows where something might lead. But, I'm at the point in my life where I could see myself settling down with my soul mate." He leaned over and kissed me on the corner of my mouth. "I'm only being so persistent with you because I have a feeling that you might be her."

"Then again, I might not be her," I stated halfhearted. If I was crazy, then I certainly wasn't the one for him or anyone else.

"There's only one way to find out," he said and stood up, pulling me up with him. "So, are we going out to dinner or not?"

I strained my mouth into a smile. "Sure. Why not?"

Mason gave me a strong hug. "Exactly. Why not?"

Less than thirty minutes later, we were being seated at a nice, cozy table at the Skyy Club. "This is a nice restaurant," I commented.

Mason opened up his menu. "I'm glad you like it."

"Do you come here often?" I asked.

"No, this is my first time here. One of my buddies told me about the place at work. He said it had a remarkable atmosphere and appetizing food."

The place definitely had charm and the aroma throughout the restaurant was mouth-watering. "Well, he was right on both counts." There was a band playing that was also incredible. "The music is wonderful also," I added.

"So tell me more about yourself, Jonquinette."

"I'm an accountant for an office supply company and that's about it. I generally go to work and come home. What do you do for a living?"

"I'm a quality control manager for a biomedical company."

"That sounds major. Are you a brainiac?"

"Not hardly. My parents kind of forced me into the profession. They thought it would pay well and get me out of their house before I turned forty."

We both laughed.

"It's true that a lot of college graduates are having problems making it solo," I said.

"Well, you seem to be holding your own."

"I don't really have a choice. My father is no longer in my life and my mother is not the type of person to live with. She would drive me plum foolish. So I definitely have to make it by myself."

I was hoping Mason didn't ask me for more details about my parents.

"What other things do you enjoy doing?" he asked.

I shrugged because I honestly didn't know.

"Do you like movies? Plays? Museums?"

I shrugged again. "I suppose I like all of the above but it has been ages since I've been to any of them," I replied honestly.

"Well, we'll have to change that. We can't have you hiding out in your apartment, missing out on the finer things in life."

How did he know I hid out in my apartment?

"This is what we're going to do. Within the next month, I'm going to take you to at least one movie, one play, and one museum. Deal?"

"Deal." I tried to cover my blush my putting the menu up closer to my face. "Thank you."

"There's no need to thank me. Thank you for agreeing to spend at least three more evenings with me."

I blushed so hard, I thought my cheeks would explode.

We enjoyed a delicious meal: rosemary chicken with tarragon sauce, garlic mashed potatoes, and steamed asparagus. Mason convinced me to dabble with a little wine so we shared a bottle of Kendell-Jackson Chardonnay. It was smooth-tasting but left me a bit tipsy.

Mason asked, "How about a dance?"

I wasn't secure about being able to get up without falling right back down on my ass but I said, "Sure."

The band was playing a jazzy version of Jagged Edge's "Goodbye." When Mason took me into his arms, I had never felt more protected or warm. I laid my head on his chest and got lost in the total experience. Then he made an extraordinary evening even more perfect by lifting my chin and fervently kissing me.

When we returned to my place, we spent an entire hour "making out." That was another first for me and I was thoroughly comfortable with it until . . .

. . . he tried to slip his fingers inside my panties, which were soaking wet.

I pushed him away and said, "I'm sorry. I'm just not ready."

Mason didn't get mad or cop an attitude at all. He kissed me on the forehead and said, "Thanks again for the lovely evening."

I grinned. "No, thank you."

He got up from the sofa and let himself out, saying, "I'll see you later," as he shut the door behind him. I remained on the sofa for a good fifteen minutes, just lying there and pondering the possibilities. It was time to pay another visit to Dr. Spencer.

20

jonquinette

It was Monday and time for my next appointment. For some reason, it felt like I was floating on air as I made my way down the hallway to Dr. Spencer's office. Mason had changed me for the better and I was determined to improve my situation even further. No matter what it took, I was going to find an inner peace.

"Did I ever tell you how I found out about you?" I asked Marcella after I was seated on her chaise lounge.

"No, how?" she replied. "I would guess that someone referred you but I don't often ask who."

"Zoe Reynard suggested that I contact you."

A huge grin came across her face, like I had mentioned her best friend or something. "Aw, Zoe. She's wonderful, isn't she?"

"From what I've seen, yes, she is."

"If you don't mind my asking, how do you know Zoe?"

I wasn't sure I wanted to go there. Then again, I was paying to see a psychiatrist so if I couldn't tell her everything, who could I tell? "I don't really know her. She's very active in these meetings I used to attend."

"I assume you mean the sexual addiction meetings at the hospital," Marcella said.

"Yes."

"When you say *used to,* does that mean you no longer go to them?"

"I haven't been for the last few weeks."

"Any particular reason?"

I took a deep breath. "For one thing, I'm not sure I'm addicted to sex. I mean, I've never had sex to my knowledge. I was just baffled and had no idea where to turn. Then one day I saw this ad in the local community paper about various support groups at the hospital. On an impulse, I checked out their website and sure enough, they had something for people with sexual troubles."

"Well, I'm just glad that you decided to give me an opportunity. A one-on-one situation is probably healthier for you anyway."

"That's an understatement." I chuckled. "I attended those meetings week after week and never said a word."

Marcella apparently didn't find it comical. She just said, "Then this is definitely best for you."

"Anyway, I just wanted to let you know how I came to find you." There was a pregnant pause before I added excitedly, "I have some news."

Marcella sat up taller in her chair. "Okay, I'm listening."

"I have this new neighbor. His name's Mason," I said with a grin.

"You're blushing." Marcella stood up and came around the desk. She sat on the edge closer to me and asked, "Does that mean there's some interest there?"

I quickly admitted, "A *whole lot* of interest, but this is a totally new thing for me. As you know, I've never had a boyfriend or anything like that."

"Then it's about time you see what having one feels like."

"Do you really think that's wise?" I asked. "I mean, under my current circumstances. What if—"

Marcella read me like a book. "You're afraid that someone else might end up dating him instead, right?"

It had become painfully evident to me that I was not alone in my body. I couldn't be. And while it was frightening to think that someone else controlled my actions, it was more frightening to allow it to continue without trying to do something to stop them.

"Right," I said. "I've thought long and hard about what you said and it's the only thing that makes sense."

"I'm glad you realize that," Marcella said.

"So what do I do and where do I go from here?"

Marcella seemed lost in deep thought for a moment. "Have you given any more thought to contacting your father?"

"Why did you bring him up?" I asked, even though I had indeed thought a lot about it.

"Sometimes people from our past can help us put together the pieces. You said your mother refuses to face facts but that your father always suspected something."

I shook my head in dismay. "I still don't understand what happened the night he got kicked out the house. It was one of those days when I simply wasn't there. I had blacked out completely and on Thanksgiving Day, no less."

"Thanksgiving?"

"Yes." I closed my eyes so I could recall the bad memories. "From what I've been able to piece together, a hooker showed up at the family dinner claiming that my father had been paying her for sexual favors for months. She also told everyone she was pregnant."

"Oh my! Was it true?" Marcella gasped.

"He denied it all," I replied. "The funny thing is, I just can't imagine my father doing something like that, especially with a hooker."

"But why would someone just show up and say that unless it was true?"

"That is something that will probably boggle my mind forever. My mother has never gotten over it. She thinks that by dating a bunch of other men, it will make her feel like more of a woman. Having someone trashy show up claiming to be his side action really messed with her self-esteem. She's been trying to get it back ever since."

"It sounds like she might need some counseling as well."

As ugly as my own situation was, even I couldn't help but laugh at that one. "Momma definitely needs some help."

"Do you think your mother would consider attending some sessions here with you?"

I snickered at the mere thought. "Not in this lifetime."

"What about your father?" Marcella asked me.

"Quite honestly, I have no idea. My father might have finally written me off by now. If I were him, I would."

"But you're not him," Marcella reminded me. "You should at least call him."

"I've never stopped loving him," I whispered. Then I looked Marcella in the eyes. "A phone call might not do it. Maybe I'll go see him."

21

jude

I couldn't take the shit one more second. Not one more second. I took over and screamed out, "There is no way in fucking hell Henry's coming back into the picture!"

"What did you just say?" the bitch doctor asked me. I didn't respond. "Jonquinette?" I got up from the chaise and started for the door. "Jonquinette?"

I turned to face her and gave her an evil grin, but still refused to reply.

"Who are you?" she asked.

"Your worst fucking nightmare, bitch!" I spewed out at her.

She sat back down calmly at her desk and folded her hands. "Well, it's nice to finally meet you. Do you have a name?"

"Hmph, you think you're so fucking smooth." I had to admit that she was just that: smooth. I would have expected her to freak out or something. "Okay, I'll play along. My name's Jude—and yours?" I sat down across from her at the desk. Nobody out attitudes me. "Oh, never mind, I already know your name. Bitch!"

"That's not very ladylike, calling me out of my name," she said. *Was she trying to piss me off or something?*

"Since I'm not a lady, who gives a flying fuck?" I retorted.

"So Jude, what made you finally come out and say hello?" She reached into her top drawer and pulled out a cigarette. "Mind if I smoke?"

"Suit yourself."

She lit one up. "Was it Jonquinette talking about reaching out to her father? *Your father?*"

"Henry Pierce is not my damn daddy!" I said. So much for playing it cool.

"Hmm, you seem to harbor a lot of negative feelings toward him."

"My, my, you are a mastermind," I stated contemptuously. "It took getting a degree to figure that out?"

"Jude, I'd really like to be your friend. Would you consider that?"

"I don't need any fucking friends."

"You know, Jonquinette thinks she's going insane. The things you've been doing aren't very nice."

"You don't know the half of it. I'm proud of myself." I crossed my legs, determined not to let the heifer make me lose it.

"Why's that?" she asked.

"Because I'm the shit. Jon's lucky to have me. Without me, she would've had her ass kicked her entire life. Without me, she would've let everyone run over her, especially the Queen Bitch, Meredith."

"Your mother?"

I sighed. "I don't know why you keep referring to that hoe and bastard as *my* parents. I don't have parents." The slut just didn't get it. "Anyway, like I was saying before you so *rudely* interrupted me, Jon wouldn't have a leg to stand on without me. Don't go throwing a pity party for her ass. You should be celebrating the fact that I *exist*."

"But the two of you can't coexist together."

"And why the hell not? We've been coexisting all this time."

"Because that's not healthy."

"So what are you saying?" I asked, getting pissed off all over again. The bitch had lost her mind and I told her, "If you think I'm going someplace, you need a psychiatrist your damn self."

She was determined to try to bond with me. The slut. "Jude, tell me about yourself."

I shrugged and said, "There's nothing to tell. I put foot to ass when need be, protect Jon from people that try to fuck her over without grease, and I love to have fun from time to time."

"What kind of fun?" she asked.

"I'll be honest. I love fucking. Fucking is the only thing worth doing in this life."

Marcella seemed bewildered. Good, I'd finally stumped her. "Do you honestly believe that?"

"Yeah."

"Why?"

"Men are such wimps. They always fold under the pressure of the pussy. I like controlling them like the little puppy dogs that they are."

"That's the word I was looking for," she said.

"What word?" I inquired with disdain.

"Control. You want to control things."

I stood up and leaned over the desk. "Don't get it twisted. I *do* control things. I'm always around. I just let Jon deal with normal day-to-day bullshit so I don't have to. If I wanted to, I could take over for good and never, ever let Jon come back. That's how dominant I am."

Marcella smiled at me. "You don't believe that any more than I do."

"Excuse me, bitch?"

"If you could truly take over for good, you would've done it years ago."

"You're beginning to bore me." I didn't like the way the conversation was headed. She didn't know shit about anything and to top it off, she wasn't shit to me so I announced, "I'm leaving."

I had made it to the door and opened it when she jumped in front of me.

"No, don't leave yet."

I poked her in the shoulder. "If you don't move out of my way, I *will* give you a beatdown you'll never forget."

"Jude, we really need to continue this conversation."

"I'm going to count to three and then I'm swinging," I told her. "One."

"Jude, please stay," she pleaded.

I balled my right hand into a fist. "Two."

"When can we talk again?" she asked.

"Three," I said and lifted my fist to steal her one in the face.

She must have known that I was serious because she moved to the side and said, "Okay, okay."

I damn near tore off her arm as I stormed past her out of the office.

There was no way I was going home. I headed straight to a bar to get my drink on. When I walked into a pub, it was boring as shit and there were only a bunch of losers hanging around. I decided I needed to do something more adventurous.

How dare that bitch doctor imply that I wasn't in control?

Huh, she was a complete idiot. Everything I had said in her office was the truth. If I really wanted to, I could make Jonquinette disappear altogether and just be Jude. But I didn't feel like working a full-time job to pay bills and I had no work experience of my own. None whatsoever.

A lightbulb went off in my head. If I could devise a way to make my own money, fuck Jon and her boring lifestyle.

I left the pub, got back into the car, and headed for "the seedy part of town." The part of town where there were liquor stores on every corner, pawn shops on every other block and most importantly, a shitload of strip clubs.

I spotted one that seemed to have heavy traffic, even for a Monday evening. A lot of desperate-looking businessmen and blue-collar workers were flooding into the joint. The name on the awning was The Bedroom. *Not very creative,* I thought.

The shitty name didn't matter to me. I only cared about the place's potential as a moneymaker.

When I got to the door, some idiot tried to tell me I had to pay a ten-dollar cover charge to come in. I informed him that I was there to apply for a job. He looked me up and down and grinned. Even with the homely looking outfit Jon had selected for the day, he could still tell my body was banging.

"Go on in," he said, moving aside to allow me to gain entry. "When you get in, ask for the owner. His name's Skippy."

"Skippy? What the hell kind of name is that?" I asked.

"Hey, it is what it is," the bouncer at the door replied. "As long as I get paid, I don't care what his name is."

I couldn't fault him for that one so I said, "True enough."

I was pleasantly surprised when I got inside and it became clearer to me why they had such a large clientele. It was a classy place, despite its outward appearance. There was a nice leather bar spanning the entire length of the club on the left and about fifty or so tables scattered around the dance floor in the center. All of the tables had plush velvet chairs and the waitresses wore cute little velvet outfits that left hardly anything to the imagination.

I stopped one of the waitresses in her tracks. "Where can I find Skippy?"

She pointed to a chubby black man seated at the end of the bar talking on a cell phone. He had on an outdated suit with a wrinkled shirt and his tie was crooked.

"Shame on it all," I said aloud. "You mean to tell me that crusty son of a bitch owns this place?"

The waitress laughed. "Yeah, Mr. Crusty runs the show."

"Where's the bathroom?" I asked.

She pointed to the back of the club. "Down that hall on your left."

I made my way to the bathroom and did some self-improvement. While I had made it past the bouncer with ease, I needed to spruce up some before I approached the owner. I unbuttoned the top three buttons of my blouse and hiked up my skirt a few inches to show more leg. I let my hair down and shook it to give it more of an untamed appearance.

Interestingly enough, there was a basket on the counter with all kinds of makeup in it. I guess the girls wanted to make sure they always looked good so they could land major tips. Lucky me. I lined my eyes, darkened my eyebrows, threw on some rouge and put on the raunchiest shade of lipstick I could find: blood red.

I puckered up, took one last glimpse at myself in the mirror and then went back out into the club.

Skippy was still in the same spot at the bar, but he was off the phone and had some hoochie momma all up in his grille. It seemed like they were having a heated discussion but I didn't give a shit. I approached them and pushed her to the side.

"Excuse me!" she said nastily.

"You're excused. No problem," I replied. I pushed up on Skippy and stood between his legs while he sat on the barstool. "I need to have a word or two with Skippy."

The hoochie momma spewed "Bitch!" at me and then started walking away. She pointed at Skippy and said, "We'll finish this later!"

"My, my, my," he said, eyeing me from head to toe. "You sure are a feisty one."

"You don't know the half of it." I nodded my head toward the bartender. "Since you own this joint, how about a free drink?"

"Normally, I don't give out free drinks but you can have one." He glanced at the bartender. "Sheila, give this young lady whatever she wants."

I told Sheila, "Hook me up with a blow job."

She laughed and said, "A woman who knows her stuff."

"A blow job?" Skippy inquired. "That's a drink?"

"Yeah. You mean you own this place and nobody's ever asked for a blow job?" I rubbed my hip against his thigh seductively. "I mean, a blow job drink. Not the real kind. I'm sure there are plenty of requests for those around here."

He grinned at me and almost started drooling on himself. "You've got some height on you, girl. How tall are you?"

"Tall enough to wrap my ankles around a man's neck and let him pummel his dick into me *all night long.*"

Skippy was about to say something when Sheila came back with my drink, which consisted of equal parts of Kahlua, Bailey's, and vodka layered into a pony glass and topped with whipped cream.

Skippy practically came on himself when I put my hands behind my back, placed my mouth over the top of the glass, raised it, and took it all down the hatch in one swallow. I put the glass back down on the bar, using only my mouth and asked, "Don't you just love a woman that swallows?"

Skippy cleared his throat. One of the strippers came up to him and before she could say a word, he told her, "Beat it!" She rolled her eyes and walked away. "This must be my lucky day but I have to ask. To what do I owe this honor?"

"Skippy, I've got a straightforward proposition. I'm interested in being a stripper. At least, I *might* be interested."

"Can you dance?"

I gave him a fierce look. "Can you get your dick hard?"

"Hell, yeah," he replied.

"Then there's your answer to a stupid-ass question."

He raised his hands in the air. "Hey, I had to ask. It's obvious you have *certain talents,*" he commented, picking up the pony glass and staring at it. "But the men come here to see women shake that ass with some degree of expertise."

I looked over at the dance floor. There was some bitch performing off "Back That Thang Up" by Juvenille. "You mean like her?"

Skippy glanced at the dancer. "Yeah, just like Kandi. She's one of our headliners."

I smirked. "Well, Kandi doesn't look the least bit sweet to me and if she's truly one of your headliners, then you've been seriously missing out."

"You talk a lot of shit," he said.

"But I can back it up."

"Come by tomorrow and audition."

"Fuck that. I want to dance tonight, right now."

Skippy shook his head. "Naw, never that. All the dancers have to do a private audition first. I can't just let you get up there without knowing that you can handle your own."

"Private audition? Is that the same thing as a trial fuck?"

Skippy eyed me suspiciously. "You sure you're not the poe-poe?"

"The poe-poe?"

"Yeah, the police. Five-O."

The idiot was starting to rub me the wrong way.

"No, I'm not the fucking police but I fucked a couple of them once." I couldn't help but snicker as I remembered the time I'd been pulled over for speeding in Jon's car. I couldn't allow a ticket to come to the apartment if it wasn't paid or even risk her finding out if I paid it so I did what I had to do and fucked both police officers in the back of their squad car to get off scot-free.

"You're a trip, girl," Skippy said.

"Can I ask you a question?"

"Sure."

"How old are you, Skippy?"

"Old enough to be your damn daddy, that's for sure."

"Then don't you have enough confidence in yourself to believe you'd be able to spot a police officer if one came in here under-cover?" I asked.

"Of course."

"Then why are we wasting valuable time with asinine questions?"

Skippy chuckled. "You've got me making all kinds of exceptions up in this bitch tonight. First the free drink and now you've actually got me thinking about letting you get up on the stage without an audition. I live by rules. They are my rules, but they are rules just the same."

I ran my fingertips over his chest. "Skippy, what's the point of having rules if you never venture to break them?"

"What's your name, Sugar?"

I hadn't thought about a name until that point. I needed something that would land a bunch of bucks. "Just call me Mercy because that's what men will have to beg me for when I start slaying their dicks with my pussy."

Skippy almost fell off the barstool when he broke out in laughter. "Okay, Mercy. You have something to wear for your big performance?"

"No, just tell the audience the truth. That I wandered in off the street and asked for a *public audition*. Like I said, I'm not sure I want to be a stripper. I just want to try it out for one night and see if I'm feeling the profession and if the profession is feeling me."

"Name your song, girl!" Skippy said anxiously.

Ten minutes later, I was taking the stage to Madonna's "Secret" and the crowd was rowdy from the first second. Skippy had personally announced me and they were all excited about a freak coming in on a whim to shed it all.

I closed my eyes and got into the tempo as it started out slowly and then picked up the pace. The song was just fast enough and just seductive enough to dance erotically to and before I knew it, men were pitching dollar bills on the stage.

I swirled my hips and started undoing the rest of my blouse until it was completely undone. I turned my back to the audience and inched it off my shoulders until it was covering my hips. Then I swung back around and let it fall to the floor. I palmed my breasts and rubbed on my nipples through my bra. They immediately stood at attention.

I reached behind me and unzipped the skirt. Once again, I turned my back to them and started working my hips out of the skirt as the DJ switched to my next request: "Always on Time" by Ja Rule. I really got into it then and so did they. They started chanting, "Mercy! Mercy! Mercy!"

I worked my way over to a young brotha sitting at a table right in front of the stage. I got down on my knees and moved them back and forth together, licked my index finger and rubbed it over the crotch of my panties. I placed my fingertip on his lips and he licked it. Then he handed me a five-dollar bill.

I spent the rest of the song making my rounds and collecting money. I even swung around the pole a time or two but didn't try to jump on the top and slide down. I wasn't geared up for that one and didn't want to make a fool out of myself if I fell. I danced to two other songs after that one ended: "Super Freak" by Rick James and "Mr. Big Stuff" by Jean Knight.

Once the next stripper, who went by the name of Pisces, took the stage, I spent about an hour doing lap dances and yes, collecting more money. I was convinced that, if I really wanted to, I could make a good living shaking my ass in men's faces.

I got dressed, thanked Skippy for the experience and told him that I may or may not be back. He seemed disappointed and claimed he would make me his star if I decided to work for him.

When I got outside, I noticed that two men were following me. They had been seated at the bar inside the club. *Is this what strippers have to put up with?* I thought. *Motherfuckers trailing them out the damn club?*

"Hey, Mercy!" one of them called out.

I swung around to face them. "What the hell do you all want? Why are you following me?"

The other one, obviously as drunk as his friend, said, "We want you to make us beg for mercy."

At first, I rolled my eyes and then I checked them out more closely. They weren't half-bad-looking and it had been a while since I'd fucked two men at once. Still, I wasn't interested so I told them, "I'm not interested but I'm sure one of the other girls would be, if the situation's right." I was implying that they could get whatever they wanted if the money was on point, and they knew it.

"Well, what would we have to do to make the situation right for you?" the first one asked.

"Not a damn thing. I'm just not feeling it tonight."

They started whispering to each other. I walked on toward the car. "Listen," one of them called out. It turned out to be the taller of the two. "Duke and I have always had this competitive spirit. He and I both claim we're the best pussy connoisseur on the planet but the bullshit talk is getting old."

I raised an eyebrow. "And?"

"And how about you let us settle the dispute once and for all?"

I laughed. "So you two want to eat me out and let me decide who's better at it?"

The shorter one nodded. "Exactly."

Now I was tired and drained but I had never been one to turn down a good pussy eating and if they were planning to battle, then they would both be trying to outdo even themselves.

I stood there trying to come up with the right price. If I didn't charge them, it would have seemed bizarre. Besides, they were undoubtedly planning to pay, and money is money.

Finally, I said, "A hundred bucks each."

"To eat you?" the taller one asked.

"Look, I don't have all night," I said. "Either you want to eat this pussy or you don't. It makes no difference to me."

The taller one glanced at his friend. "Maybe we should go back inside and find someone else."

The shorter one objected. "No, I want this one right here. If a hundred is too steep for you, I got you. It's all good because I know that I'm going to win the competition and it's worth every penny to get you to stop bragging on that tongue and shut the hell up."

He dug into his pocket, pulled out a wad of cash and paid me. I winked at him and said, "It's on."

As I lay on a bed in a pay-by-the-hour motel with my legs spread open being eaten out, I couldn't help but giggle. That damn bitch doctor didn't know what she was talking about. I was in complete control to the point that I had taken Jon's degradation to another level by accepting cash for a sexual favor. The shorter one found himself ass out. Not only did he give up the two hundred; he also gave up bragging rights because the taller one was *definitely* the best pussy connoisseur on the planet.

22

jonquinette

Never had I wished that I had started my own accounting firm more than when I went into work that Thursday and asked for Friday off. You would have thought the world had come to an end by the expression on Mr. Wilson's face.

"Jonquinette, we really need you here tomorrow," he whined. "We're backed up on a lot of things."

"Hmph, I thought we were all caught up. I only have one thing in my in box and that will take me less than ten minutes to straighten out. Fridays are slow but anything that comes in, I can surely knock out on Monday morning."

"Are you ill?" Mr. Wilson asked me.

"No, I actually need to go see my father in North Carolina."

"I wasn't aware that your father was still alive."

He said that as if I regularly discussed my private life with him.

For all he knew, my mother wasn't among the living and she lived right in Atlanta.

"Yes, he's alive," I said.

"Well, is he ill?"

"Yeah, he is," I lied, sensing that Daddy would have to be practically on his death bed in order for my day off to be a crisis.

"What's wrong with him?" Mr. Wilson pried.

I didn't want to wish anything too bad on Daddy so I said, "He runs an auto repair shop and there was a mishap."

"What sort of mishap?"

"Um, one of the cars fell off the lift. Luckily, it fell to the side but it did bang against his leg and it's broken."

What I said couldn't have sounded more outlandish and I realized it after I said it. Amazingly, Mr. Wilson believed me. He winced and said, "Ooh, that sounds painful. You should go check on him, in that case."

"Thank you."

He started walking out of my office but paused. "Now, you will be back here on Monday, right?"

"With bells on," I replied. When he left, I added, "More like with shackles on my feet."

Darnetta came in as I was talking to myself. "Did you say something?"

"Oh, no, just thinking aloud."

Darnetta sat down without an invitation. "So what's up, girlfriend? We haven't had a chance to talk much since the wedding. What happened to you that night anyway? Logan said you got sick but you seemed fine when I picked you up and all throughout the wedding."

I deliberated over an answer but knew I couldn't take too long to fabricate one because Darnetta would figure me out.

"Um, I must have eaten something that didn't agree with me."

Either that or I ate entirely too much. My stomach was upset. Plus, I had cramps."

"Hmph, please don't mention cramps. I'm on my period now and mine are killing me."

"Have you been drinking hot tea?" I asked her, legitimately concerned for her well-being.

"No, tea and I don't agree with each other. It always makes me feel bloated and I feel bad enough already."

"What about some of that over-the-counter medication for cramps?" I asked.

"I've tried every brand they make and nothing seems to help."

"All I can say is the person that invents something to stop menstrual cramps is going to be one wealthy man."

"It won't be a man who invents it," Darnetta said. "That's the quandary now. I bet you all the ones on the market were invented by people who have never felt a single menstrual cramp in their lives."

We both laughed.

"Probably true," I agreed. "Well, the good part is that we only have to suffer the madness for a few days a month."

"Yeah, but three days on a period can feel like three years sometimes." Darnetta got up and went for the door. "I'm going to call you soon so we can hook up again."

"Okay," I said, knowing good and well that I wouldn't be hanging out with her ever again. I wasn't even clear about what had happened the first time that I did.

It took me four hours to drive from Atlanta to the outskirts of Charlotte. He lived in a small town called Trinity. Once there, I drove around for more than an hour searching for my father's house. Everyone in the small town knew each other so I stopped an older African-American couple and asked them. They said Daddy fixed their cars for them and was a great man. Then they gave me directions. One or both of them must have been senile because it took me a while to figure out that they had told me to turn left on High Bridge Road when I should have turned right.

It was dusk when I finally arrived. I was shaken to see the condition of the place. From the outside, it looked like it was about to give way. While Daddy had never been one to define himself by his surroundings, this was definitely not what I expected.

I rang the doorbell and was stunned when a little girl answered the door.

"Can I help you?" she asked in the sweetest voice.

I glanced up at the house number on the porch to make sure I had the right place. "Um, does Henry Pierce live here?"

"Daddy!" the girl yelled out as she disappeared around a corner.

Daddy?

A moment later, my father appeared and had to take two steps back when he saw me. "Jonquinette?"

"You say that like it's a question. Has it been so long that you don't even recognize me?" I asked.

"Of course, I recognize you." He embraced me, then pulled me inside. "Come on in, please."

The little girl stood there swaying her hips. She was adorable with fudge-colored skin and big brown eyes. She had her shoulder-length hair in two pigtails tied with violet ribbons to match her short set.

"Jonquinette, this is Flower. Flower, this is your big sister, Jonquinette," Daddy said, making a formal introduction.

I got the impression that Flower never knew of my existence. I couldn't blame Daddy for not telling her. Since I had not responded to any of his letters, he had to assume that she would never meet me. She would have been confused to know that she had an older sister who was never around.

"It's very nice to meet you, Flower," I said, extending my hand, which she graciously accepted and gently shook.

Daddy sighed and looked at me. "I'll explain everything."

I told him, "You don't owe me an explanation."

We all migrated into his living room, which was very basic but neat. At least he hadn't become a slob over the years. He had a tattered couch and loveseat set that had seen much better days, a scratched-up coffee table, and a new nineteen-inch television sitting on top of the original box by a window. It was hot and his air-conditioning unit in the window wasn't working too efficiently. I immediately started sweating.

"Flower is a very pretty name," I told the little half-sister that I never knew existed.

She blushed like it was the biggest compliment she had ever had. "Thank you. My mother picked it out."

"Well, she did an excellent job." I surveyed the house. The dining-room table was bare and there were no pictures on any of the walls from what I could see; definitely no visible signs of a woman's touch. I wanted to know if Daddy was remarried without coming out and directly inquiring about it, so I asked, "Is your mother here?"

"Oh, no." Flower shook her head and hips simultaneously. "She doesn't live here but she's coming to pick me up Sunday night."

Daddy cleared his throat. "Flower, why don't you go get washed up for dinner."

"Okay, Daddy."

Flower pranced off and I could hear her little footsteps running up the stairs.

"No running in the house!" Daddy yelled after her.

I laughed. "Some things never change. You used to yell the same thing at me."

He grinned. "That's because you wouldn't listen and ran through the house every single day."

I picked up a department store sales paper from the coffee table and started fanning myself. "She's adorable. How old is she?"

"Six." He went over to the air conditioner and banged on it. "Sorry it's so hot in here. I'm trying to save up to get central air but it's not easy. Even with regular clients, it still isn't easy making a good living in this backass town."

"Well, Daddy, no one told you to give up being a computer programmer."

He and I both sat down on the sofa.

"No," he said. "They just told me to give up my whole damn family, which was the same thing as giving up my life."

I could tell that he was still bitter about the divorce and wanted to say something like, "You made your own bed so lie in it." But I didn't. It wasn't my objective to visit him and incite drama after so many years.

"I guess you neglected to mention her in your letters," I said, getting back to Flower.

He sighed. "I didn't know how to word it. I figured if I told you I had another daughter, I'd never get a response."

I disagreed. "Actually, it probably would've been the exact opposite. If I'd known I had a little sister, I would've wanted to meet her."

"You want something to drink? I have some orange juice and milk."

"No, I'm fine for now. I already knew you had orange juice and milk because . . ."

"Those are the only two things a person needs daily to survive," we said in unison. Daddy used to wear that saying out when I was a child. If my mother didn't have anything else in the house, she knew she better have milk and orange juice or Daddy would have a fit.

We sat in silence for a minute, feeling each other out with our eyes.

"To make a time-consuming story short, her mother, Allison, and I are just good friends," he said, evidently referring to Flower's mother. "We took pleasure in each other's company for a while and Flower was the result. We haven't fooled around in years. We just share custody and try to make sure she has a normal life."

"Unlike my life, which was never normal," I blurted out.

He put his hands on his knees, like he was bracing himself for something physically painful. "I don't know what to say."

I stroked him on the hand so he would ease up some. "No need to say anything. We'll chat about it later. I'm planning to stay for a couple of days, if that's okay?"

He smiled like he had won the lottery. "Jonquinette, you have no idea how okay that is. You've made my day, my year, *my decade,* by showing up here."

I was hoping he would still feel that way by the time it was all over, said and done. "So, what's for dinner?"

23

---

jonquinette

Daddy wasn't much of a cook; again, some things never change. He made his best attempt at making spaghetti and it needed major sprucing up. He had no spices in the house at all except salt and pepper so we made do with that.

Flower was the exact opposite of me as a child. She was conversational. Throughout dinner, she told me all about attending first grade at George Washington Carver Elementary School. She explained how he had helped out farmers by inventing more than three hundred uses for peanuts. Without having to tell me, I knew that the school had to be in the black section of town. There was no way white people in North Carolina would allow their kids to attend a school named after an African American; not the part of North Carolina we were in.

I found out that her mother, Allison, was a veterinarian and according to Flower, "the saver of all of God's creatures."

I couldn't remember the last time I had held any form of conversation with a child but I truly enjoyed it. Children are so innocent and full of life. They have no expectations, no misgivings and thus, no frustration.

Daddy was pretty quiet throughout dinner, more than likely still astonished that I had even showed up. It's like one of those things you always daydream about but become content that it would never happen. His letters over the years had pleaded with me to reach out to him but I refused. I'm glad he never showed up on my doorstep because it would not have turned out the same way. Everything works on God's timetable, not our own.

As I thought that, I realized it had been too long since I had attended church and there was no excuse for that. I would have to get back to my normal schedule and begin tithing again.

I asked Daddy, "Do you attend church?"

He looked up from his plate. "Every Sunday, like clockwork. You?"

"I try to, but I will admit that lately I have slacked off a bit."

"Well, how about we all go together this Sunday?" he asked.

Flower squirmed anxiously in her seat. "That would be great, Daddy. Then all my friends from Sunday school can meet my big sister."

Big sister! Two little words that spoke volumes and meant big responsibility. Even though I had just met Flower and had absolutely no idea how her mother would react when she met me, or if her mother even knew about me, I made a promise to myself to play a significant role in her life. I would have given anything to have a sibling, older or younger than me, to talk to when I was a child. Parents just can't understand everything, even though they were once children themselves. Every new generation faces different challenges. People just don't seem to get it.

Again, some things never change. I realized that when Daddy

whipped out a bunch of board games after dinner. He always loved to play games. Monopoly, Trivial Pursuit and Scrabble had been replaced with more modern games like Scattergories, Who Wants to be a Millionaire, and Jeopardy.

We played two rounds of Scattergories, Flower and I against him. We beat him something terrible each time until he gave up.

After that, we made old-fashioned thick milkshakes in a blender, I was surprised Daddy had one, and sat out on the swing on the front porch gazing at the stars. Flower sat between us and did most of the pushing with her feet, even though she was the smallest. She would slide down to the edge of the seat just long enough to push us off and then pull herself back up.

"Gosh, it's so peaceful here," I said, after realizing a car hadn't passed the house in more than fifteen minutes.

"Always has been," Daddy said.

"How come you never brought me here as a child?" I asked Daddy. "To visit Grandpa?"

He shrugged and didn't respond.

My paternal grandmother, who I never knew, died before I was born but my grandfather didn't die until I was in junior high. Still, I never met him, only saw pictures. Daddy had just gotten a phone call one day, came out of his home office announcing that his father had passed, and the next morning he left by himself to return to North Carolina to "give the old man a decent burial."

I remember the day he left. A torrential rainstorm occurred. Momma was vexed about him driving in such bad weather, but he told her, "I've got to do what has to be done," and left.

He came back four days later and never spoke of it again. That was why everyone found it so bizarre when he ended up back in North Carolina a couple of years later running his father's auto shop that had lain dormant since his death.

Daddy looked at his watch and then at Flower, who was yawning and had positioned her head on his upper arm. "Flower, it's after your bedtime. Go ahead and put on your nightclothes and you can take your bath in the morning."

"Okay, Daddy."

She started scooting forward to get down off the swing. I teased the bottom of one of her pigtails. "Maybe I can do your hair for you in the morning. Would you like that?"

"Yes," she replied sweetly.

"I'll be up in a few minutes to tuck you in," Daddy said.

"Okay."

She went into the house and again, I heard her running up the steps. Again, Daddy yelled out at her and then we both laughed.

Daddy rubbed his hand across his face and exhaled. "She's a handful, I tell you."

"You seem like you're doing a good job. She's an extremely happy child."

"I never thought I'd find myself sharing custody of a child."

"Not even me?" He ignored the question so I continued, "Daddy, I understand that whatever went down with you and Momma was ugly and unrectifiable, but why didn't you fight to see me? I would have loved to spend time with you. I had you for fifteen years of my life and then you just vanished."

"It wasn't like that," he said swiftly. "There are a lot of things you don't know and can't know."

"Why can't I know them now? I'm a grown woman."

"It's best to let sleeping dogs lie." He paused and said, "Jonquinette, it's not that I'm not excited about you showing up here, but why now? After all this time? I had completely given up hope."

I thought about Dr. Spencer and said, "Someone suggested I come visit you."

He seemed staggered. "Surely, it couldn't have been your mother. I've been writing her for years, too. I got one letter back telling me to burn in hell and that she couldn't wait to dance on my grave and that was it."

"Momma was heated," I said. "But she still shouldn't have said something that malicious." I took over Flower's job and pushed us off. "I didn't know you had written her letters. She's never mentioned it."

"Hmph, why would she? She hates me."

"How do you feel about her?" I pried.

"Oh, I will always love your mother. I'll admit that our marriage went through its ups and downs but I expected to be with her forever. Until that sorry-ass bitch showed up on Thanksgiving Day and ruined everything."

"What about the child she was pregnant with?" I asked.

He raised his voice. "There was no child. I never slept with that woman. In fact, I'd never even laid eyes on her. I tried to find her though, afterward, but after searching every street corner in the hooker district, I gave up. Besides, the damage had already been done and your mother wasn't trying to hear any kind of explanation. Not that I needed to justify my actions, because I hadn't done anything."

Something about the way he talked made him seem like an innocent man. "Daddy, do you swear it wasn't true?"

"I swear," he said. "I'm not a perfect man, Jonquinette, but that *I did not do*. I never cheated on your mother and I've only been with one woman since. Allison was more of a release than anything else but I'm glad I have Flower. She gives me a basis to live." He got up off the swing. "I'm going to go tuck her in. I'll be back."

"Can I do it?" I asked.

He chuckled. "You sure?"

"Yeah, if you don't mind."

He waved me toward the house. "Be my guest but I have to warn you, she expects to be read to before she falls asleep."

"I can read," I said jokingly. "Even made it through college."

"So I heard."

"From whom?" I asked.

"I have my little spies. At least one of your relatives felt some compassion for me. I even have your graduation pictures from high school and college and copies of the ceremony programs."

"Who gave them to you?" I kept prodding.

"I'll never tell. In case you disappear again, I need to know how to keep up with your life."

I touched him on the arm. "I won't disappear again, Daddy. I promise."

I spotted a tear forming in his left eye but he swiped it away before it could land on his cheek.

We didn't say anything else; I just went into the house to find Flower.

She was in her room watching a rerun of *Sister, Sister* on the Disney channel on a thirteen-inch television. She had on a black Barbie nightgown and a pair of pink slippers. I pulled the slippers off her feet and tucked her into bed.

"You don't mind if I put you to bed, do you?" I asked.

She shook her head. "Nope. Can you read me a book?"

I giggled. "Ha, how did I know you would say that?"

She wasn't a stupid child. "Because Daddy told you I would say it."

"Okay, you got me. I looked around her room, which was the only room in the house that looked like a woman had something to do with it. There were pink sheer curtains, posters of teddy bears in ballerina outfits hanging on the walls, and a few stuffed animals strewn about. "Where do you keep your books?"

Flower pointed to a toy box by the window. I got up and walked over to it.

"Any particular one you want me to read to you?"

"Hmm, how about *Isra the Butterfly Gets Caught for Show and Tell?*"

I went through the toy box and located the book by Christine Young-Robinson. After turning off Flower's television, I sat down beside her on the bed and started reading the book. She was asleep within minutes. I sat there for a while and just stared at her. I thought about my childhood and how confusing it was. My blackouts, all the accusations, all the teasing and bullying.

I started crying and looked up at the ceiling. "Dear God, please guard this child and don't let her go through the things I went through."

I pulled myself together and I was about to go back out on the porch to check on Daddy. But, when I passed his room, I heard snoring. I peeked in on him and he was fast asleep. It had truly been a long day and the serious discussion I needed to have with him could wait.

24

jude

I couldn't believe she actually went through with it; going to see Henry fuckin' Pierce. And trying to actually bond with the motherfucker at that. I thought about doing something really foul like climbing into the bed with him buck-ass naked to make the two of them think they had actually fucked each other the next morning. Only one thing saved Jon and the bastard. Flower was in the house. She was a cute little something.

Nevertheless, I needed to seriously blow off some steam, so after Henry and Flower were fast asleep, I located the keys to his Ford Ranger, the only vehicle he had except for his tow truck.

I headed into town, what there was of it, hunting for some action. I stopped by a twenty-four-hour convenience store and there were some lowlifes hanging out front drinking forties of beer. I asked them about the local night life and they all started laughing.

One of them finally told me about a "juke joint" called The Crystal Palace. His friends all looked at him like he was tripping. I should have suspected he was up to no good. The Crystal Palace was down a dark dirt road and I knew something was wrong when I pulled up beside a pickup truck that had Redneck's Toy fancily painted across the back of the bed.

I sat there and surveyed the place for a few minutes. It was fifteen minutes after one and the parking lot was packed with nothing but pickup trucks and hot rods. I had never seen so many Novas and Chargers in my life. Nor had I seen so many Confederate flags hanging or stickered in windows. Those black men at the store were trying to set my ass up.

Two white boys pulled up on four-wheelers and parked beside a pickup that had a dead deer lying on the back. I had stumbled into *Deliverance;* it was like something right out of the movie.

I didn't leave, though. The thought of walking into a place full of "good ole boys" enticed me. Whether they wanted to acknowledge it or not, all of them had probably fantasized about fucking a sister at least once.

An inebriated couple stumbled out the front door and started making out in the middle of the parking lot. My voyeuristic side surfaced and I watched them get more and more into it. My eyes followed them as they made their way over to an older model Pontiac on the side of the building. I could still see them from my vantage point.

The girl went down on him with the speed of a bullet and he came just as fast.

"Amateurs," I said aloud. "This town sucks."

I waited for them to get into their car and drive off before I got out of Henry's truck, put on my fuck-with-me-and-I'll-fuck-you-up face, and stormed toward the entrance.

"Something Like That" by Tim McGraw was playing when I

went in. The place was off the fucking chain. People were on the dance floor line dancing and a couple of scrawny white girls were on the bar swinging tits and ass they didn't even possess.

It wasn't long before all eyes were on me. No big surprise. I knew there wouldn't be any other black people in the place before I went in. No one else was bold as shit like me to walk into a club full of rednecks. If I had been male, a *brotha,* an instant ass-kicking would have been in order, but since I was female, they didn't know what to do except stare.

I went over to the bar and waved the bartender over. She acted like she didn't want to be bothered with the likes of me, but I smacked my lips and she came over taking her little sweet time. I asked for a blow job but her dumb ass didn't know what it was, so I asked her, "Are you sharp enough to make a rum and Coke? That means you put some ice, rum, and Coke in a glass. Got it?"

She rolled her eyes and then skulked away to get my drink. I watched her like a hawk to make sure she didn't try any shady shit, like spitting in my glass or being skimpy with the rum.

After she came back with it and told me it was four-fifty, I slammed a five on the bar and told her to keep the change.

The music suddenly stopped and I thought, *Aw hell, they're about to lynch me up in here, female or not.*

I was wrong. Some drunken bastard got up on their little makeshift stage and broadcasted that is was time for the karaoke contest. Now I was really laughing at their country asses. I searched the place for some bingo tables but found none. I was convinced there was a bingo hall in Trinity someplace, though.

The first bitch that took the stage was ghastly. She couldn't hold a tune if her life depended on it. I was amazed someone didn't swing a beer bottle at her head. If Dolly Parton had been in the house, she would've been justified in doing it since it was her song that was murdered. Someone needed to tell that whore to sit down, so I did. I yelled out, "Sit down, whore! Sit down, whore!" just like the people on *Jerry Springer.*

Everyone swung around to look at me. One fat motherfucker at the bar, whose head was bigger than a watermelon, leered at me and said, "Why don't you shut up? That girl can sing."

I poked his arm, which was thicker than a country ham, and replied, "If that whore can sing, I'm Halle Berry."

"Who the hell is Halle Berry?" he asked.

"Never mind," I said, after smacking my lips in disgust. Then I got curious and started acting straight-up indignant. "Have you ever heard of any famous African Americans? Martin Luther King Jr.? Malcolm X?"

He got cynical with me. "No, but I've heard of that colored boy out in California that sliced up his wife and her buddy."

I rolled my eyes. "He never got convicted."

He took a swig of his beer and said, "Just shut up and let me enjoy the show." He must not have been able to resist being nosy because five seconds later, he was asking me, "What you doing in here anyway? You can't be from around here."

"What makes you think I ain't from around here?" I responded in a countrified accent and pretended like I had chewing tobacco in my mouth.

"'Cause you ain't," he said. "The coloreds around here know better than to come in here."

"The coloreds?" I chuckled. "Why's that? I didn't see any 'For Whites Only' signs on the front door."

He sneered at me. "Some things don't have to be said for people to know them."

"I feel you. I mean, no one has to tell me that you're a fat fuck for me to know it."

His friend beside him, who was a complete contrast, and as skinny as the bar rail asked, "What did she just say to you?"

I responded by yelling over the music and horrible singing of the next contestant who was murdering another artist's song. "I said, no one has to tell me that he's a fat fuck for me to know it!" The scrawny one just stared at me like he was sizing me up. "You think you can take me? Jump, motherfucker, jump!"

"Leroy, let me handle this," the fat fuck said, holding his palm up in front of the undernourished one's face. "Missy, if I were a lesser man, I'd do something mighty ugly to you, but my daddy raised me better than to hit a woman. So I'm just gonna let this one slide."

I laughed in his face and mocked him with my country accent. "Well, I sure do appreciate it."

I was growing bored. The karaoke was giving me a headache and the drink was weak because most of the ice had melted. I was about to leave when they announced the next contestant.

"Umph, look at him!" I said aloud.

Fat Fuck turned to me and chuckled. "So you got a thing for white meat, huh? No wonder you're up in here." He nudged his friend's shoulder. "Hey, Leroy, this one over here has that 'jungle fever' in her blood."

"I have a thing for dick *period*," I said bluntly.

"Boys have dicks. Real men have cocks," he said.

I shook my head. "A cock is a chicken. A dick is a dick."

"Well, since you put it like that, I happen to have a dick," he said, licking his lips. "So does my buddy over here. How about you take the two of us on a little adventure tonight? I got a pickup right outside with a comfy bed on it."

"Let me guess. Yours is the one that says 'Redneck's Toy' on the back?"

"How'd you know that?"

I scowled. "Figures."

"So how 'bout it?"

Fat Fuck was distracting me from the hunk on the stage who was the first decent contestant, both in looks and talent. He was singing "These Boots Were Made for Walking."

"So how 'bout it, Missy?" he asked again.

"First off, you redneck fuck, your stomach is so big that I probably couldn't even get to your dick and your friend's so skinny that I'd probably need a magnifying glass to find his. I'm gonna have to pass."

Leroy leaned in closer and asked, "What did she say?"

I yelled out at him, "Get a hearing aid, pencil dick!"

I stayed for another half-hour until the contest was over. Mr. Boots Were Made for Walking lost to the first whore, who must have been sucking major dick in the men's room to win because the bitch straight-up couldn't sing. I decided to be his consolation prize and followed him outside. He was the one driving the Monte Carlo.

"Excuse me, do you have the time?" I asked him when he was about to unlock his ride.

He lifted his wrist close to his face so he could make out the dial. "It's two-thirty."

"No, that's not what I meant." I climbed up on the hood of his car, spread my legs, and lifted my skirt to give him a good visual. His eyes almost came out of his head. "I want to know if you have the time to tap this ass."

By three, we were parked side by side in the middle of a field and I was lying on his trunk with his dick inside me getting the much-needed release I craved after Jon's fucking ass decided to come to Trinity in search of resolutions she would never find.

25

jonquinette

"How did you sleep last night?" Daddy asked me the next morning when I descended the stairs.

"Like a log," I responded, since I didn't remember much about it. All I knew was that I woke up and felt like I was still exhausted. Generally that only happened to me when I had slept too well.

He grinned. "Good. The country air at night does wonders."

"Yes, it does. I kept my windows open." I noticed the sun beaming through the panes of the front door and added, "Now the country heat during the day is another matter."

We both laughed.

"I don't have much to cook for breakfast. I could go into town and pick up something."

I leaned on the banister. "Do they have a decent restaurant around here? I'd love to treat you and Flower to breakfast."

"We don't have any fancy restaurants, but we do have a pretty good diner."

"Sounds good to me. Food is food, whether it's served on china or a paper plate. Remember when you used to always tell Momma that?"

He nodded. "I'm amazed you remember."

"I remember everything."

He picked up a hairbrush off the entry table and brushed his hair back. Then he unplugged his cell phone and slipped it into his pocket.

"Flower just got out the bathtub and she's getting dressed," he said. "We should be ready to go in about fifteen or twenty minutes."

"I'll be waiting on the front porch. I've grown fond of that swing. I always wished we had one when I was a child."

"Really?" He looked at me in bewilderment. "You never told me that."

I cringed with my back to him as I went out the door. There was so much I had never told him.

"So Flower, what's your favorite subject in school?" I asked her after we were seated and eating at The Golden Spoon; the first place I had seen fully integrated with all races since I'd hit town. Good food was good food. All of the waitresses were white but I knew who was in the kitchen.

Flower's bright eyes looked up at me. "Hmm, I guess it would be math, but I'm not sure yet. I'm only in the first grade."

She was seated beside me in the booth and I admired the great rush job I had done on her hair. "Yeah, well, you have plenty of time to decide," I said, patting her on the shoulder.

"Thanks for doing my hair again."

"You're so very welcome."

Daddy was quiet. I guess he was just enjoying his two children interacting with each other.

Flower said, "I like music."

"Is that so? Do you play any instruments?" I asked.

"No, but I want to learn how to play the piano."

"What a coincidence. I played the piano when I was a little girl."

"You did?" she asked with disbelief, like she was the only child in America who had ever wanted to play it.

I thought back to how much I had enjoyed taking lessons from one of our neighbors, Mrs. Duncan, a couple of blocks over. Then Robert, the boy who lived next door to her, teased me something horrible one day and I never went back. My mother insisted that I continue, but I just couldn't. My nerves were shot.

Daddy's expression told me that he was remembering the incident also.

"Yes, but I didn't keep up with it," I said to Flower. "Promise me that once you start taking lessons, you'll never stop."

"I promise."

"Good girl."

Daddy finally interjected. "I'll find someone to teach you this week. Okay, sweetie?"

"Okay, Daddy."

Daddy took pride in introducing me to the numerous people he knew at the diner. Some of them eyed me suspiciously, like I was probably a younger lover he was trying to pass off as his daughter since the age difference was totally inappropriate.

One lady, Mrs. Mabeline Harris, spent almost ten minutes standing beside our table filling Daddy in on the latest town gossip. All I could do was be grateful I didn't live in a small town and have to deal with people constantly in my business. Not that I had any exciting business to talk about.

My stack of buttermilk pancakes and turkey sausage were delicious. I could get used to country cooking; although we did have the chicken and waffle place owned by Gladys Knight and Ron Winan back in Atlanta.

Flower grew visibly excited when she spotted two little girls going down the sidewalk on scooters. "Daddy, there's Susan and Becky," she said, pointing out the window. "Can I go play with them?"

"What about the rest of your food?" Daddy asked, gesturing toward Flower's plate of silver dollar pancakes and bacon.

"I'm full," she announced and started rubbing her belly.

Daddy and I both chuckled because we knew she was lying. Her sudden loss of appetite could only be contributed to a better proposition: hanging out with friends.

"Okay," he said. "But you make sure you stay within sight."

"I will, Daddy."

Once Flower was outside playing with her friends, I said, "Tell me more about her mother. Allison, right?"

"Yes. Like I said, she's just a friend. She was widowed a while back and it depressed her to the point that she was suicidal. That made two of us so we comforted each other to prevent the inevitable."

"Daddy, you wouldn't really kill yourself?"

"At one point, I seriously considered it. I'd lost everything that ever mattered to me, all based on the lies of one slut that I wish I could get my hands on for five seconds."

I didn't want to rehash that incident so I changed the topic. "How do you like living in the country? It's a big change from the city."

He shrugged. "I grew up here so it was just a matter of becoming reacclimated to the environment."

"And you have?"

"Well, now that I have Flower, I could never leave." He pushed his plate away and folded his hands in front of him. "I already deserted one daughter. I won't desert another one." There was a pregnant pause before he added, "Jonquinette, why did you really come here?"

I took my paper napkin and patted my eyes, fighting back tears. "Because I need your help, Daddy."

He stood up, put some money on the table and reached for my hand. "Let's go."

I started fumbling through my purse. "No, I said it was my treat."

"Jonquinette Pierce," he said with authority. "After all these years, the least thing you can allow a man to do is purchase a meal for his daughter. I do have some pride left."

I forced a smile. "I wasn't implying that you couldn't afford it, Daddy."

"I know. Let's just go."

Flower wasn't ready to leave so Daddy asked a mother of one of the other girls if she could stay and play. She agreed and said she would drop Flower off at home later that evening on the way to Bingo Night at the union hall.

When we got back to Daddy's house, I was cheerful but dreading to be alone with him at last. There was so much to say and no place to begin.

Once we were seated across from each other at his dining-room table with two glasses of orange juice, he asked me, "This is about the *episodes* you used to have as a child, right?"

"Yes," I whispered.

"They're still occurring?"

"Yes, but they've gotten worse."

He took a deep breath and clamped his eyes shut. "How so?"

"Oh, Daddy. There's no easy way to say this so I'll just come out with it. I don't think I'm alone."

"You're not alone," he said. "You have a mother who loves you, family members who love you, and you have me. I would lay down my life for you."

I shook my head. "You're not following me. You know how you keep saying that you didn't have anything to do with that woman?"

"I didn't have anything to do with her," he insisted.

"And you know how no one believed you back then?"

"Don't remind me," he hissed. "They still don't believe me but I hope you do."

I nodded. "I can't explain what happened and why that woman showed up there that day but if you say you didn't have any involvement with her, I believe you."

He slapped his hands together. "Thank goodness. I would never do anything to harm you and your momma, baby."

"I believe you," I repeated. "Now you have to believe me when I say—"

"When you say . . . ?"

"I honestly never did any of those things. I know you think I was doing them and just not owning up to them. That I had some sort of Dr. Jekyll and Mr. Hyde personality but that wasn't it. I had another personality altogether."

He was stumped. "Come again?"

"Daddy, when I say I'm not alone, I mean that I've come to realize that another person lives within me."

"Another person lives within you," he slowly repeated my words.

"Yes."

"And who is this person?"

I could tell he couldn't grasp it, simply by the look on his face and the way the words slurred out of his mouth.

"I don't know who she is. I just know that I have these black-outs and when I come back, so to speak, things have changed, people are accusing me of things I never did, I'm wearing clothes I never put on, things are misplaced or moved around my apartment when there was never anyone else there. The list just goes on and on." I didn't want to get into the sex thing with Daddy. No woman feels comfortable talking about sex with her father. Even though I realized *everything* would have to come out eventually, I wasn't prepared to deal with that part yet. Not with Daddy.

"Jonquinette, listen to me carefully," Daddy said. "You need to get immediate help. I tried to tell your mother this years ago, but she didn't want to hear it. If you need me to, I'll call someone for you. I'll go back to Atlanta with you; whatever it takes."

I reached across the table and took his hand. It was trembling, or maybe it was my hand that was actually wobbly. "I already found someone, Daddy. She's the one who suggested I reach out to you."

"A doctor?" he asked.

"Yes, a psychiatrist." I nodded. "Her name's Dr. Marcella Spencer and she's wonderful, Daddy. I really think she can help me but I can't face all of this without you and Momma."

"Does you mother know you're seeing a doctor?" he asked.

"No, but she's about to find out. I'm sick of secrets."

"So you want me to come to Atlanta?"

"Yes, but not until I have a chance to talk to Momma about it."

He smirked. "Good luck. Meredith probably won't be able to stand occupying the same room with me."

I knew he was right. "Then she'll have to get over it. Momma means well but she's self-centered and it's time for her to consider people other than herself. The two of you are my parents and, while I am grown, I still need you both."

Daddy and I spent the remainder of the day discussing the past: the good, the bad, and the ugly. When Flower came home close to dusk, we lightened up and headed for the front porch for a night of joking around on the swing.

The next day I went to church with them and cried like a baby the entire time. I hoped that I didn't scare Flower but she seemed to understand that I was cleansing my soul. Oftentimes, children identify with things better than adults.

After joining the parishioners in the church hall for their routine Sunday potluck dinner that started directly after church, I said my good-byes, told Daddy I would be in touch shortly, hugged Flower and wished I could take her with me, and headed out of town.

When I arrived back in Atlanta, hunger had reared its ugly head, so I stopped by a deli to get a chicken Caesar salad. I checked my messages and there were several from Momma, three from Mason, and one frantic one from Marcella stating that she needed to talk to me right away and that I could call her at home if it was after hours. She left her home number but it was late and I was drained. I had an appointment with her the following afternoon so I decided to wait, get some rest, and get ready to deal with Mr. Wilson and his demands the next morning.

26

jonquinette

All the next day, I was anxious to get through my workload so I could make a beeline for Marcella's office. I even called to see if I could come in an hour earlier than normal and her secretary said it would be fine.

When I got there, I couldn't stop talking about how wonderful it was to see my father. She sat there and studied me hard and I was confused that she wasn't saying anything in response.

After I had filled her in, including telling her all about Flower, my wonderful little sister, she finally cleared her throat and said, "That's extraordinary news. I'm glad you and your father have reconciled because you're really going to need him in the months ahead."

I didn't like the way she phrased it. "What do you mean?"

"Did you get my phone message?" she asked.

"Yes, I got it last night but I didn't want to bother you at home so late on a Sunday evening."

"You can call me anytime, Jonquinette. As a therapist, I recognize that my patients often need me outside of standard office hours. There are some doctors that refuse to deal with patients during late evenings or the weekends. I'm not one of them. To me, that shows a lack of true dedication on their part."

"Thanks for saying that. I appreciate it."

"No need for thanks. Like I said, it's all a part of my profession." She got up from her desk. "Jonquinette, it's such a pretty day for late September. Why don't we take a walk?"

"You mean, leave the office," I said uneasily.

She giggled. "Yes, I think the fresh air might help."

Her remark about "fresh air" tickled me. After just returning from the pure country air of Trinity, the smog, fumes, and litter of downtown Atlanta didn't seem too alluring to me.

I got up anyway. "Sure, that would be nice." I glimpsed at the wall clock. "But my hour is almost up."

"That's not a problem and don't worry about paying for extra time. I wouldn't even consider accepting it."

"Don't you have another patient?"

"No, I don't. My boyfriend wanted to do dinner tonight but we can make it a late one."

That was the first time I had heard Marcella refer to her personal life. I was always curious about what made her tick. I knew she didn't wear a wedding ring but that didn't mean she wasn't married. Numerous people don't wear their rings. Some misplace them accidentally and some misplace them on purpose. Since she said she had a boyfriend, that answered that question.

We ended up walking around the block several times. I was concerned that someone might eavesdrop on our discussion, not that they knew who we were. There was a statue in a community park and I asked if we could sit on a secluded bench nearby. She graciously agreed. There were some older gentlemen playing chess on the other side of the statue but they couldn't possibly hear us so I felt secure.

No sooner had we sat down when she blurted it out. "Jonquinette, I met her."

"Met who?"

"Jude?"

"Who's Jude?"

"Jude is one of your other personalities. She's the one that I suspect has been doing all those things. She admitted as much."

I was clueless about what to say. I just sat there and attempted to let Marcella's words sink in. *Jude!*

It felt so strange to ask the next question. "So what did she say to you, Marcella?"

"Basically, that she was your protector and that if not for her, you would've perished long ago."

"She said that?"

"Yes, that and much more. She said that she controlled you and that if she wanted to, she could take over full-time and never let you return." Marcella took my hand. "Don't worry. I don't believe she can actually do that for a second."

"But what if she can?" I asked in alarm. "What if she can make me totally fade away?"

The thought of just falling asleep, or blacking out one day, and ceasing to exist was more frightening than death. I had always had this trepidation of becoming a vegetable due to an accident or sudden illness and that was more dreadful than anything I could envision.

"Jonquinette, if there was any doubt before, there is none now. You're definitely suffering from MPD."

"What does that stand for?"

"Multiple Personality Disorder."

I jumped up from the bench and started pacing right along with the pigeons. "This can't be happening. Not now. Not when I think that I've finally found someone. Someone I could actually open up to."

"Are you referring to Mason?"

I blushed. "Yes, I mean Mason. He and I went out on a date."

"Was that your first date?" Marcella asked. "With Mason, I mean."

"That was my first date *period*," I readily divulged.

"And how did it go?"

"He kissed me."

"Did you kiss him back?"

"Yes, and that wasn't the first time. He and I had kissed once before. He had invited me to a wedding, but I didn't get the note he'd taped to my door. Darnetta, a friend from the office, had asked me to go to the same exact wedding with her. Crazy happenstance, huh?"

Marcella nodded. "Quite remarkable."

"Anyway, we both ended up there. He was the best man. At the reception we danced and then the groom needed to talk to him. I sat back down at the table and then . . ."

"Then what?"

I sat back down beside her and groaned. "I don't remember. This Jude person must have taken over somehow. The next thing I knew I was at home and Mason was banging at my door. He mentioned something about me becoming ill at the reception and leaving without telling him."

"How did that make you feel? To have him standing there recounting things you couldn't remember?"

"It scared the living daylights out of me," I replied. "I really want things to work out with Mason, but how, in all fairness, can I even date him again?"

Marcella put her arm around my shoulder and embraced me.

"We're just going to have to take this one day at a time, just like everyone else. That's the only way you can really face life; trying to deal with too many things at once makes you overwhelmed. We have to take care of the moment and then move on to the next. We can't always worry about what is to come."

I pulled away from her so I could gaze into her eyes. "That may be true in most cases and I understand perfectly what you're trying to say. But I have to worry about what is to come. If this Jude is threatening to take over my entire life, how can we stop her?"

"With treatment," Marcella answered. "Treatment and a lot of faith, hope, and love."

"Let me ask you this. What did Jude say about having sex?"

Marcella eyed me uneasily. "She mentioned it."

"And?" I pried.

"Apparently, Jude views sex, or rather the art of seduction, as some sort of power. She admitted that she's slept with numerous men."

"How many men?" I demanded to know, raising my voice.

Marcella just shook her head. "She didn't say."

I buried my face in my hands and cried for what seemed like an eternity.

After I had shed enough tears for one day, we sat and talked for another hour. Then Marcella went off in one direction to meet her boyfriend at a local restaurant after calling him on his cell phone and I went off in the other, fearful that I might not ever see her again. That night, I was almost too petrified to fall asleep but mental exhaustion finally prevailed.

jude

Disciplinarians thrive under chaos! Bring it on, bitches!

27

jude

I was just about to head out that Friday night to blow off some steam and find an unsuspecting victim to fuck. Jon had come straight home from the office, like she had done all that week since her little heart-to-heart with that bitch doctor in the park. On one hand, I was mad that the cat was out of the bag, so to speak. On the other hand, I was glad. It was about damn time that I got my props for all of my deeds, at least the good ones.

It was true that if not for me, Jon wouldn't have been able to fuction in reality. I had always been there to look after her when bullshit reared its ugly head. As for the other stuff, that was my business. Either way, I was confident that I was the gatekeeper. No one and nothing could make me go away.

While I was switching purses—the one Jon had carried to work was hideous—a knock came at the door. I tiptoed over to the peephole and glimpsed out. Shit! It was Mason.

"Jonquinette, are you in there?" he yelled through the door. "Jonquinette?"

Enough of this motherfucker, I thought. *Time to put the little puppy out of his misery.*

I flung the door open and sneered at him. "What do you want?"

He was taken aback by my attitude. "Um, it's Friday night and I thought we might take in a movie. Remember that I'm supposed to take you to a movie, a play, and a museum all within a month. Well, time is running out and I'm always a man of my word."

He stood there grinning while I pouted.

"So, how about it?"

"How about not!" I lashed out. "I don't want to go to a damn movie with you! Not tonight or any other night, for that matter!"

"Jonquinette, what's gotten into you? Did I do something wrong?"

I clucked my tongue and rolled my eyes.

"Did you get the phone messages I left for you?"

"I was out of town, visiting that bastard daddy of mine."

Mason was bewildered. "I don't understand why you're acting like this. I didn't know you were back in contact with your father."

"Maybe that's because it's none of your fucking business?" I put my hands on my hips. "And, for the record, I'm not acting. This is the real mc, so deal with it or get to stepping."

He just stood there looking brainless so I was about to slam the door in his face. He blocked it with his hand and asked, "Why are you doing this?"

I smirked. "The better question is why are *you* doing this?"

"I'm not doing anything," he stated defensively.

"Oh, yes the hell you are. You're disrupting my flow. Everything was cool until you came into the picture. Life was exactly as it should be and then you came along with your smooth talk and pretty-ass face and fucked it all up."

"You're sounding crazy," he said. "I thought we were feeling each other."

"Well, you thought wrong."

I wanted to make sure Mason never bothered Jon again. She was perfectly content with her bleak life until he entered it. His ass had to go.

"I'll tell you what," I said, pulling him by the hand into the apartment. "Let's just get it over with."

"Get what over with?" he asked.

"Fucking." I bypassed the living room and continued down the hall to the bedroom, pushing him backward on the bed and straddling his thighs. "This is your ultimate goal anyway, right? Getting Jon in bed."

I realized my slip immediately; referring to Jon in third person. Mason must have been too stunned to catch on because he didn't reference it.

"You know you want this pussy," I whispered, ripping the buttons off his oxford shirt. "I'm going to do you up real nice so you can move on to your next victim."

He attempted to push me off without getting rough but I was relentless. Besides, I could feel his dick getting hard beneath me.

"I don't consider women to be victims, Jonquinette," the little puppy whimpered. "I thought you knew me better than that."

I started licking up and down the center of his chest and then nibbled on his left nipple. "Just relax, baby," I said. "I'm about to give you the fuck of the century."

He flipped me over so that he was on top.

"Oh, you want to plummet in and out of me in this position, huh? Cool by me."

I started trying to get my panties off but he grabbed both of my wrists and pressed them up above my head.

"Stop it, Jonquinette!" he yelled out.

I ground my hips underneath his dick and licked my lips.

"Damn, I knew you were probably well-hung but shit! Let me put it in my mouth, Mason. Let me drain that long-ass pipe of yours."

"Jon, stop talking like a whore," he said. "You're acting like some one-night stand a brother would pick up in a nightclub. That's not like you."

"Oh, but it is like me. It's exactly like me. I am a whore. I've picked up so many men in clubs and fucked them that I lost count years ago."

The pain in Mason's eyes was obvious. That elated the hell out of me.

"That's right. I'm a whore. I'm not even a common whore. I'm a *major* whore. I'll give this pussy to whoever wants it, whenever they want it, and however they want it."

Mason got off me, left the bedroom, and headed down the hall for the door. I followed him. "I'll just talk to you later, Jonquinette. You must have had a bad day because I know you're lying. For some reason, you're trying to push me out of your life but it's not going to be that easy. I won't go away without a fight."

"You won't go away without a fight? This isn't fuckin' *Romeo and Juliet*. There's no family feud going on here. I don't want to be with you like that. If you want to fuck once and move on, then let's fuck. But don't harbor any delusions about this *ever* becoming more than that."

He turned and stared me in the eyes. "This is already more than that. You and I both know it."

He was really laying it on thick! You would have thought that Jon had fucked him silly by the way he was performing.

"I'm going to say this *one more time*," I said, poking Mason in the chest. "I am a whore—pure and simple."

"I don't believe that." He went out of the apartment and started down the steps. "I'll call you tomorrow."

"Since you refuse to face reality, I'm just going to have to validate it for you." I paused for a second before I went in for the kill. "Call up your buddy, Logan, and ask him if I'm a whore!"

He started back up the stairs. "What did you just say?"

"I didn't stutter. Call Logan and ask him what's up with me. Ask him what happened between me and him at the wedding reception. Ask him if he enjoyed the way I rode that big, juicy dick of his on top of that table in the back room."

Mason seemed like he was trying to maintain his composure. I knew he wanted to beat the shit of me, or rather Jon. I was hoping he would jump so that I could really fuck up Jon's relationship with him. I would have kneed his balls so hard that he would have felt the impact in the back of his throat.

Instead, he just stood there in silence momentarily and stomped down the steps.

"And don't come back!" I yelled after him.

When I went out that night, I partied like it was 1999 all over again. After downing a series of two-dollar Jell-O shots at a tavern, a couple of brothers told me about a foam party being held at an "undisclosed location." It didn't interest me in the least until they said it was a "nude foam party." Then I was down.

I trailed them in Jon's car and we ended up at what appeared to be an abandoned warehouse. When we got inside, it was cold, wet, and crazy. There was this huge Plexiglas cage in the middle of the floor, which they called "The Playpen." Fifty or more people were inside of it buck-ass-naked while a few dozen more hung around the bar area looking on.

An overhead machine was dropping gigantic bucketfuls of flyweight bubbles onto the crowd of people who were jumping around like children. I couldn't wait to get in there. One of the men I followed to the party came up behind me and asked, "Wanna get naked with me?"

I slid my tongue into his mouth and then drew his bottom lip into my mouth and bit it gently. "I thought you'd never ask."

We got naked and were welcomed into the cage by "The Goodwill Ambassador," who was in charge of helping people in and out without them busting their asses and handing out towels.

As soon as we climbed in, they started a nude conga line. It was off the damn hook. The brother I was hanging with grabbed onto my ass instead of my hips and started caressing it. His slippery hands aroused me.

"What's your name?" he asked over my shoulder. "I'm Dennis."

I broke off the line and threw my hands around his neck, jumping up and locking my long legs behind his back. Even though I wasn't feeling doing the stripper thing on the regular, I was still quite fond of the ingenious handle I'd come up with.

I kissed him on the tip of his nose, gazed into his eyes, and said, "Just call me Mercy because that's what you'll be begging me for once I slay your dick."

The brother was no joke. He carried me over to the wall of the cage and pressed me up against it. I helped him guide his slick dick into me and it was on: the biggest foam orgy one could ever imagine.

28

"Open the fucking door!" was the first thing I heard when I woke up Saturday morning. I thought I was imagining things until I heard it again. "Open the fucking door now, bitch!"

I realized it was Darnetta and wondered out loud, "What did I do now?"

I got out of bed and inched down the hallway toward the door.

"Jon, I know you're in there. Your car's outside. Now open up this fuckin' door!"

I debated about calling Mason and asking him to come upstairs, just in case things went really bad and I needed his help. But then I thought about it. Whatever Darnetta was mad about was more than likely something I would be humiliated for Mason to find out about. That's the only reason I opened the door. I didn't want my neighbors to think I had transformed from a quiet, shy woman to someone who had people banging on her door calling her a bitch.

I forced a smile and opened up. "Darnetta, what's wrong?"

Before my reflexes could kick in, Darnetta had punched me in the face. Instantly, I grabbed my nose and came back with a palm full of blood.

"You bitch!" she screamed out, storming into my place. "How could you? I thought we were friends."

"I'll be right back." I went into the kitchen to get a dish towel to cover my nose. When I came back into the living room, Darnetta was probing through my things. "What are you doing?" I asked.

"Searching for evidence."

"Evidence of what?"

"Evidence that my man has been spending time over here."

I was stunned. "Darnetta, what's this all about? I hardly know Logan. I've only met him one time, at the wedding."

"Exactly," she said, crossing her arms in front of her with an attitude. "The wedding."

It suddenly hit me. Jude had done something foul at Smitty's wedding. She'd done something with Logan. Oh no!

There was no point in denying something I couldn't even remember. The only thing left to do was express regret.

"I'm sorry, Darnetta. For whatever happened, I am truly, truly sorry."

Darnetta was so distressed that her entire body was trembling. "I've already dumped Logan. He's history."

I thought back to what Marcella mentioned about Jude using "the art of seduction" as some sort of power. I didn't want to be the cause of someone's relationship ending so I said, "Darnetta, it wasn't Logan's fault. I forced him."

"Forced him?" She smirked. "He knew what the hell he was doing when he fucked you. He told me as much. He cried like a baby and I made him get down on his knees and beg for forgiveness. Then I made him kiss my feet."

I let out a sigh of relief. "So you do plan to stay with him."

"Fuck no. Like I said, Logan's history. I made him do all of that and then I kicked him in the face. He has a bloody nose, too."

I plopped down on my sofa. "I'm speechless, Darnetta. I don't know what I can possibly do to right this wrong but I'm willing to do anything. Just name it."

She came closer and hovered over me. "The only thing you can do for me is never speak to me again. I'm not quitting my job; I need it too damn much and the economy's too bad to risk leaving before I find another one. I do intend to start an immediate search for something else, though."

I shut my eyes and wished the entire nightmare would go away. Darnetta had the biggest mouth in the company and it was just a matter of time before the cat was out of the bag at the office. She would try to pit everyone else against me by making them feel sorry for her. I'd be lucky if Mr. Wilson didn't fire me.

"Jon, you put up such a good front, acting all innocent and shit when you're nothing but a slut."

"I deserve that," I said, even though I didn't. I intended to agree with every word she said if it made her feel like she was accomplishing something.

"Well, you don't have to worry about me coming by your office anymore. I don't have jack shit to say to you, not today, not tomorrow, not ever." Darnetta went for the door. I was relieved she was leaving. She paused in the entryway. "The only satisfaction I can take away in all of this is knowing that your shit is just as raggedy as mine."

"What do you mean by that?" I asked in confusion.

She let out an evil laugh. "You'll find out soon enough."

She slammed the door behind her as I fell out in tears.

I was beginning to understand how people could turn to alcohol or drugs in desperate times. I felt like shit and couldn't imagine what Monday morning and every morning after that was going to be like at work. The classified ads came out the next morning with the Sunday paper and I intended to have my head buried in them. Ironically, Darnetta and I would probably end up submitting résumés for some of the same positions.

Alcohol and drugs were not for me so I turned to the next best thing to relieve stress and make me forget everything: exercise. I dug through my closet for my favorite pair of running shoes, found my portable CD player in an old duffel bag, threw on some biker shorts and a sports bra tank top and headed out into the cool, late-September air.

I left my apartment around eleven and didn't return until close to one. It's amazing how the body can snap back after a period of slacking off. When I hit the wall, my top pace, the air kicking in and out of my lungs felt incredible. I could feel all the impurities leaving my body through my sweat and I felt so much better, even though my life was still in shambles.

As I was sitting down on the stoop to dig my key out of my sock, I saw Mason pulling into the parking lot. Instead of cutting his engine, he just sat behind the wheel and glared at me. When I'd first spotted his car, I was excited and hopeful that he could cheer me up after the encounter with Darnetta. But, from the way he was looking at me, I realized what Darnetta had meant when she said my shit was just as raggedy as hers. Mason knew about Logan and me. Darnetta was just a battle. Mason and I were about to have a war.

While I could have waited for him to get out so we could have it out on the front steps of our building or even worse, inside, where all the neighbors would surely hear us, I chose to face the music inside his car.

I walked over to his convertible Mustang and luckily, he had the top down so I didn't have to tap on the window to gain entry. I reached over the passenger side door, unlocked it, and climbed in without an invitation.

"We need to talk," I said.

He glowered at me. "Don't you think you said enough last night?"

I almost choked on my breath. "Last night?"

"Yeah, last night." He didn't say anything else for a moment. He turned up the radio and started flipping stations until he came across "She's Out of My Life" by Michael Jackson. He laughed and said, "How appropriate."

I turned off the radio. "Mason, I need you to listen to me carefully."

"Oh, Jonquinette, I think I've heard quite enough. First, from you last night and this morning from Logan." He took his seat belt off and finally cut the engine. "I went over to his place and confronted him after you told me all about it."

"I told you all about it?"

He glimpsed at me with disdain. "Yes, after you told me all about it sometime between admitting that you were a whore and stating that you just wanted to fuck me and get it over with."

I slid down farther in the seat and tried to mask my eyes with my right hand.

"Oh, that's right," Mason added. "You're not just a whore. How did you put it? You're not just a common whore, but you're a major whore. Did I say it right?"

I shrugged. I hadn't a clue what Jude had said.

"Respond to me, dammit," Mason demanded. "You got into my car and said we needed to talk, so talk."

I had absolutely nothing to lose so I decided to tell Mason the truth.

"What I'm about to say is going to sound crazy, probably because it is."

"Everything you said last night was crazy."

"Last night, *I* didn't say anything."

Mason pondered over my statement in silence.

"Mason, the person you spoke with last night wasn't me."

"That's the most ridiculous pile of shit I've ever heard!"

"I'm very serious. I'm going to say what I have to say and then I'm going to leave you alone. I'm only confessing to all of this because I don't want you to misconstrue my actual feelings or think you did something to make me act as I have."

Mason sighed. "Okay, say your peace."

"I've never been with a man before in my entire life. I've never had sex. Not with Logan or anyone else."

He chuckled. "All right, whatever."

"All these years, I knew something was wrong with me but I never wanted to face facts. They started when I was just a child."

"What started?"

"The blackouts."

"Blackouts? You can't be serious."

"I'm dead serious. I have these episodes when I lose chunks of time—sometimes large ones but mostly smaller ones."

"Are you saying what I think you're saying?" he asked in dismay.

"I have a multiple personality disorder, Mason. Whatever transpired last night was between you and Jude, not you and me."

"Jude?"

"Yes, that's what she apparently calls herself." I laughed nervously. "I've never met her but I heard it through the grapevine."

"Hmph, well, I met her."

I sat up in the car seat. "So you do believe me?"

"I believe that you weren't yourself last night. I won't go as far as to say that you were a different person. I've seen that sort of thing in movies but never in real life."

"Well, it's not as uncommon as you might think. Last week, I searched the internet and there are thousands of websites dedicated to the topic. I even read some testimonials from other people who have the disorder."

Mason cleared his throat. "This is incredible."

"There was even this one woman who had more than forty personalities who spanned in age from infancy to the elderly, both male and female."

"Say I buy into this, Jonquinette. What can you do about it? Do you need to be in some sort of hospital?" he asked.

"Goodness, I hope that I don't need to be hospitalized. I am seeing a doctor. She's as sweet as can be."

"Well, that's a positive sign, right? The fact that you sought help?"

"Yes, it's positive. I only wish I'd done it years ago."

"So she's treating you?" Mason inquired.

"She's a psychiatrist so thus far, we've just done a lot of talking. I just found out that she met Jude during one of my sessions. Jude came out because she was pissed off about my trying to bring my daddy back into my life."

"Then your daddy knows?"

"I told him." I shifted in the bucket seat. "However, he already knew something was wrong. He always has. My mother just never wanted to hear about it or accept it."

"But she accepts it now?"

I shook my head. "She doesn't know about the latest developments, but I plan to tell her the first chance I get." I stared at Mason, who was sitting there looking into space. "I just want to thank you."

"For what?"

"For at least listening to me and hopefully, for not judging me."

"I have to confess. Last night threw me for a total loop, especially when you, I mean Jude, told me about what happened with Logan at the wedding. But—"

"But what?" I asked.

"Even though you were acting raunchy and told me about fucking everything that moved, it was strange because I still wanted to be with you. It went against everything I've ever believed in, but I still craved you."

I blushed uncontrollably. "Really?"

He took my hand and kissed it. "Really." He leaned over and kissed me on the cheek. "Now that we've discussed this, I don't want you to have to go through this alone."

"I'll have my parents."

"Yeah, but you'll also have me."

We sat there in Mason's car for a good while and I started telling him about all the childhood memories, or lack thereof, that I had. He was mesmerized and so was I. To think that he was still talking to me after what Jude had done was all I needed to know to make a final decision. Mason was the man for me. The only man for me.

29

jonquinette

I woke up early the next morning, miraculously, rejuvenated. Mason had come upstairs with me the night before and stayed with me for several hours. We didn't really talk, at least not with words. We cuddled on my sofa and watched *One Week* and *Love and a Bullet* on cable, starring Treach, who was phenomenal.

Mason must have let himself out because when I woke up, I was covered up with a fleece blanket and the volume on the television was turned down.

It was just after seven A.M. and I was excited, since it meant that I could make it to the eight o'clock church service on time. I was determined to get my life on the right track and getting back into the habit of going to church was a good start.

Even at that time of the morning, church was packed. I managed to squeeze past a heavyset gentleman and take a seat next to an elderly woman on the next to the last pew. The music ministry moved me to the point where I jumped up and started stomping my feet. Normally, I would've been too embarrassed to draw attention to myself but something was changing. It was a new dawn.

When it came time for the first Scripture reading, the woman beside me let me share her Bible because I had forgotten mine at home. After the Scripture had been read, Reverend Townsend stood up in the pulpit and told the members of the congregation to shake hands with all of the people surrounding them.

Everyone got on their feet, with the exception of those who could not, and greeted each other warmly. When I shook the elderly woman's hand, I took a good look at her face and couldn't help but wonder how old she was. She had a ton of wrinkles but there was something youthful about her appearance.

The rest of the church service was very moving. The minister gave a sermon that I really needed to hear. The topic was "Believe in Yourself." He reminded us all that every day our beliefs guide our actions and it is up to us to make the impossible become possible. It validated what I had been feeling with Mason the night before. I believed that I could overcome my situation with the right support circle in place and enough faith.

After church service ended, I did something that I had never done before. I actually stayed and talked to people in the fellowship hall. It was the church's anniversary so there were many people lingering around, preparing for a big celebration dinner later that evening, which I didn't plan to attend.

I had just finished talking to a woman named Jasmin, who wanted me to join the YAMS, the Young Adult Missionaries, when the elderly woman came up to me and took my hand.

"What troubles you, child?" she asked me.

I laughed nervously. "What makes you think I'm troubled?"

"I've lived a long time," she replied. "And when you are

blessed to be here as long as I have, you start to see things. You can read faces. I have been reading yours all day."

She had me curious. "What does my face say?"

"That you're hurting. That you came here today looking for help, searching for answers."

"You're right. They say church is the place to find yourself. I'm here to find myself."

"The Lord works in mysterious ways, child," she said, patting me on the arm. "He never gives us more than we can handle. I've buried three husbands and two children and every time, I thought that I would never survive the pain. But, guess what? I did. For whatever His reasons, He called them all home before me and one day, I will see them all again."

"Can I ask you a question?"

"Sure, child."

"I know you're never supposed to ask a woman her age, but I'm really curious about yours. You have this glow about you, almost childlike, but yet you are so experienced and wise."

She grinned at me. "I'm flattered. And please, I passed the point of being offended when someone asked my age decades ago. I'm ninety-three."

I was stunned. "Ninety-three?"

"Yes, I've been here a long time. I still have four surviving children, nine grandchildren, and thirty-eight great-grandchildren."

"That is amazing." I suddenly felt ashamed. The woman had so many people who loved her and I had never truly been loved. "I'm not married," I said in embarrassment. "In fact, I've never really had a relationship, but I'm kind of getting close to someone now."

"Don't fret, child. You still have plenty of time left. I can feel it in my bones. You're going to be here for a long, long time."

A tear formed in the corner of my eye. *Not if Jude has anything to say about it,* I thought.

"I can tell something is troubling you," she continued. "But trust me, this too shall pass and life will go on. There were times when I begged the Lord to put me out of my misery, especially when I saw my youngest child kill himself right in front of me."

"Oh my gosh! What happened?" I asked and then regretted it immediately. I didn't want her to have to rehash bad times. "Never mind. That is none of my business."

"It helps me to talk about it sometimes. Chad had everything going for him. He owned his own business, had a home, a nice car, and everything to look forward to. Then he hooked up with the wrong woman and she had him so taken with her that when she decided she wanted to move on to something better, he couldn't handle it. Chad came to my house one night, a Saturday night. I remember because I was on my way to play bridge. He came in, sat down on my sofa, told me how much he loved me and always would, and then he took a pistol out of his jacket and shot himself in the side of the head."

Something made me want to throw my arms around the woman and hug her. "I'm so sorry."

She embraced me back. "You have nothing to be sorry for." She let go and looked me in the eyes. "Just do me one favor."

"Sure."

"Don't let your troubles break you down. Be thankful for every day, every single day, because you never know when it will be your last." She wiped a tear from my right cheek. "Even at my age, I still embrace life. I come to church every Sunday and praise the Lord, every Saturday I play bridge at the local hall, and every Tuesday I have dinner with my man."

Now I was really shocked! "Your man?"

"Yes, can you believe it?" she asked jokingly. "Even at my age, I can still pull them."

"Is he your age?"

"Honey, finding a man my age would be like searching for an ear of corn in a watermelon patch."

We both laughed.

"No, I have a younger gentleman who comes calling. He's just a baby: seventy-four."

"Wow, I never thought I'd hear a man in his seventies being called a baby."

She giggled and ran her fingers through her silver hair. "Me either, but thank the Lord that I'm here to be able to do it."

"So every Tuesday you have dinner together? That's so romantic. I'm so happy for you."

"I'm happy for me, too, and dinner is not all we have," she said suggestively. "I make the same meal every week: smothered pork chops with gravy, collard greens, creamed corn, and sweet potato pie. He always brings a bottle of sparkling cider and a bouquet of roses. We sit and talk, we eat, and then we make love."

I was so amazed at her openness and I realized why she looked and felt so great for her age. The woman was loved by a man and she loved him back. That was something I had never had but something I was determined to get.

The hall was thinning out so I decided it was time for me to head on home. "Would you like for me to walk you out? Do you need a ride someplace?"

She shook her head. "I'm fine. I live a block away and I enjoy the walk. One reason why I've lived so long is because I've always been active. I watched way too many of my friends wither away and most of them would have lived a lot longer if they hadn't just given up. Just because you age doesn't mean you have to act old."

"I totally agree with you."

She gave me one last hug. "Take care of yourself, child, and maybe we can sit together again sometime."

I smiled. "I'd like that. I'd like that very much." She started walking away. "Wait! I don't even know your name."

She turned around. "Just call me Nanna. That's what everyone calls me: my family, my friends, and the people here at this church. I'm like a mother to everyone."

"Thanks, Nanna," I said. "My name's Jonquinette and it has been a real pleasure. You've helped me in ways I could never explain."

She chuckled. "We all help each other."

30

jonquinette

My conversation with the old woman after church truly motivated me. I found myself so hyped up later that night that I couldn't get to sleep. I lay in bed staring at the ceiling for what seemed like an eternity, but sleep would not come. I tried drinking a pot of green tea. Still nothing. I tried reading myself to sleep with V. Anthony Rivers' novel *Everybody Got Issues*. I ordered the book offline because of the title, not only catchy, but true. Still nothing, though. I couldn't go to sleep.

I finally figured out that I needed to talk to someone about my plans to speak with Momma the following day. I thought about going downstairs to Mason's but I didn't want to appear too needy. At least, not with him. So, I called the one person who was well aware that I was needy and then some. It was ten after midnight.

The phone rang twice before a groggy female voice picked up and said, "Hello."

"Marcella?" I asked to make sure I had copied the right phone number down from my answering machine.

"Jonquinette, is that you?"

I was astonished that she recognized my voice so quickly. "I'm sorry for calling you at home so late on a Sunday but I really need to chat with you."

I heard some movement on the other end of the phone and then she said, "I already told you, you can contact me anytime. What's wrong?"

"I just feel so bemused and I'm scared about what I plan to do tomorrow."

"Which is what?"

I paced the floor with my cordless phone for a few seconds before answering, "Confronting my mother."

"Do you need to talk in person, Jonquinette?"

"I would be grateful for that," I responded without a second of hesitation. "Can you meet me at your office?"

"No."

"I'm sorry, you're right. It's ridiculous for me to expect you to come out this time of night."

She took me off guard by saying, "I'll come to you. Give me an hour."

Always true to her word, Marcella was knocking at my door exactly fifty-six minutes later. I had spent that time straightening up and trying to look more organized than I normally was. This was Marcella's first time at my place and my mother always taught me that people can tell a lot about a person by the way they live. Being that Marcella was my psychiatrist, I expected her to really inspect and analyze everything about my residence. I rearranged my magazines so that they were in monthly order, my DVDs and CDs so that they were in alphabetical order, and my books as well. It was silly, really, but it helped me pass the time.

Marcella came in wearing a sweatsuit and a pair of sneakers. She looked youthful in the outfit. I was used to seeing her in business suits and heels. I had on a pair of pajamas and a fluffy pair of slippers.

I hugged her with appreciation when she came through the door. "Thanks so much for coming."

"Don't mention it, Jonquinette."

I led her into the living room where I had prepared a plate of cookies and another pot of tea, since I figured we would be up into the wee hours of the morning.

After we were seated on the sofa, Marcella asked me, "So what makes you assume that speaking with your mother will be a confrontation?"

That was an easy question. "Because I know how she is." I poured us both a cup of tea and put a spoonful of sugar in mine. "I haven't discussed my mother much but when I said she was self-absorbed, that was an understatement."

Marcella took her cup from me and put two teaspoons of sugar in hers. "How so?"

"My mother thinks the entire world revolves around her. She doesn't identify with the fact that everyone else has problems of their own."

"You mentioned her being bitter about the divorce." Marcella took a sip of her tea. "Um, this is delicious."

"Ha, bitter is putting it lightly. When that hooker showed up at Thanksgiving dinner and humiliated her in front of her entire family, she was distraught. She probably thought it was a fate worse than death."

"Tell me more about your mother's background."

"My great-grandparents were murdered when she was a child and I don't think she ever recovered from their loss. Her parents are retired. They were both janitors and she was ashamed of it."

"Do you see your grandparents?"

"I try to visit them in Florida at least every two years, but when I go down there, they always seem introverted. It's like I don't exist. They never go out with me when I'm there and they don't even offer to let me stay with them, even though they have the space."

"So where do you stay?" she asked.

"At a hotel down the street," I replied. "Plus, Florida brings back a lot of bad memories for me. Being tantalized and browbeaten. I don't have any fondness for the place, but I do adore my grandparents."

"Does your mother have a close relationship with her parents?"

"Good question. She talks to them on a regular basis; that much I know for sure. Whether I would classify them as being close, I don't know." I picked up a cookie and nibbled on it. "So much has happened this weekend. I'm not sure if I can handle anything else."

"What happened this weekend?" Marcella asked excitedly.

"You better brace yourself."

Marcella sat up straighter on the sofa. "Okay, consider me braced."

"Darnetta showed up here yesterday morning and punched me in the nose."

"Darnetta? The coworker you mentioned? The one who invited you to the wedding?"

"Yes." I paused to take another sip of tea. "Apparently, a whole lot happened at the wedding when Jude took over."

"Such as?"

"Jude seduced Darnetta's man." I searched Marcella's face for a clue as to what she was thinking, but couldn't read her thoughts. "She did it with Logan right there during the reception."

"Let me get this straight. Jude had sex with the man in public?" she inquired.

"Well, in a private room someplace, but basically, yes."

"So what did you say to Darnetta?"

"I did the rational thing since I knew she wasn't making it up. I apologized for Jude's behavior—my behavior."

"Did she accept your apology?"

"Absolutely not. In fact, I still need to go through the want ads so I can start applying for other jobs in the morning." I got up and started pacing the floor. My anxiety had kicked back in full throttle, just thinking about going to work. "Darnetta is a drama queen and she's going to do everything within her power to make me out to be the devil incarnate at the office."

"That's unfortunate."

"That's also not all," I uttered.

"What else?" Marcella asked.

"From what I've been able to piece together, the way Darnetta found out was by walking in on Mason and Logan arguing about it."

"Logan told Mason?"

I shook my head. "No, Jude told Mason."

"Jude?"

"Uh-huh. Mason came over here Friday night to ask me out to a movie and Jude convinced him that I was a whore and to prove it, she threw the incident with Logan up in his face."

"How did you find that out?"

"Mason told me." I sat back down beside her, remembering the wonderful night we had spent together. "He's such a good man."

"I take it that things went well between the two of you."

"I told him everything. He actually listened to me and even tried to comfort me afterward."

"That's definitely a good thing."

"Yes, it is." I began to think about the possibilities between Mason and me and how much I wanted to see what could actually develop. Then I thought about Jude and how she could ruin it all. "Jude's getting out of control. Or maybe it's the exact opposite. Maybe she's in control." Marcella was silent. She seemed like she was in deep thought. "She's really going to take over completely, isn't she?" I asked.

Marcella said, "Not if I have something to say about it." She took my right hand and held it tightly. "Jonquinette, I need to speak with Jude."

"Meaning?"

She touched me on the cheek with her free hand and stared me in the eyes. "Jude, I know you can hear me. Come out. I promise I won't hurt you."

I tried to pull myself away from her. "This is crazy, Marcella."

She refused to let my hand go. "Jonquinette, you're not the one destroying your life. She is and that's why she's the one I need to get across to."

I couldn't help but laugh. "So you think she's just going to come out like that? On demand?"

"No, but I do think she'll come out to prove that she can whenever she wants to." All of a sudden, Marcella started screaming. "Jude, you said you can run the show, so run it!"

I sat there waiting for something to happen. I pictured it being something straight out of a movie. Time seemed to slow down to a snail's pace as we both just waited and waited. Nothing happened.

Marcella smirked. "Well, Jonquinette, it looks like you're the dominant personality after all."

jude

That bitch had gotten on my last damn nerve. Talking so much shit, as if I couldn't appear whenever I wanted to. I had just been sitting back, enjoying the fireworks, and trying to see how Jon would handle the drama. After all, I'm the one who set the wheels in motion when I told Mason about fucking Logan. I was kind of bored and wanted to see the proverbial shit hit the fan.

"Jon's not dominating shit!" I lashed out at Marcella after her taunting me to come out.

"Jude? Is that you?" she asked, staring in my eyes like there would be something different present in them instead of just looking like Jon's eyes. There may have been anger in them but that was about it.

I poked her in the chest and snarled at her. "You really think you know every damn thing, don't you?"

"I know enough." Marcella sat back on the sofa and appeared to be sizing me up. "So how have you been, Jude? I understand you've been a bad girl the last couple of days."

"I understand you've been a bad girl," I said mockingly.

She grinned and folded her hands on her lap. The bitch was acting too calm, cool, and collected for me.

"Don't patronize me," I stated with disdain. "If you're asking whether or not I showed my ass, you're damn right I did. Mason needed to get to stepping and get the fuck out our lives."

"You may feel that way but your plan backfired on you, Jude. Didn't it?"

I had to admit to myself that Mason's apparent acceptance of Jon's situation threw me for a loop. I assumed that his ultimate purpose behind constantly coming on to her was sex, but he was acting like he actually cared. Most men would dump a sister with a quickness if she boned one of his friends. As far as having multiple personalities, most would probably run for the hills.

She sat there, smirking, waiting for a response.

Finally, I replied with much confidence, "It appears it may have but it's not over until it's over."

Marcella reached over and took my hand. "Why are you trying to hurt Jonquinette, Jude?"

"I'm not trying to hurt Jonquinette." I yanked my hand away from her and stood up. "She's trying to hurt me and I can't have that. What Jon should have done was keep her damn mouth shut in the first place. It was okay when she was going to those meetings at the hospital." I went over to the window and looked out over the parking lot of the complex. Mason's car was out there. The bastard!

"Hell, they were even somewhat entertaining," I continued. "I enjoyed listening to those pathetic people talking about how sex had ruined their relationships and sometimes, even their lives. Jon never said anything in the meetings and I was cracking up inside. Then Miss Thang had to go and start yapping off at the mouth. She started this shit, not me. Don't get it twisted."

Marcella got up and followed me over to the window, lurking over my shoulder. "Before you did your dirt anonymously. Now you're doing things to directly affect Jonquinette and the way people look at her."

"Fuck the way people look at her!" I screamed at her without turning around. "This is my world!"

"Jude, Jonquinette realizes all that you've done for her and she's grateful for your protection all those years." She placed a hand on my right shoulder. "But now, she has other people who understand her and we're going to protect her from now on." She slid her hand down my arm, grabbed my elbow, and swung me around. "She doesn't need you anymore. Don't you think it's time for you to go away?"

"Go away?" I stared her directly in the eyes and said, "You must be out of your fuckin' mind! I'm not going any damn place! If one of us is going somewhere, it sure as shit isn't going to be me!"

"Jude, Jonquinette deserves a normal life. If you truly care about her, then you'll let her move on."

"Move on?" I chuckled. "So what is to become of me? What is supposed to happen to my life?" I pulled away and walked into the kitchen to find some real food, not those damn cookies Jon had set out on a plate.

Marcella didn't come all the way into the kitchen. She just stood in the doorway while I searched the cabinets for something decent to munch on. "Jude, I don't profess to know all the answers and I know this is hard on you, but both of you can't go on like this."

I slammed one of the cabinet doors. "Why can't we both go on like this?" I opened the fridge, sniffed the milk to see if I could at least have a bowl of cereal. It was sour so I poured it down the sink.

"Look at what's happening," Marcella said. "Like you just said out there, things are changing. Jonquinette is not going to just sit back and let things be anymore. You're getting angry, lashing out at people, and she's becoming a stronger person."

I closed the refrigerator door, leaned on the counter and put my hands on my hips. "Um, how can I put this." I tapped my foot. "Jon is not becoming a stronger person because Jon has always been weak as shit. That's the reason I'm here; to make sure people don't fuck her over."

"Do you think I'm trying to fuck her over?" Marcella asked.

"That's yet to be determined, but I know that I'm not going anywhere. You can just forget that shit."

Marcella came into the kitchen and took my wrists into her hands. "Listen, will you at least agree to talk to me again, on a regular basis? Maybe we can come to some sort of terms."

I yanked my wrists away. "What is all this touchy-feely shit? Are you a dyke or something?"

She frowned and replied, "No, I just want you to know that someone does care about you. I care about you, Jude. I care about both you and Jonquinette. You're not alone and I don't want you to ever feel like you don't have someone to talk to. I understand, clearly, that there are two of you and both of you need love."

I shook my head and snickered. "Whatever, bitch!"

"See, that's what I mean. Your hostility toward me is just a front. You really crave to be loved. Isn't that why you have sex with so many men?"

"Oh, so you want to go there, huh?" I asked. "I guess it's time for the motherfucking gloves to come off."

She stood there and took a challenging stance. "Fine by me. If I can't get through to you by talking calmly, then we can get loud. However, that's not going to solve anything."

"And me coming into your office, lying on your chair like I'm some sort of fucking diva, and spilling my guts will solve something?" I asked sarcastically.

"It's a start. Tell me, Jude. Why do you really have sex with so many people? Why do you consider that important?"

"You tell me. You're the doctor." I ripped open a bag of chips that was sitting on the counter. I was craving something salty. "Oh, what was it you told Jon? That I use it as a power play?" I laughed. "You're too funny. You do realize that everything you say to her, I hear."

"Yes, I know that you're always around," she admitted. "So you know how much your adventures are hurting Jon. She came to me because she thought she was insane. You regard that as protecting her?"

I didn't like the direction the conversation was going. It was time to end it. "It's time for you to leave," I informed her.

"Jude, aren't you going to answer my question?"

"No, I'm not going to answer your stupid-ass question." I went out of the kitchen and opened the front door. "Get out!"

"Jude, this isn't going to improve anything. You're always ending our chats abruptly."

"Chats? This isn't a fucking chat. We're not two girlfriends catching up on things or lollygagging around. This is a fucking argument and I won't engage in it any longer. It's useless. You think that you can convince me to go away? Well, like I said before, that shit is not happening!" I opened the door wider. "Now get the hell out!"

"Would you allow me to talk to Jon again?"

I laughed. "Jon's not here right now."

"Can you allow her to come back out?" she asked.

"You are one sick cookie. If you think I'm going let you sit here and fill Jon's head with more of your bullshit tonight, you are sadly mistaken." I went down the hallway toward the bedroom. "If you're not going to leave, then I am. I'm getting dressed."

"No, don't do that," Marcella stated in a panic. "It's late and you need to stay here. I'll leave, if you really want me to."

I couldn't help but be amused. I glimpsed at her and she was standing in the doorway looking pathetic. "Aw, I get it. You know that if I go out, I'm going to fuck someone and you're trying to spare Jon that embarrassment."

She lowered her eyes to the floor but refused to respond.

"Well, you're right," I continued. "If I leave here, especially at this time of morning, I'm going to go out and fuck the first thing moving." I decided to rub it in. "In fact, I might do it anyway, even if you do get the hell out right now. That trips you out, right? Knowing or rather not knowing what I might do next?"

"You're truly enjoying this, aren't you? Destroying this young woman's life."

"I'm not destroying shit. I'm simply living mine."

Marcella left without saying another word, thank goodness! I went out on the balcony and watched her pull away slowly. I retrieved my bag of chips from the kitchen, came back out and sat on one of the two lounge chairs Jon had out there. About fifteen minutes later, I saw a brother that I had seen many times before leaving the building. It was way over in the morning and he had obviously just finished making a booty call to the sister in Apartment 1-C. She was the uppity bitch with a weave who always thought she was too special to even speak to Jon. One of those women who thought her shit didn't stink and that her pussy was worth millions.

I decided to kill two birds with one stone because I had never liked that bitch in 1-C.

"Hey, you!" I called out to him as I stood up on the balcony so he could see me.

He looked up just as he was hitting the keyless entry button on his key chain to unlock a black Mercedes SLK 320. "Yes?" he asked.

I didn't say anything. I just ripped off Jon's pajama top, followed by her bra. Then I stepped out of the pants and underwear. I stood there naked, just staring at him seductively. Then I closed my eyes and started swaying my hips to imaginary music and palming my breasts. I heard the beep again as he locked the car, followed by his footsteps coming back up the walkway toward the building. The shit was just that easy.

31

jonquinette

I hesitated before I knocked on Momma's door. I had no idea how I would break the news but it had to come out. I needed her, more than ever.

She saved me the trouble of knocking when she suddenly swung the door of her condo open. She was startled and slapped her right hand across her chest.

"Hello, Momma," I said, faking a smile.

She took a deep breath and sighed. "Jonquinette. What a pleasant surprise."

"You really mean that?"

"Yes, of course I mean it. I was on my way out to the store but come on in." She turned and walked back into her place, leaving the door ajar for me to follow her. "In fact, I've been getting frustrated because you haven't returned any of my calls."

It was true that she had left several phone messages, both at home and at work, but I just couldn't bring myself to call her. Dealing with the drama from Darnetta and Mason had been bad enough and I didn't think I could deal with a lot of drama from Momma.

"I'm sorry," I told her. "I was out of town for a while and then when I got back, some things happened."

Momma eyed me suspiciously. "What sort of things?"

"Can I sit down?" I asked as I walked into the living room. Her place was immaculate as always. I was hoping I wouldn't catch her at a bad time, with a man in the house, and it appeared that I had lucked out.

"Jonquinette, stop acting like you're some sort of stranger." Momma laughed. "Of course you can sit down. My home is your home."

I plopped down on the sofa and she took a seat in the armchair directly across from it. "What if I am a stranger?" I asked her.

She leaned her head to the side in confusion. "Excuse me?"

"I said, what if I am a stranger?"

Momma seemed irritated. "You're not making any sense. You're my daughter. I gave birth to you, so how could you possibly be a stranger?"

I picked up a photo frame off her end table. It was a picture of the two of us at my college graduation. In retrospect, I guess it was a picture of the three of us. Momma didn't say another word to me. A heavy silence just hung in the air like thick smoke.

"I live inside this body and I feel like I'm a stranger," I finally said.

She laughed again, this time uneasily. "You must be over-heated. You're acting delirious." She got up from her seat and started walking away. "Let me go into the kitchen and get you something cold to drink. I made some freshly squeezed lemonade, your favorite."

I tossed the picture onto the sofa cushion, jumped up, and grabbed her by the elbow. "Momma, lemonade isn't going to cure this."

"Cure what?" she snapped at me.

"My illness." We stared at each other while I searched for the words to say. "Momma, did you never figure it out or did you just choose to ignore it?"

She yanked her arm away in anger. "I have no idea what you're talking about."

She took off toward the kitchen anyway and I was right on her tail. I refused to let her walk away from the situation. "I won't cut any corners with this. Momma, I have MPD."

Momma took two glasses out of the dishwater and started to get an ice tray from the freezer. She paused and asked, "MPD? What the hell is that? Some sort of venereal disease?"

"No, Momma. MPD stands for Multiple Personality Disorder."

She dropped both the ice tray and one of the glasses on the floor. The glass shattered everywhere. "Bullshit! Bullshit!" she screamed.

Momma grabbed a dishrag and bent down to clean up the mess. She wouldn't even look at me. "Momma, I'm serious."

"You can't be serious. You're not some lunatic."

"No, I'm not. I just have an illness and I plan to get help for it." She continued to busy herself with the cleanup efforts like it was no big deal. "That's why I came to see you today. I need you to be there with me. I can't go through this alone."

She finally stopped in her tracks, stood up, and got close enough to me to breathe on my cheek. "Who filled your mind with this nonsense?"

"I've been seeing this doctor, Dr. Spencer, and she's the one who broke it down for me. She explained it and then when I spoke with Daddy, he—"

My mother's voice went up ten notches. "Wait a minute! When did you speak to Henry? Did he call you?"

"No, he didn't. Actually, I went to see him."

Momma looked like she was suddenly on the brink of tears when she said, "You little ungrateful bitch. How could you betray me like that?"

I knew the mention of my father would get her upset. Momma always expected me to choose her side over his. I was determined to make her see the light, though. "Momma, going to see Daddy wasn't about betraying you. He's my father. I have a right to spend time with him."

"Your father disrespected me. He went out and got that bastard child and totally disgraced both of us."

"Daddy said none of that was true." Momma stormed back into the living room. I was getting sick and tired of following her, but I wasn't about to give up. "He doesn't know why that woman showed up there that day, but he said he'd never laid eyes on her before."

She smirked at me. "And you believed him?"

I put my hands on my hips and stood my ground. "Yes."

"You know what I can't believe?" she said with a snarl. "I can't believe you're turning your back on me."

That's when I felt myself getting angry. My mother had always been selfish, thinking the entire world revolved around her. "Momma, can't you understand that this is not about you!" I screamed at her. "For once, pay attention to me! What *I* need!"

She slapped me across the face and I was stunned. Momma had never hit me before, not ever.

"How dare you?" she asked. "I've taken care of your needs your entire life. When that motherfucker deserted us, I took on sole responsibility for you."

"Momma, Daddy didn't desert us," I said, beginning to cry.

"You pushed him away. Maybe you're the one that needs some of that lemonade. You seem to be delirious."

Momma went into the foyer and opened the front door. "I won't listen to any more of this." She stood there, obviously waiting for me to exit. When I didn't budge, she yelled, "Get out!"

I sat back down on the sofa, determined to say everything I needed to say before I left. "You have to listen. Think about it. All those times when I said I didn't do those horrid things. All those times you probably had conversations with me that didn't seem quite right. Remember our dinner a while back?"

Momma remained by the door. "Yes, you were talking crazy then, too."

"No, it was because I wasn't there. Momma, I woke up the next morning with a carryout container full of red meat and had no recollection of ever meeting you for dinner."

She slammed the door. "What?"

"When I called you up to apologize, I was calling to apologize for not keeping our plans." She came over and sat down beside me. "I know all of this is hard to comprehend, but listen. I need you to listen because all my life, I've been scared to open up and tell the truth."

Something changed in her face and her demeanor. For once, my mother felt compassion for me. She took my hand and squeezed it gently. "I'm listening, Jonquinette. Tell me everything."

"There have been countless times, dating back to my childhood, when I simply wasn't there. I would black out and when I came back, that's when I would find out what I supposedly did."

Momma shook her head but continued to hold my hand. "This is crazy."

"There's more." I sighed. "For years, I've been waking up with signs of sexual intercourse. Sex that I never had."

Her left eyebrow went up in the air. "How can you have sex and not know it?" she asked incredulously.

I knew all of it was too much to believe. Hell, I could barely believe it myself and I was living it. "Momma, it happened and it's going to continue to happen if I don't do something to stop it. To stop her."

Momma let my hand go. "Her?"

"Apparently, she calls herself Jude."

"Jude?"

"Yes. Jude."

"How do you know this?"

"Because Dr. Spencer met her. She "came out" in her office when I was contemplating about reaching out to Daddy."

Momma laughed uneasily and ran her fingers through her hair. "Came out?"

"Took over. Took control." I took her hand again. I needed that connection, even if she didn't. "It seems that she hates Daddy for some reason and that was the trigger that made her show herself."

Momma looked confused. "Why would she hate Henry?"

"I don't know. Maybe because he wanted to get help for me when I was younger and she was all about self-preservation."

"So how long has this Jude person been around?"

"According to her, since damn near the beginning."

A look of revelation shot across Momma's face. "Then since she hates Henry so much, do you think it's possible . . ."

It suddenly hit me at the same time it hit Momma. "She could've been the one who set him up." I let her hand go, jumped up and started pacing the floor. "That's it! That's why I don't remember anything about Thanksgiving Day. Jude was in control and somehow, she did it. She planned the entire thing. Now that I think about it, I had some money stashed away in my sock drawer and when I searched for it the following weekend to go clothes shopping, it was gone. That must have been what she used to pay the woman."

"She probably paid that whore money to show up and say she was screwing Henry," Momma said, jumping up also. "Oh my God, that means our marriage ended for nothing. All these years wasted."

Momma broke down in tears. I held her tightly in an embrace. "It's okay, Momma. Don't cry. Please don't cry."

She looked at me with glazed-over eyes. "So what do we do now?"

"We get help. All of us."

32

jude

I seriously needed to relieve some stress. This was just getting to be too much. I had seen a late night infomercial for an online dating service several times, after returning to Jon's apartment from a fuck hunt.

I sat down at Jon's computer and signed on to her account. The computer was slow as shit because she refused to get a DSL line or a cable modem. I clicked on the internet and signed on to my free account that she knew nothing about. My latest screen name was DurtyDeedz.

I made a quick stop by Blackgentlemen.com to see if any new bachelors had been added. All I could say was, "My, oh my!" The commercials for the website are what motivated me to check it out. I was shocked to see the way it was laid out. It was a free site, but I didn't want to join. I rather decided to tour the site as a guest. They had me check two boxes; one telling my sex and the other telling which sex I was searching for. I checked female and then male and hit continue. Then they asked if I just wanted to hang out and meet people, seek out a committed relationship, or just try something wild and freaky. Of course, I chose the wild and freaky button. It then asked me what age group I was interested in, what my zip code was, and what my sexual interests were. I entered 30344 as my zip code and selected the domination and submission button. What the fuck!

I was surprised to see a ton of matches come up with pictures included on the site. Now being on a bachelor or bachelorette site is one thing, but being on a site and announcing to the world that you are into domination and submission is another thing altogether. It was cool by me because it just made me hornier to know I wasn't the only freak of the week. The real trip was the fact that at least half of them were married. It's a small world and I could imagine the beatdown some of them must have gotten when their wives, or worse, one of their wives' friends spotted the ad and then spread the word to all the other friends, associates, and family members.

I scanned the ads, mostly checking out the pictures, since most of them were jacked up and easy to eliminate. I finally spotted a thirty-nine-year-old male named DickinUDown. He said he was five-eleven with a muscular body and that he didn't smoke but he drank sociably. He also said that he was open to conventional sex, sex with a couple, sex with no intercourse, and domination and submission.

He was looking kind of fly in his picture, even though it was sort of blurry. I decided to email him and get straight to the motherfucking point.

To: DickinUDown@pitbullsonline.com
From: DurtyDeedz@cumntastethis.com
Subject: Cum and Dick This Down

Dear Dickin,

I saw your ad on the dating website and I am not one to mince words or play games. You live in Atlanta and so do I. Let's hook up and see what can happen when we get "durty" together in the Durty South. I prefer to remain a mystery so all I'm willing to tell you at this point is that I have "the three F's." I'm freaky, fine, and I have a fat ass.

If you get this email right away, you are looking at the opportunity of a lifetime. I'm willing to meet up with you in a private place and fuck the living daylights out of you. Why, you ask? Because I'm bored, horny, and sick of not being able to find a decent fuck the traditional way.

It is now ten after four. You have until exactly six this evening to respond. After that, this offer expires and I'm moving on to the next man that catches my eye on the site.

Keeping It Real,
Durty

I stayed online but went to the kitchen to fix something to eat. There wasn't a damn thing in there. I went through Jon's purse to see if she had any cash and there was nothing so I hit up her reserve that she kept hidden in a sock in her lingerie drawer.

I got a twenty out and then called the closest pizza place to request a delivery. I wanted a pizza with all the red meat they could find on it. While I waited for the pizza, I turned on *Jerry Springer*. That's my motherfucker right there. If they ever try to take Jerry off the air, I'm putting my foot to someone's ass.

I had just sat down when the email chime went off on the computer. I got back up and went to read it.

To: DurtyDeedz@cumntastethis.com
From: DickinUDown@pitbullsonline.com
Re: Cum and Dick This Down

   All I can say is Damnnnnnnnnnnnn! What's up, my freaky
honie? There is no need for you to search any further. I am
definitely down for whatever. Just let me know when and where to
meet you so I can check out those "three F's." I will be there, ready
and waiting. I'm doing my tongue warm-up exercises now and then
I'm going to jack off a few times so I won't cum for at least an hour
when I tap that ass. Holla back at me with a quickness.

                                                            Dickin

   Humph, he was beginning to sound like he was full of shit. I
talked a lot of junk but I could back my shit up. I wasn't so sure
about him, but what the hell. Might as well find out. I responded
right away.

To: DickinUDown@pitbullsonline.com
From: DurtyDeedz@cumntastethis.com
Re: Cum and Dick This Down

   All right, Dickin, it's on. Meet me tonight at eight in front of
the Paradise U.S.A. motel. If you don't know where it is, get the
directions off Yahoo. I have nothing else to add. See you when I see
you.

                                                            Durty

   I glanced at the time in the right-hand bottom corner of Jon's
computer screen and realized the pizza place was getting danger-
ously close to their thirty-minute guaranteed delivery time. Shit,
free pizza is even better than good pizza.
   With a mere two minutes left, there was a knock at the door.
As I went to open it, I said, "Shit!" After I opened the door, I said,
"Triple shit!"

The brother standing there in front of the doorway was just that: fine as triple shit. He was tall, dark, clean-shaven, and had lips to die for.

He just stared at me for a second, checking me out. I spun around and poked my ass out at him so he could get a better look.

"Do you like what you see?" I asked him.

"Uh, yeah, I love what I see," he responded hesitantly. "Um, here's your pizza."

"Could you be a sweetheart and bring it inside for me?" I grabbed my right wrist. "I have that darn carpal tunnel syndrome, fooling around with that computer mouse and all."

"Sure, I can bring it in," he replied.

"Thanks." He followed me into the dining room. "You can just sit it down right here on the table."

"No problem." He looked at the receipt taped to the side of the box. "That'll be sixteen-fifty."

I had tucked the twenty into my bra. Instead of reaching down to get it inconspicuously, I put on a show. I unbuttoned the shirt I had on and exposed my bra, then whipped out my titty so he could see my nipple and took out the money. I handed it to him, without covering myself up. "Here you go. Keep the change."

He licked his sexy-ass lips. "Thanks."

I started squeezing his arm. "You look like you work out. Do you?"

"Whenever I get a chance."

"You work out at home or at the gym?"

"Mostly at home but sometimes I go to the gym."

"Which one?" I asked.

"The Body Sculpture."

"Oh yeah, I've heard of it." I licked my lips back at him. "Do all the men who work out there look as fine as you? If so, I might need to start hanging out there."

He blushed. "Um, I'm not sure. I'm not one to check out other men."

"So you don't know if they're as well-hung as you, then?"

"What makes you think I'm well-hung?" he asked me.

"Just an assumption. You seem like the type of man that would have major holdings." I slid my hand down his arm and onto his crotch. "Oh yeah, my assumption was right."

He started laughing. "This is wild!"

"Do you have other deliveries to make?"

He nodded. "Yeah, but they won't give them to me until I get back to the shop." He looked at his watch. "I should really get going."

I stood on my toes and nibbled gently on his chin. "Couldn't you tell them you had car trouble or something?"

He lowered his mouth onto mine and darted his tongue into my mouth. "I suppose I could do that, if I had the right motivation to do so."

"Well, then, let me give you some motivation."

I sat down on a dining-room chair and started unzipping his pants. He looked like he could split bricks with his dick when I took it out.

"Um, chocolate on a stick, my favorite," I said. I remembered seeing some whipped cream in Jon's refrigerator. "Sit down on the table. I'll be right back."

When I came back, he was completely nude and spread-eagle on the dining-room table.

"Now that's what I'm talking about," I said. I squeezed some whipped cream on the head of his dick. "Feed Momma the dick."

I took my time licking the whipped cream off his dick as he moaned and groaned. Then I deep-throated him until he exploded in my mouth.

"Mighty tasty," I commented afterward.

"Glad you liked it," he replied.

I took off my clothes and climbed onto the table from the opposite direction, placing my pussy over his face while I took his dick into my mouth again. We sucked on each other for a while and then I moved down, smearing my pussy juice over his chest and abdomen. I climbed on top of him backward and sat on his dick. As I rode him, it sounded like someone slurping up a thick milkshake through a straw.

Once I had my way with him, I told him, "You can get dressed now."

He agreed, after peeping his watch. "Yeah, I better go. But listen, I get off at eleven. Want me to come back?"

"No, I have plans," I answered.

"Well, what about tomorrow sometime?"

"I have plans then, too. And before you ask, I have plans the day after that and the day after that." I wanted to make sure he got the hint so I added, "In fact, I have plans for the rest of my natural life."

He shook his head as he put on his clothes. "Damn, you don't have to be that cold."

"Let's just keep it simple. You came over here, we were attracted to each other, we explored it, and now it's over. You can go back to delivering pizza and I can finally eat mine."

He had the audacity to cop an attitude with me. "Okay, whatever. I'm used to whores like you."

I smirked at him. "Let yourself out. I have to go take a shower. Whores like me keep busy schedules. I have to go get ready for my next fuck of the night."

I left him standing there looking stupid, the little hound dog.

I debated about keeping my appointment with DickinUDown. I had already met my dick quotient for the day. Then again, he was into domination and submission and that was a huge turn-on. I stopped by an adult shop and picked up some items, then headed over to the Paradise U.S.A. motel.

I waited for more than thirty minutes for him to show up and was about to leave when I spotted a raggedy car pulling into the lot. It was so raggedy, I couldn't even tell the make and model of the vehicle. A man got out the car who looked nothing like the photo on the dating site. Big surprise, huh?

Something just told me it was him. I sighed and shook my head. I watched him stand there, scanning the parking lot nervously for a while and then I got out of Jon's car. "Dickin? Is that you?" I asked.

"Yeah, it's me!" he yelled in response.

He came closer to me and I almost hurled. First off, he was anorexic. Secondly, he looked more like fifty-nine than thirty-nine. Thirdly, his ass was reeking and I picked up on that in the breeze when he got within twenty feet of me.

I was pissed. This motherfucker was about to learn a valuable lesson about lying to people on the internet.

"Damn, you are fine and freaky with a fat ass," he said after he was all up on me.

"Why don't you just shut up and go pay for a room?" I folded my arms in front of me and leaned on the side of Jon's car. "I don't have all night."

He cleared his throat. "I thought you were paying for the room. You invited me."

I rolled my eyes at him. "I'm out of here."

He grabbed my arm. "No, wait. I got you. I got this. Just give me a minute to get my debit card out my car."

I didn't respond. I just watched him retrieve his card, go into the motel office, and walk back out a few minutes later with a key.

I got my shopping bag out of Jon's trunk and met him in front of Room 112. Once we were inside, I handcuffed his ass, gagged him, put a leather hood over his head, broke out my flogger and tore his ass up. His stupid ass asked me if I wanted to fuck him afterward.

I leaned over and whispered in his ear, "Update that damn picture on the internet. If you don't, the next sister might not be so nice." I gathered my things together and left. I still had time to catch the late night episode of Jerry.

33

jonquinette

The day had finally arrived and it had been a long time coming. To think that Momma and Daddy had been apart because of me, at least because of a part of me, was too much to bear. Despite what some people believe, we only get one life. Jude had ruined their life together, apparently because she felt threatened.

Daddy didn't feel comfortable staying with me since I only had one bedroom, so I registered him at a hotel less than two blocks from my apartment. I debated about how to structure the reunion. Part of me felt it would be better for Daddy and Momma to see each other again for the first time in a public place. At least then I wouldn't have to worry about them getting too loud. Daddy wasn't the type and Momma was too uppity to allow complete strangers to see her arguing.

The other option was for them to do it in private so that they could really open up with each other. On the flip side, they could have ended up killing each other. I asked Marcella about it and she said that a private atmosphere would probably be better. She even offered to lend us her office. I didn't think they were ready for that, though.

I wanted it to be someplace peaceful so I decided to take them to a park for a picnic, something we hadn't done together since I was a child. Daddy got into town around nine o'clock on a Saturday morning but he couldn't check in to the hotel until three in the afternoon. I took him out to breakfast at a waffle house and it was a good thing because it gave us an opportunity to get a game plan together before Momma was added to the mix.

"How's Flower doing?" I asked him after we were seated in a booth.

He grinned at the mere mention of Flower's name. "She's doing great and she sends her love."

"And I send my love back."

"She was upset that she couldn't come with me but I explained to her that it was more important for her to be in school and that I had no idea when I would be back."

"Aw, well let her know that she is welcome to come see me during one of her school breaks or summer vacation. I would love to have her."

"Wouldn't that be too much for you to handle?" he asked.

"No, because I will take off work whenever she is coming," I replied. "Speaking of which, who's manning your shop while you're gone?"

"Nobody, but it's fine. While I hate to lose business to the competition, the townsfolk will just have to take their cars on over to Jose's place. That's the only downfall of running a one-person business. When you can't be there, the business is not functioning."

"Have you ever thought about hiring someone?"

Daddy laughed. "I don't get enough regular business for that. I make enough to get by but just like other types of service-oriented companies, income is solely based on demand and not on recurring customers."

"True, I guess you can never depend on people having car trouble."

He shook his head. "Not on a schedule, that's for sure."

"I won't say that I'm rich or anything, Daddy, but if you need some extra cash, I do have some savings."

He put his hand up to wave me off. "I wouldn't hear of it. Jonquinette, if I really get strapped, I can always go back to programming. I enjoy the repair business but I do have other skills."

"I realize that, Daddy." I didn't want him to think I was implying that he couldn't survive on his own but I also wanted him to know that he supported me for the first fifteen years of my life and for that, I owed him something. "Just don't hesitate to ask me for something, if you need it."

It hit me that I was sitting there talking about life as if mine were normal. There was no guarantee that I would even be around. Jude could possibly get rid of me at any second. I was intentionally beating around the bush, avoiding the matter at hand, and decided to stop it. "Daddy, what are your feelings about seeing Momma again?"

He shrugged. "Part of me is excited as I think I've ever been in my entire life."

"And the other part?"

"The other part is scared to death."

"Have you decided yet?" the waitress asked. I hadn't even noticed her walking up to the table.

"Daddy, you know what you want?" I asked, glancing down at the menu for the first time.

"I'll just have a buttermilk waffle with a side of country ham," he said.

"Um, I'll take a three-egg omelet with cheddar cheese, mush-rooms, and green peppers," I said, placing my order. "And we'll both have orange juice. Two large, please."

The waitress took the menus from us and said, "I'll be right back."

I resumed our conversation. "I can understand you being scared. I'm kind of scared about how things will go down my-self."

Daddy chuckled. "I can imagine. All I can say is the last time we saw each other, which was in the courtroom for our divorce, she looked like she wanted to kill me with her bare hands."

"I'm sorry I couldn't have been there for you that day, in court."

"Jonquinette, that was the last place you needed to be. I'm sorry I couldn't have been there for you during the rest of your educational years and after." He lowered his eyes to the table. "I feel like such a failure."

"Daddy, you are anything but a failure. You are a kind, loving, compassionate man whose life was screwed up because of circum-stances beyond your control. The bottom line is this is all my fault. All mine."

"Jonquinette, you can't go blaming yourself for this. This is not your fault. You have an illness and that is not something you can control."

"Yes, but why did this have to happen to me? To our family?" I asked him, in search of answers.

Daddy didn't respond, but a troubled expression came across his face.

"Sorry," I said. "I can't expect you to know the reasoning be-hind all of this any more than me. I just don't understand."

"That's what the doctor is for, right?" Daddy asked. He grinned, I'm sure to try to reassure me. "I haven't met this Dr. Spencer yet but she sounds like a good person."

"She is a great person."

"Then let's just wait and see what happens. We'll take this one day at a time."

"That's the only way to take life," I agreed.

The waitress returned with our food and it hit the spot. We had about four hours before we were due to meet Momma at the park so I took Daddy sightseeing. Even though Atlanta was only four hours from him, he'd never actually seen the city. He'd only bypassed it on the highway going from Florida to North Carolina.

We got to the park at two o'clock on the dot. I spotted Momma's car in the parking lot.

"She's already here," I told Daddy.

He searched the immediate area for her. "Where? I don't see her."

"I don't see her. I just see her car." I parked next to Momma's Buick and cut off my ignition.

"I was about to say," he said, "I know it's been years but I would hope that I could still recognize Meredith."

"Oh, you'll recognize her." I giggled. "Momma hasn't really changed a bit. She's just as glamorous as ever. Never a hair out of place."

"Even though Meredith was always a bit too materialistic for me, I have to give it to her. She always, always looked good. There was never a day that I wasn't proud to have her on my arm."

"Aw, Daddy, are you saying that Momma was your show-piece?"

He blushed. "I wouldn't go as far as to say all that, but I'd rather have a pretty woman on my arm than an ugly one any day."

"I bet Flower's mother is pretty," I said. "You can tell that by looking at her daughter."

Daddy shrugged as he undid his seat belt. "Allison looks okay. She's not Meredith, though. My one and only true love."

I glanced over at Daddy and prayed he didn't have hopes of actually getting back together with Momma. Forgiveness was one thing; falling back into the groove like nothing ever happened was something totally different.

I took my seat belt off and got out of the car, meeting Daddy in the back by the trunk. I unlocked it and took out the picnic basket and blanket. Daddy took the basket from me and we headed down a path toward the shelter area where Momma was supposed to meet us. When we got within seventy yards of it, we saw her sitting on the top of one of the four wooden picnic tables. She had on a casual velvet pantsuit and her hair was pinned up.

I yelled out, "Momma! We're here!"

She didn't turn around at first. She seemed hesitant, like she was almost scared to face Daddy. I could hear him let out a heavy sigh from beside of me and then he became so quiet that I wasn't even sure he was breathing.

Then he whispered, "Maybe this wasn't such a good idea after all. You think we could arrange for us to go to separate therapy sessions? I'm not backing out of helping you, believe me, but I'm getting a bad feeling here."

I reached over and touched him on the arm. He was trembling. "It's okay, Daddy. Part of living life is facing our fears. Marcella taught me that."

He put his hand on top of mine. "I guess you're right. Let's go ahead and get this over with, then."

As we approached Momma, she still didn't turn around.

Daddy stopped dead in his tracks. "Listen, do me a favor. Go feel out the situation for me."

"Feel out the situation?"

"Yeah, see if she still feels like seeing me. If she doesn't even want to turn around, I don't want to put her on the spot. Or myself for that matter."

"Daddy, this has to happen and it is what it is. But, if it'll make you more comfortable, I'll go make sure the coast is clear."

"Thanks, Jonquinette."

Daddy leaned against the nearest tree he could find, probably to prevent himself from falling, and I went on to Momma.

"Hey, Momma," I said, after I got right beside the table where she was sitting.

She glimpsed nervously at me. "Hey, sweetheart."

"Why wouldn't you turn around?" I asked.

She shrugged. "I guess I'm just trying to prolong the inevitable."

"Daddy's over there standing by a tree because he doesn't think you want to be bothered with him."

"It's not that. It's just that it's been ages since I've seen him." She moved a piece of hair that had fallen and placed it behind her ear. "What if he thinks I've aged badly?"

"Momma, you haven't aged at all."

She laughed. "Honey, we've all aged. Some of us just age better than others."

"Well, consider yourself one of those then, because you look exactly the same to me."

"That's because you see me all the time. It's like when a grandmother doesn't see her grandchildren for a few months and when she sees them, they look completely different from the last time."

I found myself getting agitated. Why was I having a discussion with my mother about her looks when this was about something ten times more serious?

"Momma, I'm not trying to be nasty or anything, but Daddy isn't here to see whether or not you still look fly. He's here because I asked him to come and help me get cured. Nothing more, nothing less."

She glared at me with disdain. "You just don't get it."

"No, Momma, *you* just don't get it. All my life everything has been about you. What Meredith thinks. What Meredith wants. Well, today and the next several months, or however long it takes, will be all about me and why this is happening to me."

She suddenly got loud with me. "Are you implying that this is somehow my fault? Your mental issue has nothing to do with me."

"It might not have anything to do with you or it might have everything to do with you, but I'm not trying to place guilt. I'm trying to be normal for once in my life."

Neither one of us saw Daddy approaching until he was right on top of us.

"Meredith, hello," he said uneasily.

She finally turned to look at him. Then she turned away from him and stared out into the woods. "Hello, Henry."

He inched his way even closer and sat the picnic basket down on the table. "How are things?"

"Things are okay," she said, still not making eye contact. "How are things with you?"

"Okay."

"So I hear you have a daughter."

"Yes, her name's Flower. She's six."

"Six. Wow!" Momma must have figured out that her body language was ridiculous. She got down off the table and turned around so that they were face-to-face. "Time has been good to you, Henry. You've gotten more character with age."

Daddy blushed. "Time has been extremely good to you, Meredith."

"Why, thanks."

I laid the blanket over the next table and said, "I'll just use the blanket as a tablecloth instead of someplace to sit. We can have lunch under the shelter since it looks a bit overcast."

"That's fine," they both said in unison. Then they made eye contact and broke out in laughter.

"I didn't cook," I confessed. "I'm not even that good at making sandwiches so I took the easy way out. I had my favorite deli prepare a scrumptious selection for us." I started pulling items out of the basket and putting them on top of the blanket. "Let's see. We have an array of fresh fruit: strawberries, grapes, and assorted melons. Then we have some panini sandwiches with roasted chicken, peppers, and chipolte mayo along with macaroni salad and freshly baked oatmeal raisin cookies."

"Oh my," Daddy said. "My mouth is watering just thinking about digging into that."

We all sat down and got reacquainted as a family. It was a good and bad experience. It was all good until we got to the part about Jude, which led to the Thanksgiving Day episode, which led to the hooker, which let to bad memories of the divorce and everything that came with it and after it.

The afternoon ended with Momma and Daddy both in tears. For a change, I was the only one who was acting strong. I comforted both of them; one in one arm and one in the other.

There was a shocker, though. Momma asked if she could take Daddy back to his hotel to check in instead of me. He had left his car at my place and she said that she would bring him to get it after he'd gotten his key and was settled in. The next morning, Daddy's car was still out in front of my apartment building, which made me wonder. When I came back from the eight o'clock church service, it was gone.

34

jonquinette

"Now make sure you don't peek," Mason whispered in my ear as he led me down the landing of our apartment building. "You'll ruin the surprise."

"I'm not going to peek." I was so tempted to mess with the makeshift blindfold that he had made from a necktie, but I just took baby steps so I wouldn't fall on my behind on the way down. "Won't you give me a little hint though?"

"No, no hints. You women are so strange. You get excited about surprises but then always want to know what they are before they are given to you."

I giggled. "Human nature, and I don't think that reaction is limited to women."

"You may have a point." Mason stopped at the bottom of the steps and I could hear him fumbling around with a set of keys as he unlocked his apartment door. "I guess, in retrospect, I could have just blindfolded you once we got in front of my door since there was no surprise on the steps."

We both laughed.

"I was thinking that but I wasn't about to say anything. It's cool. It just adds to the experience, almost falling down a flight of stairs to my death."

Mason kissed me on the cheek. "You're too funny."

I heard his door creak open and he led me inside his place.

"You realize this is my first time in your place? It's not like I'm going to recognize if something has changed," I informed him.

"I know this is your first time here and that's a shame. But all of that is about to change because I plan to invite you over more often."

"I might be late from time to time because I often lose my car keys."

Mason was silent for a minute and then started laughing. "Like I said, you're too funny."

He removed the blindfold and it took a moment for my eyes to adjust to the lighting. When they did, I was floored. "Mason, I don't know what to say."

"Don't say anything," he replied, taking my hand and walking farther into his place.

His apartment was awesome. He had it laid out in all dark leather tones complemented by animal patterns. But that's not why I was so shocked. Mason had the entire place decorated like it was Valentine's Day. He had several vases containing red and yellow roses placed around his apartment with a handmade banner hanging over the dining-room entry that said, Happy Valentine's Day, Jonquinette!

He chuckled and said, "I'm not the best at making banners and my letters are crooked, but it's the thought that counts."

"I can't believe you did all this. It's nowhere near February."

He kissed my hand gently. "I wanted you to know that come

what may, I plan to spend Valentine's Day with you next year. I'm committed to making this work and I will stand by you, through thick and thin."

"That's so sweet!"

"Ah-ha, speaking of sweet, I have a lot of sweets for you."

I blushed. "You do?"

"Yes, and I also have dinner prepared for you, but we're going to do things a little differently."

"How so?" I asked, overwhelmed by the total experience.

"We're going to eat backwards."

"Eat backwards?" I laughed. "Never heard of that. You mean we sit at the table backwards and try to eat? As clumsy and uncoordinated as I am, I'll make a mess."

"No, that's not what I mean." He chuckled and kissed my hand again. "We're going to start with dessert and work our way back. First, we will have dessert, then the main course, the salad, and finally the appetizer."

"Now that sounds very interesting." I took a good whiff of the air. "Something smells yummy."

"Hopefully, it will be."

"Did you cook?"

"Um, no, I cannot tell a lie. I did not cook one single thing." Mason snapped his fingers and three people came flooding out of the kitchen carrying trays—two men and one woman who were all dressed in black suits with white shirts and black ties.

"You are too much!" I exclaimed.

For the next hour, Mason treated me like royalty. The "staff" as he continuously referred to them, served the food on fine china and crystal. What was missing were utensils. Mason informed me that it was a commonly known fact that food eaten by hand is sexy. I wasn't going to argue with him and we ended up feeding each other.

We started out with Chocolate Heart Layer Cake with

Chocolate-Cinnamon Mousse along with Heart-Shaped Dried Cherry and Chocolate Chip Scones and strawberries sprinkled with sugar and marinated in wine. Then we had Chicken in Red Wine Sauce with Root Vegetables and Wilted Greens followed by Red Leaf Lettuce, Watercress and Cucumber Salad with Buttermilk Dressing. Lastly, we had Skewered Scallops with Orange-Sesame Dipping Sauce as an appetizer.

To say the least, I was stuffed after dinner. The "staff" cleaned up everything and departed. At some point, I must have fallen asleep and I was terrified when I woke up. I hoped that Jude hadn't taken over for a period of time, said or done something crazy, and ruined my perfect date with Mason.

I was relieved when I saw Mason coming down the hallway grinning at me. "Hey, you! The food did you in, huh?"

I giggled. "That's an understatement." I decided to be honest. "I'm glad to see that nothing went wrong."

"What could possibly go wrong?" he asked, sitting down beside me on the sofa.

"I thought you-know-who might have reared her ugly head."

Mason ran his fingers through my hair. "No, there's no one here but you and me."

"How can you tell?"

"Come again?"

"Realistically, how can you tell that I'm really Jonquinette and not Jude?"

He shrugged. "When I met Jude, and to my knowledge I've only come across her once, it was obvious that something was wrong."

"How so? I mean, besides the obvious with her declaring herself a major whore and all of that."

"She had a different air about her, a different way of carrying herself."

"What do you mean?"

"She had this attitude like she ruled the world and you're more, more . . ."

I decided to help him out with an appropriate word that wouldn't sound too demeaning. "I'm shyer."

"Yes, that's one way of putting it. I knew the things she was saying and the way she was acting just wasn't you."

I changed the topic. "So what's next or is our date over?"

"No, our date is not over. In fact, we're headed out."

"We are? Do I need to go change?" I asked, looking down at the pair of jeans and simple sweater I had on with a pair of penny loafers. "All I need is about fifteen minutes."

"No, you look great and there's no need to get dressed." He stood up and twirled around. "Check me out. It's not like I have on a tuxedo or anything."

Mason had on a pair of khakis and a button-down alabaster shirt. He was sexy as hell, too.

As we left our building and walked to his car, I began to wonder if things would lead to something sexual that night and if I were even ready for it. In my mind, I had never experienced sex, even though my body had obviously engaged in it countless times. Would I be able to "hang" as some people called it? Would I even halfway know what I was doing in order to please him? I was scared to death.

We ended up at a large office building downtown and I was wondering what in the world we were doing. "Mason, what is this place?" I asked as we pulled into a spot in the empty parking garage.

"Don't worry. This is where I work."

"You're taking me to your job?" I asked incredulously. "At this time of night?"

"Shh," he whispered, placing his index finger over my lips. "Just relax and go with the flow."

We were greeted by the night guard at the desk who gave Mason a high-five and we then took the elevator up to the eleventh floor. Mason directed me into his office and told me to have a seat.

"So, what are we doing here?"

"We'll only be in my office for a second." He opened a closet and disappeared inside. I glanced around; his office was impressive, to say the least. He had a magnificent picture window that spanned the entire wall and a mahogany desk with a high-back black leather chair. There were two computers on his credenza and a flat plasma television was hanging on one of the walls.

He came back out holding a duffel bag. "Let's go."

We got back on the elevator and headed to the roof. "I don't know about this," I said after I saw which button he pushed. "I'm not a big fan of heights."

He gripped my hand. "It's all good. Don't worry."

I forced a smile. "If you say so."

He kissed me on the cheek. "I do say so."

When we got to the roof, it was a gorgeous night and I could immediately see why he took me up there. There was a spectacular view of the city skyline.

"I've never seen anything this beautiful," I told him.

"That makes two of us." He slipped his tongue into my mouth and I eagerly accepted it. While we had kissed many times before, this time was different. There was something permanent about it. I could have stayed that way, in his embrace, for an eternity, but he broke the kiss. "Let's dance."

"Excuse me?"

"We never got to finish dancing at the now infamous wedding so I figured we could finish the dance here." He paused and studied me. "That was you that I danced with at the wedding, right?"

"Yes, I remember everything until the point when you walked off with Smitty."

"Cool." Mason opened his duffel bag and pulled out a battery-operated lantern and boombox combination. He turned on the light, directing it toward where I was standing, and then took a CD out of the bag and put it inside the boombox. "Without You" from Charlie Wilson's *Bridging the Gap* started playing.

Mason came to me and put his arms around my waist and started singing to me about how the sun doesn't shine without me. I was weak in the knees. We were lost in each other and the music for the next two hours. I could not have imagined a more perfect evening. There was no way to top it off. At least, that's what I thought until we went back to Mason's place.

He asked me, "Is it okay if I run you a bath?"

My nerves were shot. It was time to make a decision and it was an easy one. I just prayed I would measure up.

"Sure," I responded.

"I don't have to join you. I'll leave that up to you. I just want to pamper you and make you feel special."

"You've been doing that all night, Mason."

He brushed his lips across mine. "That's because I'm in love with you, Jonquinette."

I closed my eyes and exhaled. "I never thought I would hear anyone say that to me."

"Well, now you have."

"I don't know how to respond," I said.

"Then don't." Mason disappeared in the back and I heard water running. A few minutes later he came back, took me by the hand, and led me to the bathroom where he had prepared a bath with vanilla-scented oil. There were rose petals scattered across the surface of the water. Candles in champagne-shaped glasses were surrounding the tub wall and there was soft music coming from his bedroom.

"Would you like for me to undress you, Jonquinette?" he asked me seductively.

"I-I-I'd like that," I finally managed to get out. "But only if I can undress you too."

I wanted Mason to know that I didn't want to bathe alone. I needed to be held, caressed. I needed him, and only him, to make love to me. I wanted to know what it felt like, especially since I had no idea how much time I had before Jude decided to rid the world of me forever.

Walter Beasley's "I Had a Dream" started playing as Mason pulled my sweater over my head. I slipped out of my penny loafers and made eye contact with him as he unfastened and unzipped my jeans. He sat down on the side of the tub so he could maneuver them over my hips and then I stepped out of them.

He grabbed my waist and kissed my nipples through my white cotton bra. They were as hard as black pearls. He lowered my bra straps and reached behind me to unclasp it. I ran my fingers through his dreadlocks and kissed his forehead as he took one of my now bare breasts into his mouth and suckled on it.

I heard myself moaning and thought about all the times I had fantasized about such a moment throughout the years of mastur-bating in my lonely bed at night.

Mason kept exploring both of my breasts with his tongue while he lowered my panties down around my ankles so I could step out of those as well. So there I was nude, in front of a man, for the very first time by my own choice. Instead of feeling humiliated or uncomfortable, I felt liberated. At that moment, I knew I could go through with it. I wasn't leaving there until Mason and I had made love.

I pulled on his dreads so that he would look up at me. "I want to make love to you tonight."

He grinned with that incredible smile of his. "Then you shall. I would like nothing more."

"Let me undress you now."

Mason stood up so I could unbutton his shirt and slide it off his shoulders. It fell into the tub but neither one of us made a move to retrieve it. We just continued to stare at one another. I fumbled with Mason's belt to get it loose and then helped him take off his pants. He had on a black sheer thong and I saw a dick for the very first time.

Walter Beasley's *Rendez-Vous* CD continued to play as he took the thong off and climbed into the tub. He grabbed my hand and helped me to step in. He sat down and I straddled him. We began kissing again, this time more intensely. I could feel his dick between my thighs, teasing my pussy lips. I had never known so much pleasure. That was a far cry from a towel or sheet causing friction against my clit, which was all I was used to.

Mason started sucking my breasts again and turned on the jets in the tub. The water pulsating against my skin only added to the experience. I moved back off him slightly and reached down to caress his dick. It felt wonderful to the touch. Mason also reached down into the water and started fingering me gently. The volume of my moans increased and I had an orgasm just from him touching me with his hand.

He glanced up at me and asked, "Did you just do what I think you did?"

I snickered. "Um, yes, I believe I did." I laid my head on his shoulder and hugged him with both arms, letting go of his dick. "Mason, don't laugh at me. Remember all of this is new for me."

He grabbed my chin and gazed at me lovingly. "I would never laugh at you, Jonquinette."

He took a towel and a bar of soap, lathered it up and started bathing me, slowly and tenderly, never breaking eye contact. Before I knew it, I had completely lost control of my senses. I started sucking on his neck and then his chest. He pulled my head back toward his legs by my hair, squeezed the towel so that water cascaded down the center of my chest and then starting sucking my nipples. Again, I had an orgasm.

We finished bathing and Mason refused to use a bath towel. Instead, he licked me dry. Then he carried me into the bedroom and laid me down on his king-sized bed. It was covered with silk animal-print sheets and a matching down comforter. He lifted my left foot to his mouth and proceeded to suck my toes, one at a time. After he was done with my left foot, he went to work on my right one. I was speechless. I just laid there shivering and enjoying every second of it.

Mason worked his tongue up my calves and then my thighs. He took a brief hiatus when he got to my pussy. He just blew on the hairs, which tickled. I suppressed a laugh. He said, "I'm going to taste you now," and that's exactly what he did.

The heat of his tongue swirling on my clit and darting in and out of me made me want to scream with delight. I grabbed a pillow and smashed it over my head, muffling my moans. Mason yanked it from me. "No, I want to see you and I *definitely* want to hear you."

He began to eat my pussy again and I grabbed the headboard, trying to handle what he was giving me. I lost count of how many times I climaxed and I was practically hallucinating by the time Mason felt he had accomplished his mission.

"Are you ready?" he asked me, positioning his dick between my legs.

"I've waited all my life for this," I whispered in his ear. "But I need to say something to you first."

"What's that?"

I caressed his cheek. "I'm in love with you also."

"Do you really mean that, Jonquinette?"

"Yes, I do. I really mean it. I never thought I would find love

after all these years. I'd given up. You've made me believe that anything is possible."

He kissed me on the lips. "Anything is possible."

Without saying another word to each other, Mason entered
me and we made love for the first time. I prayed it wouldn't be the
last.

35

jude

I called in sick. Fuck work! Instead, I went to the Queen Bitch's apartment to check up on things. She and Henry seemed to be getting a little bit too close for comfort. All the damn work I did to get them to break up, hiring that whore, setting the entire Thanksgiving fiasco up, and after all these years they were speaking again. The world had truly gone to shit! Queen Bitch Meredith needed to take her ass back to whoring and golddigging and forget about Henry.

After driving over there, I got the shock of my life when Flower opened the Queen Bitch's door.

"Jonquinette!" She flung her arms around me like she was Dorothy and she'd finally made it back home from the Emerald City. "I'm so happy to see you!"

Flower was a cutie. I can't deny that, but what the hell was she doing in Atlanta? I decided to take the safe route and play nice with her. If I had really said what was on my mind, I would have scared the little chick.

"Hey, Flower. You're looking beautiful today and that's an adorable outfit," I said, trying to think of what timid-ass Jon would say in a similar situation.

Flower twirled around like she was a runway model. "Thanks, Miss Meredith bought it for me."

"Miss Meredith, huh?" I was getting a really bad feeling. "I should have known. It looks like something she would pick out." The outfit did have Meredith written all over it. It was much too fancy for a young child and must have cost a grip, which meant Meredith was trying to kiss up to the little one. "Is *Miss Meredith* home?"

"Yes, she and Daddy are in the kitchen baking cookies."

"Stop the madness!" I exclaimed, rolling my eyes to the ceiling and following Flower into the condo.

"Huh?" Flower asked. "What does stop the madness mean?"

"It's just a saying." As we got farther into the living room, I noticed several shopping bags from high-end stores strewn about. "Someone went on quite a shopping spree, looks like."

"Yeah, Miss Meredith said she wanted me to have some city clothes. She thought my clothes were too old."

Humph, no big surprise! That sounded just like the type of bullshit that would come out of Meredith's mouth.

I noticed that the Disney Channel was on. "Flower, why don't you finish watching television while I go into the kitchen and see what Mommy and Daddy are doing?" I cringed when I called them Mommy and Daddy, but I really didn't have a choice. I was on a fishing expedition and I was just now baiting my hook. After Flower sat down, I said, "Be right back."

"Okay, Sis," she said.

That stunned me. She was referring to Jon as her sister already, like they'd known each other for years.

I got to the doorway of the kitchen and almost lost it when I saw the *Leave It to Beaver* action going on. They both had on aprons. Henry was taking a batch of chocolate chip cookies out of the oven while Meredith was stirring a pitcher of iced tea. Give me a break!

Part of me wanted to turn around and storm out the door but I had to get the real deal. I cleared my throat to get their attention.

"Jonquinette, Precious, we didn't hear you come in!" Meredith exclaimed.

Precious? She was really tripping.

"Flower let me in," I said. "Imagine my surprise when she answered the door."

That's when Henry chimed in, grinning from ear to ear. "We were just about to call you and invite you over. I went to pick up Flower yesterday and drove her right back."

"What about school?" I asked.

"Aw, she can miss a couple of days," Meredith replied. "Henry thought it was important for her to go ahead and meet me."

I shifted from one leg to another. I was getting more pissed off by the second. "And why is that important? For Flower to meet you, I mean."

They both eyed each other uneasily. Then Henry said, "Jonquinette, we have so much to tell you." He held up a cookie. "Have a cookie, straight out the oven. Your momma made them from scratch."

I didn't take the cookie. I looked at Meredith instead. "Since when did you start making cookies from scratch?"

"Oh, Jonquinette, please! You remember when I used to bake you fresh sweets all the time when you were a child," she lied without missing a beat. She never baked shit when Jon was a child.

"Oh yeah," I said. "And they were delicious." If she was going to stand there and tell bold-faced lies, I might as well join the party. "So, what is it that you have to tell me?"

First Henry sat down at the kitchen table and then Meredith. I thought I was seeing things when they started holding hands.

"This can't be!" I said loudly. Then I caught myself. "Okay, I take it that the holding of hands means something momentous."

Meredith sighed. "Um, yes, it does. Henry and I have been doing a lot of talking these past several days. Making up for lost time, so to speak. This has been a complicated time for all of us but something good has come out of it."

Henry interrupted her. "What your momma is trying to say is that we've decided to make another go at it."

"You're kidding!" I exclaimed. "You can't be serious!"

Henry said, "We've never been more serious in our entire lives." He leaned over and kissed Meredith on the cheek. "In fact, we're going to get remarried sometime in the spring, after we make sure that your therapy is going well and things have settled back down some." He held on tighter to her hand. "Besides, none of this should have ever happened. We want you to know that we don't blame you. It was that other person, that Jude wench, that caused all of this trouble and we're going to make sure we put a stop to that."

If it was actually physically possible for smoke to come out of someone's ears, it would have been coming out of mine right that second. No! That motherfucker didn't call me a wench! I took a few deep breaths before I went off on both of them.

"Does that mean you'll be moving here to Atlanta?" I finally asked. The thought of him moving closer to Jon was revolting but I had to pose the question.

Meredith replied, "No, I'm planning on relocating to North Carolina."

I had to refrain from break dancing, I was so damn happy all of a sudden. While I wasn't thrilled at the prospect of the two of them getting back together, not having to worry about the Queen Bitch stopping by Jon's place unannounced or worrying the hell out of her did have its appeal. "Really? Cool!"

Meredith seemed staggered. "Wow, we weren't expecting that reaction. We assumed you would be upset."

"Upset about what?" I went closer to them with my arms wide open and they both stood so I could hug them. "I'm thrilled for the two of you. After all, what's meant to be is meant to be."

"But we feel kind of guilty about leaving you here in Atlanta alone," Meredith continued. "We were hoping you might consider moving also."

She had lost her fucking mind!

"That's impossible, Momma. I have a good job here, my place, and most importantly, Dr. Spencer." I couldn't believe those words had just left my mouth but I had to make it sound legitimate. "I'm also kind of seeing someone now and I want to find out where that can go."

Meredith and Henry both yelled out in unison, "Seeing someone?"

Okay, Jude, I told myself. *Make it look good!*

"Yes, his name is Mason and he's one of my neighbors."

"I don't believe I've ever met him," Meredith said.

"You've never met any of my neighbors, have you?" I asked, thinking back and trying to recall whether or not Jon had ever introduced her to any. "Besides, he hasn't been living there that long."

"Is he a nice man?" Henry asked. "I don't want you mixed up with some rascal."

"He's not a rascal, Daddy. He's extremely nice and really has it going on."

"Well, if he can afford an apartment in your building, he must be halfway decent," Meredith commented.

"He's more than halfway decent," I said. "He's an incredible man."

Henry cleared his throat. "Does he know about, umm, does he know . . ."

"About my situation?" I asked.

"Yes. Your situation."

I really didn't want to respond to that. I was still trying to deal with the conversation Jon had with Mason in his car and him coming up to her place afterward. Not to mention all the other shit they had been doing together.

"Well, does he know, Jonquinette?" Meredith inquired. "It's okay, Precious, you can talk to us."

There she went with that damn Precious again!

"Mason knows everything. He's accepted it and plans to help me through this. So, you see, while it would be nice to have the two of you around, I can manage. I'm a grown woman, even though I act childish at times, and I have to start living my own life. I've got Mason now, and I can understand your logic behind moving to North Carolina. Flower needs both of her parents nearby during her upbringing and I'm sure her mother has no intention of moving to Atlanta."

Meredith seemed uncomfortable when I mentioned Flower's mother. That was her stupidity because she knew that she didn't birth her. Thank goodness because the poor child would have been doomed if she had.

I knew what both of them were thinking, even though they weren't talking about it. Jon had never had a boyfriend, not ever, and now all of a sudden she had one in her mid-twenties. Not to mention during such a tumultuous period in her life.

I decided to elaborate. "It's weird, finding a man that I mesh with after all these years. He took me completely by surprise. I met him in the hallway one day, the next week he stopped by with a pie, and it's been a whirlwind romance ever since." Meredith didn't seem like she was quite buying it so I added, "Momma, that's one reason why you haven't heard from me too much lately. I've been seeing a lot of him. We even attended a wedding together."

That was a flat-out lie and if it were drama day for me instead of fishing expedition day, I would have really said, "He and I ended up at the same wedding and to make sure I had some ammunition to use later on, I fucked the best man."

I chuckled as they both stared at me. I wondered what their reaction would have been if I had really blurted that out.

Flower came into the kitchen. "Are the cookies ready yet, Miss Meredith?"

Meredith ran over to the stove like she was Flower's nanny or some shit like that. "Yes, they are, sweetie. Why don't you go wash your hands in the little girls' room while I make you a plate of cookies and a glass of milk?"

Flower pouted. "I want some of the tea Daddy made."

"Okay," Meredith conceded. "But just one glass of tea. We wouldn't want you to consume too much sugar. You're a growing girl."

Flower looked at me and asked, "What does consume mean, Sis?"

"It means eat, drink, take in," I replied, irritated.

Just when I was about to make a speedy exit, Meredith dropped a bombshell.

"Um, Jonquinette, we were going to call you earlier to ask you for a favor."

"What favor?" I asked, hoping the Queen Bitch wasn't going to ask me to do something ridiculous.

"Henry and I have tickets for a play this afternoon at the Neighborhood Playhouse and we were wondering if you could watch Flower for us."

I glimpsed down at Flower, who grabbed my arm excitedly. "Yeah, Sis, can I hang out with you?"

Henry said, "We'd really appreciate it, Jonquinette."

It became painfully clear that Meredith and Henry were caught up in their own little world and not thinking clearly. If Jonquinette were really Jonquinette at the moment, which she wasn't, and agreed to watch Flower, what did they think would happen if Jude showed up and took over, which I already had. After all the negative things that had been said about me, why would they risk the possibility of me ending up baby-sitting Flower? Stupid asses!

All three of them anxiously awaited my answer. I had planned to go find some dick action that afternoon to relieve some stress. Baby-sitting would definitely put a damper on my plans, but Jon would never think of telling them no so I had to suck it up and say, "Sure! I'd love to spend the afternoon with Flower!"

Within thirty minutes, Meredith and Henry were glowing as they pranced out the apartment arm in arm. Jon still had a key to Meredith's place and there was no way I was going to sit there and watch kiddie television all day.

I took Flower to the park and hated every minute of it. A bunch of brats running around, full of hopes and dreams that their lives would be wonderful when they became adults. If they only knew the real deal. I wondered how many of them were the opposite and tried to pick out the ones that looked sad—the ones who looked like they were mistreated, abused, or just had issues to deal with period. Since it was too early for school to let out, most of them were five and under. I saw one little boy off by himself. He was sitting up underneath a slide as other kids took turns plummeting down it above his head. For the entire time we were there, he didn't talk to another child or play with another child.

His mother was sitting on a bench with a baby in a stroller. She barely paid him any attention. She would shove the pacifier back into the infant girl's mouth whenever she cried and glimpse at the boy every ten minutes or so. The rest of the time she had her head buried in a novel. Someone could have snatched him easily and she wouldn't have noticed until they were in a car five or six miles away. Damn shame.

Flower was mighty talkative and I have to admit that she began to grow on me. After all, it wasn't her fault that Henry had donated the sperm to create her. She was inquisitive, asking me about everything under the sun. She was good-humored and in high spirits and had good manners. I took her on the miniature train ride, let her ride the merry-go-round, and then we played two rounds of putt-putt. She beat me something terrible because Jon never played and I normally had better things to do, like fucking.

After she was worn out from playing, I took her to Paschal's to grab a bite to eat. We ordered fried chicken, collard greens, and creamy potato salad and threw down on all of it. I should have taken the opportunity to eat some red meat, since Jon refused to, but I couldn't go to Paschal's and not jump on the fried chicken.

Flower opened up to me and talked a lot about her mother. Allison seemed like a decent human being so at least she had one parent she could count on. Then Flower turned the tables on me and started asking a lot of questions about Jon's childhood. I lied and said that it was the greatest and that Jon was popular and had tons of friends and all the boys were in love with her. What a crock of bullshit!

When I got back to Meredith's condo with Flower, they still were not back. I let Flower watch television while I snooped around. The Queen Bitch had enough sexy lingerie to clothe a whorehouse full of women. She had one sexy little red lace number that I just had to snag since the tag was still on it. I crammed it into Jon's purse, already making some plans for later that night.

They finally came back in about nine, which still gave me plenty of time to go searching for dick. The way they were all lovey-dovey made me sick and I couldn't take it anymore. I planned to go out, fuck some fool, and then ponder over whether or not I would *allow* them to get back together or break that shit up again. There wasn't a doubt in my mind that I could put a stop to it, if I so desired.

It was too damn easy to just pick up a man. No man was likely to turn down pussy if the woman looked halfway attractive. I wanted a challenge so I went to this gay club called The Milk Farm, which I took to mean that there were a lot of men up in there milking each other's dicks. Shame on it all.

When I first walked in, some of them might have assumed that I was a transvestite but upon closer inspection, you could see their chins practically hit the floor. I had always assumed that some women hang out at gay bars for whatever reason, but this one was all male except for me. They were grinding all up on each other, tonguing each other down, and my pussy was getting wetter by the second. True sex fiends get turned on by anything sexual, even two dogs humping.

I hopped on a vacant barstool and waited for the bartender, a midget in a thong and leather hat who walked on top of the bar instead of behind it. He snarled at me and asked me what I wanted. I said, "A blow job just like everyone else in here." I laughed at my joke but he didn't like it. "Don't front. I'm sure you know how to make it."

He teetered away to get my drink.

The two men, or queens rather, that I was sitting between

were hideous. I wouldn't have fucked either one of them for bone marrow. I started scanning the club for other prospects. I realized that it would prove too difficult to pick out which ones were prospective fucks. The ones that went both ways. The ones who were married and in there on the downlow. That was the beauty of being me. Because I didn't really exist, at least not on paper or as far as anyone was concerned, I could do whatever the hell I wanted, whenever the hell I wanted, and no one could touch me. Too many people hold back from doing the things they yearn to do. They are too busy worrying about what so-and-so might think. On the other hand, I didn't give a fuck what people thought.

That's why there was no hesitation on my part to do what I did next. The midget finally came back with my drink. I did my little hands behind my back trick and gulped it down. Just then, the DJ put on "Fever" and it was on. I climbed up on the bar, started dancing to the music, and singing. Then I started stripping.

Of course, the assholes were the initial ones to start yelling shit like, "You need to sit down, bitch!" "Get that slut off the bar! No one wants to see a whore stripping!" and "Did it suddenly get a little fishy in here!"

I ignored them all. I was waiting for that one person who defended me because I knew he would be the one open to what I had in mind. Sure enough, right before the song ended, I heard someone yell out, "Leave her alone! Let the diva do her thing!"

The strobe lights on the ceiling were irritating and I shielded my forehead with my hand so I could make out someone in the back. The only thing I could see was that he was extremely tall and dark-skinned. The song ended and no one applauded but one smart aleck said, "Great! Now get the hell out and go to a club where people like kitties!"

I played it cool and sat back down at the bar. Within five minutes there was a tap on my shoulder and it was him. Men are so damn predictable. It turned out that Hugh, which I'm quite sure wasn't his real name, was married with four kids and trying to find himself. He said that he had experimented with men in college and had never gotten his curiosity out of his system. I asked him did he take it up the ass or give it. He said give it and that was cool with me because I had no intention of fucking a man who would take one up the ass. I made sure he had a condom, invited him to step in the back into a bathroom stall, and then I let him experiment with a freak and give it to me up the ass. Poor Jon was going to wake up the next morning wondering what the hell!

36

jonquinette

When I arrived in the parking garage at Marcella's office building, it was difficult to find a space. There was a convention meeting at the hotel across the street so a lot of people had used Marcella's building as an overflow parking area.

I had to go all the way up to the sixth level and park on the roof. It was nippy, even for mid-October, and I went to search in my trunk for a jacket. I found one and was closing my trunk when I heard someone say from behind me, "Well, hello again."

I didn't recognize the voice but when I turned, I was face to face with Zoe. "Hello."

"It's nice to see you again," she said. "And I'm glad we ran into each other here. I take it that means you decided to use the card that I gave you."

I smiled uneasily. "Yes, I did. Thanks for the recommendation."

"It's not a problem." She came closer and sat a shopping bag that she was carrying down on the ground. "I just finished up a session with Marcella."

I glanced at my watch. "And I'm next up to bat." We both giggled. "Marcella really is wonderful and she's helping me out tremendously."

"That's good." She offered me her hand. "We've never formally been introduced. I'm Zoe Reynard."

I shook her hand. "I already knew your name, from the meetings and all. I'm Jonquinette Pierce."

"Beautiful name."

"So is yours."

There was an uncomfortable silence for a moment and then Zoe said, "I'm not trying to get into your business but I feel like I have to say something."

"Go ahead."

"Life throws us a lot of curveballs. We can run from them or we can catch them and throw them back."

"I never thought of it quite that way," I said. "Curveballs, huh?"

"I don't know if you've ever heard me actually give a testimonial at a meeting, but to make a long story short, sex almost killed me: *literally*."

I lowered my eyes to the ground to avoid eye contact. "I'm sorry to hear that."

"I fought back. I was determined not to give up my life that easily, even when everything seemed hopeless. Looking back on it, I can't believe how many people were hurt, some even killed, because of my actions."

"Killed?" I asked in disbelief, looking back up at her to see if she was serious.

"Yes, killed, because of my issues with sexuality." She leaned on my trunk. "I used to blame myself. I just couldn't deal with it."

"But you're okay now?"

"Most of the time. I won't sugarcoat it. The memories will never go away, not ever. If I have to eventually pay for my sins, then so be it. I've come to terms with that. For now, though, I just intend to live life with my husband and kids. They give me all the love and encouragement that I need."

I didn't want to be nosy but I felt like I just had to ask. "What caused you to be like that? Addicted to sex?"

"Are you really addicted?" she came back at me.

"My situation's a little bit more complicated than that," I responded. "I wouldn't say that *I'm* addicted to sex. It's more like someone else that I'm extremely close to is addicted to it or rather uses sex to prove a point."

Zoe seemed confused. "I won't ask you to elaborate. To answer your question, there were some incidents dating back to my childhood that triggered everything after that."

"Incidents?"

"Yes, incidents that I had buried. We often bury things in our minds. The human body is a very intricate thing, an amazing thing, and sometimes we are things and have done things we can't remember."

I laughed. "In my case, that's definitely true."

"Did you have something happen in your childhood?" she asked me.

"I had a ton of things happen in my childhood. I was bullied, tormented, teased, and treated like crap by all the other kids."

"What about your parents?"

"I have two loving parents, but they had issues because of me. In fact, something I did made them divorce."

"I'm sorry to hear that."

"Yeah, well, they are meeting me here today." I thought about Daddy's car being at my place overnight and added, "I'm hoping that there may be some chance for them to reconcile; even after all these years."

"If it's in God's plans, they will," Zoe said, looking up at the sky.

"So you're religious?" I asked.

"I didn't used to be, at least not much, but I am now. My husband and I take our children to church every Sunday and pray together every night."

"That's good." I glimpsed at my watch again. "I really have to go before I'm late. I wish we could continue the conversation some other time."

Zoe took a business card out of her purse and handed it to me. "Call me."

I scanned the card. "You're an arts dealer, huh?"

"Yes, all African-American art." She smiled and touched my hand. "Take care, Jonquinette, and if you ever need anything, just reach out to me. Marcella understands a lot and I'm sure she will help you get through this, but she's never walked in our shoes." She picked up her bag. "When you feel comfortable enough, I hope you will consider coming back to the meetings." She eyed me uneasily. "You and your friend."

As Zoe walked off to get into her car and I walked to the bank of elevators, I wondered about her last comment. Had she figured me out that easily?

marcella

Working with Jonquinette Pierce had turned out to be much more than I had bargained for. Just like every professional I welcomed challenges in my career, but this one had taken on a personal edge. I had only one similar experience in my entire career. When I was fresh out of medical school, I interned at a psychiatric hospital in New York State under the guidance of Dr. Michael Driggs. He was one of the most respected psychiatrists in the country and had recently succumbed to colon cancer.

Dr. Driggs had a patient named Constance who suffered from Multiple Personality Disorder. I sat in on his therapy sessions with her and it was nothing short of amazing. While Constance had already pretty much figured out that she had at least three other personalities, it turned out that she had at least forty. Day after day, month after month, we met them one at a time. Dr. Driggs introduced me to the technique of integration, where he basically had lengthy discussions with each personality to see what their individual issues—or grievances, so to speak—were and how they could be solved. Constance had been the victim of severe neglect and physical abuse as a child. Because of that, she developed various personalities to deal with situations that she could not deal with. There was Bernie, who was an older gentleman. Bernie emerged when Constance felt threatened. He spoke in a heavy tone and his body language was intimidating. Rhonda was the little child who emerged when Constance was feeling lonely and abandoned, which she had been by her parents at the age of four. She ended up in foster homes and unfortunately, each one of the homes harbored a form of evil. Her first set of foster parents used to beat Constance with a belt and lock her in the cellar for days on end. The second set used to make her eat dog food while they dined on fine cuisine, courtesy of state funding. She and the other six foster children in the home eventually ran away together, seeking help from the local police, and the state had no choice but to find new homes for all of them and press charges against the couple who had made them suffer.

The list of traumas in Constance's life went on and on until she simply could not function in society. She checked herself into the hospital, pleading desperately for help and some form of supervision. She did not trust herself or what she might be driven to do next.

As I sat in my office waiting for Jonquinette and her parents to arrive for their first joint therapy session, I couldn't imagine what had triggered her MPD and how Jude had been created. Other than the fact that she had been bullied as a child, which didn't sit quite well with me, there was no other obvious reasoning behind the events that had transpired.

Jude herself didn't realize that she was crying out for help by sleeping with various men. She assumed that promiscuity was a display of power but nothing was further from the truth. Self-degradation is no better than someone else doing the degrading. I had a general idea of how I planned to proceed with Jonquinette's healing process, but first I wanted to meet her parents and see how they interacted with her.

Jonquinette showed up first. I was glad that she came in separately because it gave us an opportunity to chat alone.

After she came into my inner office and sat down, I asked her, "So how are things?"

"I can't tell you how much better I feel," she said.

"Really? Why is that?"

She leaned up and whispered, "Mason and I did it. We made love."

She giggled with delight and I faked a smile. I wasn't so sure getting sexually involved with Mason Copeland at that point in time was such a great idea. It might just serve to complicate matters.

"Jonquinette, if you are happy, I am happy for you."

"Thanks!" She leaned back in the chair. "Oh, guess who I just ran into in the parking lot."

That was a no-brainer since she'd just left my office. "Zoe?"

"Yes. She's so sweet. She even gave me her card in case I want to talk."

"That's great. Zoe is a very compassionate woman and you may need to hear some of the things she has to say."

I meant every word of that previous statement. In many ways, Zoe and Jonquinette were identical and in many others they were not. Zoe had a sexual addiction while Jonquinette, or Jude rather, used sex to make a statement.

Jonquinette glanced at my wall clock. "Humph, I wonder why my parents are late."

No sooner had she said that when a knock came at the door. A stunning-looking couple entered and my first thought was that they seemed way too happy for two people who had just found out that the only child they shared together was ill.

Jonquinette jumped up and made the introductions. "Dr. Spencer, these are my parents, Henry and Meredith Pierce."

I shook both of their hands. "It's very nice to meet you."

Henry replied, "Same here. I just wish it was under better circumstances."

"Please have a seat," I said, directing them to my leather couch. Jonquinette sat down on the chaise and I sat in an armchair.

Meredith said, "Sorry we're late. Henry just got back from dropping Flower back off in North Carolina."

"Flower was here?" Jonquinette asked, obviously stunned.

Meredith laughed uncomfortably. "Don't be silly, Precious. Of course, Flower was here. You spent the day with her."

Jonquinette's mouth fell open and the rest of us came to the same conclusion simultaneously.

Henry said, "Oh shit! You mean my baby girl spent the afternoon with that wench!"

No one responded and Jonquinette decided to lie down on the chaise instead of just sitting there.

Meredith said, "Jonquinette, does that mean that you don't know about our news?"

"What news?" Jonquinette asked.

Henry cleared his throat. "The news about your momma getting back together with me."

I studied Jonquinette's reaction. She clamped her eyes shut and sighed. "No, I didn't have a clue."

Meredith folded her hands on her lap but I could still see them trembling. She glimpsed at me uneasily. "I guess we should talk about that later. We're here for Jonquinette."

I waited for Jonquinette to make any comments about the revelation. When she remained silent, I moved on. "As you know, Jonquinette is suffering from Multiple Personality Disorder, otherwise known as MPD. It is also commonly referred to as Dissociative Identity Disorder. Ideas about MPD date back to the 1800s. This is not a new concept."

Meredith asked, "So what exactly is it and how can we stop it?"

"Basically, Jonquinette has at least one alter personality who was created to free her from the memories and experiences that were too difficult for her to rationally deal with."

Henry said, "So are we talking about a mental illness? Is she insane?"

I shook my head. "No, Jonquinette is not insane. That was her assumption at first as well. Jonquinette is perfectly capable of leading a normal life without having to drown herself in pills or being hospitalized. What she has done, in a nutshell, is devise an innovative survival technique."

Meredith shifted in her seat. "You said at least one alter. Does that mean there are more?"

Even as I made eye contact with her mother, I could sense Jonquinette staring at me. "That is a possibility but as of now, the only one we need to concern ourselves with is Jude. She's obviously the most powerful and the one causing all the problems."

Henry shook his head in dismay. "I still can't believe that wench was left alone with Flower."

Jonquinette sat back up on the chaise. "I have no idea what you're talking about, but why would you let me baby-sit Flower knowing my situation."

Jonquinette's parents glared at each other as I could sense their guilt.

Jonquinette continued, "Until we get this all straightened out, don't dare do that again. Flower is a sweetheart and if she meets up with Jude while she's angry, there's no telling what might happen." She paused and asked, "You couldn't tell it wasn't me?"

"No, not that time," Meredith quickly responded. "I won't lie. Looking back on things, there were times when I should have known something was terribly wrong. Like that time when we had dinner recently and you called me a whore."

Henry glared at Jonquinette. "You called your momma a whore?"

Jonquinette smacked her lips. "It wasn't me, Daddy. You're still missing the point. I've never intentionally set out to hurt anyone. I would never call Momma a whore. That's disrespectful and you didn't raise me that way."

"But did we raise Jude that way?" Meredith asked. She covered her face with her hands. "This is so confusing."

Jonquinette got up off the chaise and walked over to the sofa. Her parents made room for her to sit between them. Each took one of her hands.

"You're right," Jonquinette said. "This is confusing." She looked at me. "Marcella, what's next?"

"We get to know each other," I responded. "That's all I want to do today. You've told me a lot but only your parents can fill in the blanks of the times you don't remember. I have several questions I need to ask."

Henry gripped Jonquinette's hand tighter and glanced into my eyes. "Ask away."

I had blocked out the next three hours for Jonquinette and her parents and we made good use of every minute of it. We talked about her childhood and Jonquinette seemed troubled to the point where I thought she might lose it a few times as she heard firsthand accounts of things she never did.

37

jonquinette

"Are you ready?" Mason asked me when I opened my door. "We have a tight schedule to keep."

I blushed. "Yes, I'm ready. Just let me grab a lightweight jacket."

I was kind of worn out from the therapy session but nothing would have stopped me from spending quality time with Mason. In many ways, being with Mason was probably the best therapy of all.

First, we went to the Atlanta History Center. I learned so much about a city where I had lived for several years. Mason said it was a shame for people to live someplace and have the tourists actually visit more of the museums and attractions. We walked the thirty-three acres of gardens, woodlands, and nature trails after visiting the inside exhibits. Watching the children running through the gardens made me suddenly think about actually having a child one day. In a perfect world, it would happen.

We left the Center and headed to the High Museum of Art. There was an exhibit of African-American art, so we had chosen the perfect day to go there. We walked up and down the ramps, taking in all the beautiful paintings and sculptures. There were several by an artist named Quinton Matthews. I had heard that name someplace, maybe in a news story, but couldn't recall all the details. Either way, his work was magnificent. In fact, I was so moved by the intricate details of his work that I stopped by the gift shop and picked up a reproduction of one of them entitled *Forever in Love*.

I was getting tired but was determined to hang, so when Mason suggested going to Zoo Atlanta next, I was all for it. We went to the zoo in Grant Park and saw the giant pandas, Lun Lun and Yang Yang, the zoo's main attraction. Afterward we went to the petting zoo and had a ball playing with the animals. When we left, I just knew we were headed home but . . .

. . . We drove out to Stone Mountain Park and it wasn't crowded at all for that time of year. I had always wanted to go there but had no one to go with. Ever since I had lost the baby fat back in high school, I had managed to stay in good shape by watching my diet for the most part. Mason was in great shape, as I had found out firsthand when we made love. I still blushed every time I thought about it. We opted against the cable car and the 1.3 mile hike up the side of the mountain was a breeze. We walked through a canyon of boulders that were covered by chewing gum. It was quite a hilarious sight.

We got to the top, more than 1,600 feet above sea level, and took in the spectacular view. We found a cozy spot where no one else was hovering around and made out for about thirty minutes. It was incredible.

It was getting close to sunset so we decided we needed to head back down while the visibility was still good. We did have time to go pedal boating right quick and we ended up having a race with a couple of teenage boys. We beat them big-time and were out of the boat and chilling on the dock by the time they were tied up.

Mason and I went back home just long enough for us to go to our respective apartments, shower and change. Then we headed back out again. I took three vitamins first. The shower almost put me out, I was so exhausted.

We ended up at Cherry, an eclectic sushi bar on Peachtree Street. We had the Tuna Tataki, which was mouthwatering and shared a glass of American wine. We topped it off with a bowl of cherry cobbler, which we also shared. The inside of the place was classy and completely decorated in red. Apparently, it used to be a residence that dated back to the early 1920s.

By that point, I was tired, full, and ready to go back home and cuddle. But Mason wouldn't hear of it. He said, "You need to make up for lost time, Jonquinette. There are so many things you should've already experienced that you haven't. Let me help you create more memories. Positive memories."

I blushed and said, "Okay, let's go for it."

"Then let's go relax and have some fun," he said, taking my hand and pulling me out the restaurant.

Our last stop of the evening turned out to be anything but relaxing. We ended up at The Punchline, where Sir Laughs-a-Lot was performing. He was one of my all-time favorites. I fell in love with his humor way back when he used to star on *Bet You I Can Make You Laugh*. Mason had called ahead and made reservations so our little wooden table was close to the front. I almost lost my drink when he told a joke about a woman running into her doctor's office screaming and complaining about having too much hair on her breasts. When the doctor asked her how much the hair was growing, she said from her breasts down to her penis. That was too funny.

We spent a couple of hours laughing so hard that we were brought to tears and then Mason asked, "Ready to go home?"

I eyed him seductively. "Your home or my home?"

He kissed my forehead. "Choose."

"Well, since you treated me to a bubble bath last time, reciprocity is in order. Want to christen my tub?"

"Absolutely."

That's exactly what we did.

38

marcella

It was time. I was determined not to let Jon-
quinette and her parents leave my office until I exposed the truth.
I had grown to care about Jonquinette, as I did all my patients. But
there was something fragile about her that I felt the need to
shield. It was actually ironic. I was beginning to identify with the
reasoning behind Jude's actions. Jonquinette was the kind of spirit
that people would naturally be drawn toward to shelter.

They all arrived at the same time, instead of separately like the
previous session.

"Come on in and have a seat," I said as they walked in single
file. I went to the outer office and told my receptionist to put the
phones on night and go ahead and leave for the day. There was no
point in her staying since I had no more patients scheduled and I
was not going to take any calls.

When I came back in, they were all seated: Jonquinette on the chaise and her parents on the couch.

I sat in the armchair and placed a tape recorder in the middle of the coffee table. I hit Record.

"Is this really necessary?" Meredith Pierce asked sarcastically. "Who's going to end up hearing that?"

"No one will hear it, unless I have your permission. This is simply for me to take notes with and possibly to play back for Jonquinette." I glanced at Jonquinette and added, "Just in case she misses something."

Jonquinette nodded. "I understand what you mean. You plan to call Jude out, don't you?"

I didn't hesitate to answer. "Yes, I do."

Henry started panicking. "Say what? You're going to summon that wench? This is crazy!"

"Please, Daddy!" Jonquinette exclaimed. "You promised you would help me."

"And I will, but I'm not so sure about this," he replied. He eased back on the couch and seemed to calm down some. "All right, if this is the way it has to be, then let's get it over with."

I decided to let them know right away that, "There's a possibility that Jude won't come out at all. She revealed herself to Mason once that we know of and to me once, but that's about it. She was obviously around when Flower was visiting but she pretended to be Jonquinette and not herself."

Henry shook his head. "I still can't get over that. Something tragic could have happened."

Jonquinette glared at him and looked irritated. "Well, I hope that never happens again."

Meredith spoke up. "It won't happen again, Precious. Your daddy and I have already discussed that at length."

"Why don't we all just relax," I suggested. I turned to Jonquinette. "Jude, I know that you can hear me. You're always around."

Meredith sighed loudly. I looked at her and put my index finger to my lips. "Please, remain perfectly quiet for now. We don't want to irritate her."

"Who gives a shit if we irritate her?" Henry lashed out suddenly. "This entire situation is that wench's fault."

Jonquinette jumped up off the chaise, walked over to the couch and slapped Henry across the face. "I've had just about enough of you calling me a wench, you motherfucking bastard!"

Both Henry and Meredith were shocked. Henry rubbed his face and looked like he wanted to say something but didn't. Instead he glanced at me like he was searching for answers and I nodded for him to remain quiet.

I stood up. "Jude, it's nice to see you again."

"Save the bullshit, you bitch! I told you before that I wasn't going anyplace so all this therapy shit is a waste of time. The Queen Bitch and her flunky can't make me go away either."

Meredith asked with disdain, "Who are you calling a queen bitch?"

"You, bitch, you!" Jude screamed. "All of Jon's life, all you've ever cared about is yourself. Look at you now. Jon asked the two of you to help her and what do you do, start fucking again and talking about marriage as if that will solve something. Well, fuck all of you!"

"Jude, try to calm down," I said, walking closer to her and putting my hand on her shoulder. "Let's just sit back down and talk about this calmly."

"No, hell no! Hell fucking no!" Jude started pacing the floor. "I decided to come out for one reason and one reason only, to inform all of you that you can't win. You'll never win!"

"Why are you doing this?" Meredith asked, on the brink of tears. "Why are you doing this to my baby?"

"Your baby?" Jude put her hands on her hips. "Jon never mattered to you, not really. All you cared about was putting up a pretense. You wanted everyone to think that you had the perfect marriage and the perfect little daughter, even though you didn't. You only care about material things, just like your two fucking sisters."

Meredith started crying harder. "I can't take this. I love Jonquinette. I always have. You're sick."

"I'm not sick, you bitch!" Jude sat down in the middle of the coffee table with her legs spread open facing them. She lifted her skirt and started fingering herself. "Does this make you sick, bitch? I decided to be a whore just like you. The only difference is your golddigging ass has been fucking men for what they can give you all these years and I fuck them for the hell of it."

Henry stood up and headed for the door. "I won't sit here and watch this a second longer."

Jude said, "What's wrong, *Daddy?* You can't handle it so you're just going to cut and run out on us like you did all those years ago?"

Henry turned around and glared at Jude. "This is all your fucking fault, wench! You set me up! I never even met that prostitute."

Jude started laughing. "Okay, fine. Since you've all figured it out already, I confess. I did it and I'm damn proud of it, too. You tried to get help for Jon, which meant trying to get rid of me, and I had to do something to stop you."

"Is that why you stabbed me?" He got all the way up in Jude's face. "It was you who stabbed me, wasn't it?"

An expression of fear came across Jude's face. It was brief but I saw it. I'm not sure if Meredith and Henry even picked up on it.

Meredith stopped crying and looked from one of them to the other. "Stabbed? Henry, what are you talking about?"

Jude took two steps back from him. "Yeah, what do you mean by that?"

"Don't get cute with me, you cunt!" Henry started unbuttoning his shirt. "You know exactly what I'm talking about." He took his shirt off and pointed to a tiny scar over his shoulder blade. "I'm talking about this."

Meredith stood up, came over to him, and touched it. "That's where you accidentally cut yourself with a pocket knife. I remember when you came home with it bandaged up."

Henry smirked. "That was the story I made up to cover up for who I thought was Jonquinette. Now I know it wasn't her at all."

"What are you talking about, Henry?" Meredith prodded.

"I didn't want the police to file charges against her. I knew that after all the incidents in her past that they'd allowed to slip through, one more might cause them to lock her up in juvenile detention."

Jude hissed at him. "You're a lying bastard! I never stabbed you!"

"You showed up at my office one day, stormed in like a hurricane, and started talking crazy. Just like you are now, as a matter of fact. I told you that it was time to get you some help. Your solution was to pick up a letter opener off my desk and stab me in the shoulder with it. I bet you were aiming for my heart but I moved out the way just in time."

We had definitely reached a crossroads. I remained silent and allowed the situation to play itself out.

Jude grabbed my shoulders and started screaming. "I didn't do that, Marcella! I didn't!"

I didn't respond. I just pushed her away from me. Part of me wanted to embrace her but I needed her to get angry. I had to allow whatever was destined to happen to occur.

Meredith grabbed her chest and looked like she was about to faint. "My baby stabbed someone! Her own daddy! Oh my God!"

She fell on her knees and started crying all over again. "This is my fault. I should have listened to you, Henry! We should have gotten her help way back then!"

Jude yanked Meredith back up off the floor by her hair. "Get up, Queen Bitch! He's lying through his teeth. It never happened. He cut his own ass with a pocket knife, just like he said. He's just trying to fuck with me for some reason but I won't tolerate it." Jude shoved Henry, practically knocking him back onto the chaise lounge and repeated, "I won't tolerate it!"

"Jude!" I called out to her. "Jude! Look at me!" When she turned to face me, I said, "What if he isn't lying?"

"But he is lying," she insisted. "I didn't stab him and Jonquinette sure as shit didn't. She wouldn't have the nerve. Besides, I've always been here and I would know if she'd done something like that. Hell, I would've been happy about it. I'm telling you, if I'd stabbed the bastard, I would admit it in a heartbeat. In fact, if you have a letter opener, I'll stab him now. He deserves it for lying on me."

"Look," Henry stated angrily. "I'm telling you that Jude stabbed me. It's all water under the bridge now and I still have no intention of pressing charges but this all needs to come out. I'm sick of lying."

Something changed on Jude's face. A calmness came over it. Then that was replaced with fury. "Sick of lying?" She faced Henry. "You're sick of lying?"

"Yes," he responded. "The truth needs to come out."

"I couldn't agree with you more," she said in a voice that I didn't recognize.

Henry didn't seem to notice the voice change but Meredith did.

"What happened to your voice?" Meredith asked.

Jude smirked at her but didn't respond.

"Nothing happened to her voice." I walked up behind her and whispered in her ear, "Who are you?"

She turned, gave me a smile that was more scary than pleasant, and brushed past me. She sat down in the armchair where I had been sitting and pressed the Stop button on the tape recorder. "We won't need this anymore."

I wanted to make a move to turn it back on but decided against it. It was obvious nothing critical would be said as long as it was on.

I asked again, this time louder, "Who are you?"

Henry exclaimed, "You mean there's another one?"

"Shh! Don't say anything!" I cautioned him. "Why don't you tell me your name? I know you're not Jonquinette and you're not Jude, so who are you?"

She rubbed her eyes like she was tired. "I don't have a name," she finally responded.

"Everyone has a name," I insisted.

"Not me."

"Then make up one," I said. "I need to call you something."

She thought about it for a moment and said, "Just call me Jetta. I think that sounds mad cool."

"Okay, Jetta. Tell me, were you the one who stabbed Henry in the shoulder?"

Jetta grimaced. "Damn right, I did it."

Henry asked, "Why did you stab me?"

Jetta ignored him and started staring at Meredith. "You thought you knew everything that was going on in your house, didn't you?"

"What do you mean?" Meredith asked. "Please tell me what you mean."

"Did you ever suspect?" Jetta kept her eyes fixated on Meredith but nodded in Henry's direction. "Did you ever realize that he was a pedophile?"

Henry collapsed onto the chaise while Meredith pulled herself up off the floor. She walked over to us and got close enough to smell Jetta's breath. "Pedophile?"

"Yes, you know what that is, right? A person, or sick fuck as I prefer to call them, who has sexual desires for children." Jetta glanced at Henry. "Now he's sitting over there trying to play the pitiful act; probably thinking of a lie to tell, some excuse for why he did it."

"What did he do, Jetta?" I asked, realizing we had finally made progress.

I had always felt there was at least one more personality living inside of Jonquinette. Jude professed to be all-powerful but something or someone had to be keeping her from taking over Jonquinette's life completely. Now I knew her as Jetta.

"He molested Jon. What do you think he did?" she replied. "That's why I allowed Jude to do what she did. I don't even think she realizes what he did to Jon. She just hated him because he was trying to get rid of us. What she did was actually ingenious." Jetta chuckled. "Wish I had thought of it. Instead, I tried to stab him to death but that didn't work and I'm glad it didn't. After it was over, I realized my mistake. I didn't want Jon to end up in prison, along with Jude and the rest of us in tow, so I'm glad I missed his heart."

Meredith looked at Henry in confusion. "Henry, is any of this true?"

"Yeah, *Henry,* is it true?" Jetta asked sarcastically. "Tell her the truth, *Henry!* Tell her about the bath-time *fun* when Jon was just four years old. Tell her about the *fun* in the shed in the backyard. That's what you used to call it, right? *Fun?*"

Henry broke down and started sobbing. I went over to the chaise and sat beside him, rubbing his bare back. "By helping Jonquinette, you can also help yourself."

"God help me!" he screamed out. "God help me, I did it!"

Meredith gasped. Jetta appeared sated and sat down.

"I molested my baby," he continued. "But I couldn't help it." He pleaded with Meredith with his eyes. "Meredith, baby, I know

I can never make up for what I did, but I tried. I did get help. I went and talked to someone and he helped me. That's why I was trying to get you to get some help for Jonquinette, too."

Meredith suddenly jumped on top of Henry and tried to choke him, knocking both me and him off the chaise. I tried to pry her hands off his neck. He was just willing to sit there and take it.

"This is totally your fault!" she screamed. "I'm going to kill you!"

Henry continued sobbing, Meredith continued choking and I continued trying to get her hands off him. "Jetta, help me," I said. "You know this is wrong. It can't all end like this."

The situation seemed hopeless. Henry started gasping for air and I was stuck underneath him with all his weight on me trying to accomplish an impossible task.

The next thing I knew, Jetta screamed out, "Momma! Momma, quit!"

It wasn't Jetta though. Jonquinette was back.

She pulled Meredith off Henry by the waist. "What are you doing, Momma?"

"Meredith, it's Jonquinette!" I yelled out. "It's Jonquinette. Don't let her see this. She's been through enough."

Meredith's eyes became glazed over as she let go of Henry's neck. She collapsed backwards on the floor and whispered, "God help us! God help us all!"

39

jonquinette

After I was filled in on what had happened when Jude took over in Marcella's office, I couldn't find any words to express my feelings. I heard the tape, which cut off at the point where Jetta decided it would be cut off. Jetta? Things were getting more confusing by the second. But I wasn't so much shocked about Jetta as I was about what she had accused Daddy of doing. In fact, I tried to defend him but he admitted that he had molested me as a child.

He said that his father had molested him, which is why he never took me to visit my paternal grandparents. After the Thanksgiving Day fiasco, Daddy came to the conclusion that he deserved to be alone and that karma had caught up to him. He returned to North Carolina and reopened his father's auto repair shop as a means to punish himself for his own sins. A constant reminder of his sins would be his fate.

Marcella, Momma, and I listened intently as he described everything he had been through. He said it was a vicious cycle because his father, my grandfather, had been molested by his own uncle as a child. I still couldn't imagine not remembering the things my father related in that therapy session. How he would do things to me when Momma wasn't around, mostly when she was out spending money on things we didn't need.

Marcella explained that Jetta had taken the abuse for me and Jude had become my protector, even though Jude never knew about the abuse. She also speculated that while she rarely made an appearance, Jetta was the one who really controlled things. She prevented Jude from making me completely disappear.

My main concern wasn't even for me but for Flower. Daddy assured me that he hadn't molested her but admitted that he had experienced some urges. Marcella told him that he had no choice but to come clean with Allison, Flower's mother. She told him that there was always the chance that he would relapse in a moment of weakness and shatter yet another young life.

Needless to say, Momma called the wedding off. She left, stating that she was catching a cab home so she could take a tranquilizer and lie down. I told her that I would come by later to check on her. I couldn't take any more for one day either. I told Daddy and Marcella that I had to leave. Marcella asked Daddy to stay behind so they could talk.

I also caught a cab home since Daddy had driven to Marcella's office. When I arrived, Mason was just returning home from work. He saw me get out of the cab and must have been able to tell that I had been to hell and back. He came to me and I collapsed into his arms in tears.

Mason and I spent the next few hours talking about everything that had been revealed earlier that day. As usual, he wasn't judgmental at all. On the contrary, he cried when I told him about

Daddy and the pedophilia. He also expressed concern for Flower and I told him that I would go to my grave protecting her, if I had to. In fact, I planned to call her mother the next day and tell her everything myself. I didn't want to risk leaving it up to Daddy.

Mason pampered me by running me a bath and giving me a deep tissue massage afterward. I was steadily learning that he was a man of many talents. Mason made love to me slowly from behind up against my bedroom wall—so passionately that I wept, because I couldn't imagine him still wanting me after finding out yet something else devastating about my past.

It was late when I had Mason drop me off at Momma's condo, close to two in the morning. I used my key and entered without knocking. She was knocked out in her bed and I stood over her for a moment, listening to make sure she was still breathing. For a second, I was scared that she had taken an overdose. That, I would not have been able to handle.

I climbed into bed and took her into my arms. She woke up, saw me, and asked, "Is it you, Jonquinette?"

It was a shame that she had to ask. "Yes, it's me, Momma. Get some rest."

We both fell into a much-needed sleep.

The next morning, Daddy was banging on the door by nine. He was taken aback when I answered instead of Momma. His eyes fell to the carpeted hallway. "Jonquinette, I'm so sorry, baby. How can I ever make it up to you?"

"You can't." I turned and he followed me into the living room. "Momma's still sleeping and I have no intention of waking her up. The longer she stays asleep, the longer she doesn't have to deal with reality." I rolled my eyes at him and sat down. "I guess I'm an expert at that, huh? Falling asleep, or rather letting someone else take over, so I don't have to deal with reality."

Daddy sat down across from me. "I just wanted to come by to say that I'm leaving today. I planned to stop by your place next."

"Well, now you don't have to waste a trip," I stated sarcastically. Then I caught myself. "Daddy, I won't pretend that I'm not angry. That would be nothing but a performance. I am angry but, at the same time, I understand that you are just as much a victim as me."

"That's still no excuse," Daddy said. "I hurt you and that's unforgivable."

"In time, I hope that I can forgive you, but I know that I'll never forget. At least, now that I know."

We sat there in an uncomfortable silence for a moment.

"Daddy, I want you to know that I plan to call Allison sometime today and tell her everything."

"Please, let me do it," he stated in a desperate tone. "I should be the one to tell her."

"Maybe, but I have the *right* to tell her. I have to make sure that nothing happens to Flower. While you mean well, I have to do this so that I have peace of mind."

He nodded. "I understand, Jonquinette."

"I'm glad that you do."

"Can we still spend time together?" he asked. "We lost so many years. All I want is a chance to get to know you again."

I shook my head and sighed. "Daddy, I need to get through this first before I can answer that. I thought about it long and hard last night and I think being in constant contact with you would hinder my healing process. We both need to heal separately before we can heal together."

"Marcella alluded to the same thing after you and Meredith left her office yesterday. She gave me the contact information for several doctors in North Carolina. I plan to find one who can see me immediately."

"That's a wonderful thing." I stood back up. "Daddy, I don't mean to be rude but I can't think of anything else to say to you right now." I glanced at the bedroom door. "Plus, I don't think it would be wise for you to be here when Momma wakes up."

He stood and headed for the door. "I agree." When he got to the doorway, he turned and said, "Would it be too much if I asked for a hug? Just in case it's the last one."

I hesitated at first and then embraced him tightly. "Good-bye, Daddy."

When he let go of me, I spotted a tear in the corner of his right eye. "Good-bye, Jonquinette."

I watched him saunter down the hallway and closed the door as he pushed the call button for the elevator.

40

marcella

I decided to conduct the next therapy session at Jonquinette's apartment. I wanted all of the personalities to feel comfortable and it was the obvious choice. I spoke to Jude first. She greeted me at the door. I knew it was her right away from the way that she grinned at me and carried herself.

"Good morning, Jude," I said.

"Good morning, Marcella. Come on in. We've been expecting you."

"You sound mighty cheerful this morning."

Jude shrugged. "What can I say? If you can't beat them, join them."

"So you realize there are others?" I asked.

"I know there's at least one. When Jonquinette came back into your office, so did I, and I heard everything she heard."

"I take that to mean that you never knew about Henry's molestation of Jonquinette?"

Jude shook her head. "No, I didn't. I just always knew I didn't like the bastard. It seems that my actions have now been justified." She laughed. "At least I didn't attempt to outright kill him. If I had, I wouldn't have missed."

I chuckled. "No, I don't suppose you would have."

Jude walked over to the window and peered out. "I've been giving this a lot of consideration. Jon's been through a lot."

"Yes, she has, and you've been there for her when she needed you most."

"But now she doesn't need me anymore. Is that what you're getting at?"

"You tell me. Does she still need you?"

"I hate to admit this but I suppose not. That doesn't mean I'm going away completely, though. I might just stop doing all the bad things I've been doing and let Jon make all the decisions."

"So you admit that you've been doing bad things?"

"Of course. I won't even attempt to sugarcoat it. Jon was boring, simple as that. I had to do something adventurous to make life bearable. But now that she's dating this Mason dude, who's all right by the way, things are looking up."

"You like Mason?"

"He's growing on me, slowly. He's romantic and that's a good sign. I believe that he loves Jon and I know for a fact that she loves him. Who am I to interfere with what could be the love affair of the century?"

"I'm delighted to hear you say that, Jude." I walked over to her and placed my hand on her shoulder. For once, she didn't yank it away from me. "Jude, I know that this is hard on you. You're a person just like Jonquinette and Jetta."

"I meant what I said before," Jude stated, turning to look at me. "I never set out to hurt Jonquinette. I love her. But, I had to do what I had to do and as far as the sex, that was my escape."

"I understand perfectly."

"Marcella, I've made up my mind. Yes, I've *definitely* made it up. I'm going to let Jon live her life the way she wants to." Jude actually seemed excited as she spoke the words. "She deserves it. She's been through enough." She paused and added, "I can't speak for this Jetta person, though. I don't even know her ass but I like her."

We both laughed.

"I don't think Jetta will be surfacing anytime soon, Jude. She spoke her mind and accomplished what she set out to do. At least, that's the way I view it, but I could always be wrong."

"No, Marcella, you're right," Jude said smugly. "I have confidence in you. But don't get it twisted." She poked me in the arm. "If someone starts fucking with my girl, I will be back to handle things."

"I have no doubt that you will," I stated honestly. "I'll try to make sure that no one fucks with Jonquinette ever again."

Jude hugged me, which truly shocked me, and whispered in my ear, "Good looking out."

She headed down the hall to the bedroom. "I'm tired. I need to lie down for a while."

"Are you okay?" I called after her.

She turned and winked at me. "I'm just fine. We all are."

I decided to stay at Jonquinette's apartment to see what happened. Mason knocked on the door and I introduced myself to him. We chatted quietly in the living room for a few minutes, but I refused to go into details since I was still sworn to protect the privacy of my patients. I listened to him comment on things that Jon had obviously revealed to him but I refused to expound upon them.

Mason seemed like a wonderful man and I could see why Jonquinette was so in love with him. Most people would not deal with such a difficult situation but Mason swore that he had no plans to go anywhere. In fact, he told me that he one day planned to marry Jonquinette. I encouraged him to put that on hold until she had time to heal. He agreed to wait.

I let him out and sat down on the sofa, staring at the ceiling and pondering the events of the past several days. I wished Dr. Driggs was still alive so I could seek his advice. I had a call in to another dear friend of mine in Florida. He was on vacation but his secretary assured me that I would be his first phone call upon his return. Either way, with or without another doctor to consult, I was determined to help Jonquinette.

An hour later, I heard the bedroom door creak open and I sat up, waiting to see who would emerge. As soon as she came around the corner, I knew it was Jonquinette. She looked refreshed and had this glow about her.

"How about we go out to dinner?" I suggested. "It would be a good thing for us to get out of this environment for a little while."

Jonquinette smiled. "I'm starved. Where shall we go?"

"Um, how about Justin's? I heard the food's fantastic and I've never been."

"Me either. Sounds good to me. Let me just get a coat."

"Great. We'll take my car."

Jonquinette and I had a lovely dinner at Justin's and talked about the future, *her* future.

epilogue

Ever since the onset of my integration, I must admit that it's been difficult to accept that I am all alone now. It's weird because I never really knew them. I just knew that sometimes I simply wasn't there.

I was finally able to become strong enough to stand alone. A lot of it had to do with making sure that Flower didn't suffer the same fate as me. All those years, Jude and Jetta existed to protect me. Now it is my time to protect Flower.

Daddy is getting the help that he needs. It is still difficult to forgive and it is impossible to forget. So much pain was caused by his actions—a chain reaction to pain that he endured at an early age himself.

Flower's mother won't allow Daddy to see her at all. She said that, in time, she might agree to supervised visits. I decided not to press charges. There was nothing to be gained by that because Daddy has an illness. He's not a criminal.

Mason and I are still going strong. He has hinted around about marriage but I'm not ready. I have so much more I have to figure out about myself, now that I'm in complete control of *all* of my actions. Darnetta is still mad at me and not speaking but that's her prerogative. There will be no more apologies coming from me and I refuse to allow her to make me find another job. If she truly hates me, she can find one because times are hard.

I still go to see Dr. Spencer. I plan to keep my weekly appointments for as long as necessary. Marcella said there is a chance that one or more alters might surface again, but only for a little while and not to the degree that they did before. They would not have the same hold on me. She was honest with me by saying that it could take several years for me to become fully integrated. She said that my alters are still present but all of us are just living together in harmony. I found that difficult to comprehend but I didn't doubt it. I let her know that I was in it for the long haul. Too many people think they don't need counseling, when it's obvious that they do. It is not a sign of weakness, like so many tend to think. It is a sign of empowerment.

Jude and Jetta, wherever you may be, thank you from the bottom of my heart.

NERVOUS

ZANE

An Atria Books Discussion Guide

ABOUT THIS GUIDE

The suggested questions are intended to help your reading group find new and interesting angles and topics for discussion for Zane's *Nervous*. We hope that these ideas will enrich your conversation and increase your enjoyment of the book.

A Conversation with Zane

Q: Jonquinette is a fascinating character with a complex disorder. How did you research the psychiatric problems afflicting her? Did you talk to any doctors or patients who have experience with this condition, or read any interesting real-life accounts?

A: I love the Jonquinette character, and her multiple personality disorder (MPD) intrigued me. I did most of my research via the Internet and read a lot of medical information about the causes, symptoms, and cures. I was also stunned by the number of sites operated by people suffering from the disease. I thought that it was rare until a search engine came back with hundreds of sites. Out of all my characters, Jonquinette took the most thought to create and bring to life.

Q: In some ways, *Nervous* is about conflicting impulses that can arise in a person, even if they only have one personality. Like Jonquinette, do you think we all have to learn to balance desires for sex and love, forgiveness and retribution, and submissive and assertive behavior?

A: I think that balancing life is a task that people endure on a daily basis. What is too much and what is too little? Do we give of ourselves freely or proceed with caution? Do we just forgive, forget, and move on, or do we try to get back at those who harm us emotionally or physically? Jonquinette had to deal with all of those feelings when it came to opening her heart up to Mason, forgiving her father instead of having him arrested, and learning how to take control of her situation.

Q: In the Introduction, you wrote that the idea for this novel came from a short story. What aspect of the short story so intrigued you that you had to write this novel? What was it that you wanted to expand and explore?

A: The short story entitled "Nervous," from *The Sex Chronicles: Shattering the Myth,* was one of the stories that I received the most feedback on, particularly from women. In a sense, most women have two sides to them: the one that wants to be respected and the one that wants to explore new things without being judged. *Addicted* had originally started out as a short story in my head but I thought the character was much deeper than just a few pages, so I put it aside and wrote the novel later. I felt very much the same way about the main character in the short story "Nervous." She deserved a closer look and it was amazing to give her a name and a voice.

Q: The conversation Jon has with the wise old woman at church seems to mark a turning point for her. Did you have a particular model for that character? The church itself seemed to play an important role in Jon's life. How do you think church helps care for its members?

A: I felt compelled to put that in the book because I am a "PK," Preacher's Kid, and the church has always played an important role in my life. Whenever I hit a hard place, going to church lifts me back up. I believe there are no mistakes or accidents in life and I believe that God intentionally closes some doors, in a sense saying, "Don't go there!" Then he opens up the right ones. As for the model for the older female character, there was an older woman who once helped me make some difficult life decisions and I used her as the model. I actually wrote a short story based on my relationship with her called "Sometimes Young People Do Listen." She is a very special person to me.

Q: You've taken your erotica to a wide audience, first through the Internet, and then through a traditional publishing house. Who do you think your readers are? Who do you write for?

A: I think my readers are just about anyone who likes to read books that keep reality in perspective. The sex is a major part of my writing—but I think it is more about me writing about things that people have done, would like to do, or have always wondered about doing. I write for myself; it is my escape into the unknown. It relieves my stress. It makes me happy. Being able to do what I love doing for a living only makes the sun shine brighter, but I would still write if no one ever read it. In fact, I probably have more written that has not been seen in public than has been.

Q: What do you think about the way pedophiles are handled by the state? Do you believe, as Jonquinette does, that they should be treated instead of prosecuted?

A: I believe that has to be dealt with on a case-by-case basis. However, I really don't believe that prison rehabilitates anyone. In my opinion, it only increases anger, depression, and the willingness to go outside of the law. I believe that pedophilia is a disease and that more concentration needs to be placed on breaking the vicious cycle than on locking people up like animals. I am tackling that concept in a book that I am editing called *Breaking the Cycle*. The madness must stop somewhere and sometime, and there is never a better time than the present.

Q: What writers do you admire? Who inspires you to write?

A: Quite honestly, the majority of people have probably never heard of most of the writers who I admire. The ones that people have heard of include Stephen King, Jeffery Deaver, and Patricia Cornwell. I am actually a huge mystery buff and even write mystery novels. Those are some of the ones collecting dust on my various hard drives. I admire and am inspired by all of the authors that I publish under Strebor Books International. However, if I had to name my favorite author of all time, it would have to be D. V. Bernard, a young brother from New York City, who wrote *The Last Dream About Dawn* and the upcoming *God in the Image of Woman*. He blows me away every time. I just hope he one day gets the recognition that he deserves.

Q: How has your writing changed since you started? Is there any aspect of the craft that you are more aware of now than when you started?

A: As an author, I strive to make every book better than my last book. I strive to grow in some way and hone my craft. At first,

I hated writing dialogue. Now I find that to be one of my greatest strengths. I faced my challenges head-on, concentrated on them the most, and overcame them. I am more aware of a lot of the technical aspects of writing—how long a novel should be, the importance of backstory, story line structure, and most important, the knowledge that character development, or the lack thereof, can make or break a story. That is the main reason I can't finish certain books, and I tell authors all the time: if you do not develop your characters properly and make the reader feel a closeness to them, the reader will not care when things begin to happen to them—good or bad.

Q: Why did you choose to write erotica? Have you ever been drawn to write in other genres? What is it about erotica that you want to draw out in your writing?

A: Actually, I never chose erotica. It chose me, but that is a story for another day because it is a long one. I think of my story lines first, I flesh out my characters, and then I add risqué sex. I write in several other genres and hope to publish some of those numerous novels—under another pseudonym—in the near future. As for erotica, I believe different people have different ideas about what it means. To me, erotic stories do two things: make people horny—the obvious one—and make people lose themselves in the story. I don't like stories that jump straight into sex. Who cares? Anyone can have sex or just write about some nameless person sexing another nameless person down. One of the contributors to *Chocolate Flava: The Eroticanoir.com Anthology* sent me a story about two people, hooking up again after several years, in a hotel room getting busy. I rejected it but told her to try again. I wanted her to tell me who the people were, why were they so happy to see each other again after many years, why had they been apart for so long, etc. She came back to me a few days later with an incredible story that ended up in the book. To me, that's erotica.

There is one main reason why I do write erotic fiction and will continue to do so. I have made many women realize that they are not alone. A lot of women grow up believing that men should be the sexual aggressors, that men should be the experimental ones, and that women should just settle and be satisfied with the luck of the draw. I want women to know that it is more than okay—it is essential—that we speak up and express our sexual needs, wants, and desires. Men are not psychic. Only a woman can tell what turns her on or off. Men do it all the time and ask for specific sexual acts. It is time for the tides to turn and if I can aid in making it happen, then I'm game.

Q: You seem to be a strong advocate for psychiatric care and counseling. Do you feel that these services are not as available or as widely sought as they should be?

A: I believe they are available but that they are not sought out enough—particularly in the African-American community. I actually know three black female psychiatrists personally and there was a convention for black psychiatrists at the D.C. Convention Center some years back. That means they are plentiful. However, needing help with mental issues has often been considered a stigma, a sign of weakness, because we are supposed to be beyond that. Everyone is the same inside and we all bleed the same, so to make the assumption that other races can be mentally off balance but we can't is absurd. Women of other races often leave luncheon dates announcing that they are running late for an appointment with their therapist, but you would be hard-pressed to find a sister openly admitting to it. It is sad, really, because so many choose to suffer—sometimes for an entire lifetime—instead of seeking help.

Questions and Topics for Discussion

1. What is your first impression of Jonquinette? Is she friendly, responsible, reserved, assertive? Does Jonquinette surprise you at any point in the novel, or do anything that seems unlike herself? Do you think she surprises Jude? Although the integration of her personalities gives Jon the greatest control over her life, her character develops in more subtle ways over the course of the novel. How does she change, and how does her development make the integration possible?

2. How would you characterize the dynamic between Jonquinette and Jude? Sometimes it seems like Jude sees herself as Jon's protector. Do you think that is always the case? Jude acts like she knows what's good for Jon. When she's in control, she disparages Jon's diet, her glasses, and her clothing choices. How are Jude's choices determined by her own biases? How much does she take care of Jon, and how much does she take care of herself?

3. What do you think of the way Jude handles Mrs. Greer's dog, Shadow, and the girls in her gym class? Jude is much more assertive that Jon, but she is also much more violent. Why does Jude make such dramatic and destructive gestures? How does her approach to these situations foreshadow her later approach to sex?

4. As soon as it looks like Jonquinette has taken an interest in Mason Copeland, Jude becomes fearful that he and Jon might form a serious relationship. She says, "No serious relationships. Just sex and I was the only one entitled to that" (page 45). At first it seems like Jude goes on sexcapades because Jon is repressed, and Jude expresses her inhibited sexuality. But here, Jude reveals that she prefers to have Jon be chaste so that she can control their love life. Why do you think Jude wants to control this aspect of their life?

5. Similarly, why is Jude so opposed to the idea of meaningful sex? In the beginning, it seems reasonable that she might not want to form attachments, since her lovers might discuss her adventures with Jonquinette. But since she's well aware that Jon knows, vaguely, what she does with their body, this can't be the only reason. What other reasons does she have for maintaining her anonymity?

6. What part does Flower play in this story? Jonquinette quickly becomes attached to the child. She says, "All those years, Jude and Jetta existed to protect me. Now it is my time to protect Flower" (page 281). How does her relationship with Flower allow her to come into her own? How does her protective stance toward Flower show how she has grown?

7. After Jonquinette becomes aware that her dad molested her as a child, she has a tough decision to make. She says, "I decided not to press charges. There was nothing to be gained by that because Daddy has an illness. He's not a criminal" (page 282). Do you agree with Jon's decision? Do you think Henry is a criminal? Jon has the responsibility of making this decision for herself as an adult. Do you think her mom would have

made a similar decision if she had learned about the abuse when Jon was young?

8. Jonquinette's mother, Meredith, is unwilling to get psychiatric care for her daughter, even after it's clear that she needs assistance. After Marcella Spencer helps Jon figure out how her disorder is affecting her life, Jon decides to ask her mom to participate in her therapy. She asks her mom, "Momma, did you never figure it out or did you just choose to ignore it?" (page 203). How do Meredith's responses to her daughter's condition indicate that she didn't want to believe her daughter was ill? Is there reason to believe she just didn't know? Why is Jon herself so nervous about getting help? Why does she finally decide to make an appointment with Marcella Spencer?

9. What do you think of Jon's decision to reopen communication with her dad? Knowing that Jude often acts as Jonquinette's protector, and forced Henry out of Jon's home, how do you feel when Jon goes to visit Henry despite Jude's displeasure? Do you think their reunion is a necessary step in Jonquinette's recovery?

10. Although Jonquinette meets a number of unpleasant people in her life, sometimes it seems as though the most difficult personality she encounters is Jude, her own alter ego. Although Jude is the fighter, Jon wins the battle for their body. What does she have to do to convince Jude to let her control her own life?

11. In some ways, the battle between Jonquinette and Jude is one-sided. While Jude is aware of Jon's life, Jon knows nothing

about Jude, her life, or her desires. How does this affect their conflict? What does it say about Jude that she manipulates and controls Jonquinette?

12. Jude accuses Meredith of many awful things. She calls her selfish, a gold digger, and a whore. Why does Jude hate Meredith so much? Jonquinette seems to love her mother despite her flaws, and she certainly treats her with respect. What do you think of Meredith? Do you think either Jon or Jude has an accurate impression of their mother? How do their opinions about her reflect on their own personalities?

13. Was it wise of Jonquinette to hook up with Mason before her integration? His involvement in her life provoked Jude into creating quite a scene at the wedding. Still, do you think Jon could have convinced Jude to let her keep control without Mason's love and support? What role, if any, did Mason play in her recovery? Might his presence in her life actually have jeopardized her healing process?

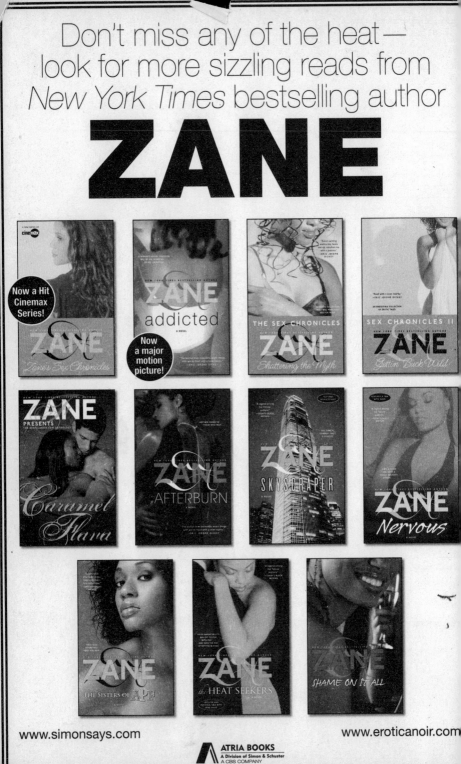